҂҂҂҂҂҂

Getting Published

Getting Published

The Acquisition Process at University Presses

PAUL PARSONS

UNIVERSITY OF TENNESSEE PRESS ❦ KNOXVILLE

The paper in this book meets the minimum requirements

of the American National Standard for Permanence of Paper

for Printed Library Materials.

The binding materials have been chosen for

strength and durability.

Library of Congress Cataloging-in-Publication Data

Parsons, Paul, 1952–

  Getting published : the acquisition process

  at university presses /

  Paul Parsons. — 1st ed.

  p. cm.

  Bibliography: p.

  Includes index.

  ISBN 0-87049-611-5 (cloth: alk. paper)

  ISBN 0-87049-612-3 (pbk.: alk. paper)

  1. University presses.   2. Scholarly publishing.

  3. Authors and publishers.   I. Title.

Z231.5.U6P37   1989

070.5'94—dc 20   89-31711   CIP

To Mary Helen

ꝏꝏꝏ

Contents

ღღღ

Tables

❦❦❦

Acknowledgments

Researching and writing this book was a delightful experience because the people in scholarly publishing are delightful individuals. They are intelligent, energetic, and, thankfully, talkative. I owe much to those American university press directors and editors who opened their presses and their minds to scrutiny.

No book is a solo act. An author benefits from the encouragement, guidance, and criticism of others. In my case, I am indebted to sociologist Lewis Coser, Beacon Press director Wendy Strothman, and other leading scholars and publishers for their valuable feedback while this work was in progress.

This book's gestation period spanned five years, from conception to birth. Paul Ashdown of the College of Communications at the University of Tennessee at Knoxville was there at the conception, and he provided not only encouragement but also incisive questioning at just the right times to keep this project on course. I also am indebted to Kelly Leiter, George Everett, and Malcolm McInnis. In my current position at Kansas State University, I offer a special word of appreciation to my director, Carol Oukrop, who did all within her power to enable me to complete this book on schedule. My graduate assistant, Julie Andsager, provided valuable assistance in fact checking.

Finally, gratitude goes to University of Tennessee Press director Carol Orr, acquisitions editor Cynthia Maude-Gembler (now at Syracuse University Press), copyeditor Mavis Bryant, and marketing director Jennifer Siler. I have been fortunate to work with such good people.

Introduction

Scholars accumulate information in the research phase and then synthesize that information in the writing phase. Yet their task does not end there. For scholarship to benefit the community at large, the end product must be made available to others. The scholarly process, then, also must include securing publication. For many scholars, this final step is a mysterious one.

This book explains the practices and philosophies controlling the selection of manuscripts published by university presses. Specifically, it analyzes how editors go about the task of choosing what to consider for publication and what to discard, and how the peer review and editorial committee mechanisms ultimately choose the works to be published. This is not a "how-to" book. No book can offer a step-by-step procedure to follow in order to secure publication of a manuscript. The publishing process is too diffuse and too arbitrary. But scholars—particularly those who have yet to develop their own academic or publishing "networks"—are in need of information about how scholarly publishers go about their business.

My interest in scholarly publishing began, rather typically, when I wrote a manuscript suitable for a university press and then wondered how the acquisition process worked. I had worked as a reporter for United Press International and as an editor with the Associated Press for eight years, when I was awarded a Fellowship in Religious Studies for Journalists at the University of North Carolina. Thanks to the fellowship, I began a fact-finding odyssey that eventually took me inside fundamentalist Christian schools in thirty states. In my eventual quest for an outlet for the investigative study, my attention focused on university presses as publishers of serious, although usually not bestselling, works. The book was published by a university press that specializes in religious studies. Later I served on the other side of the publishing fence, in an advisory capacity in my discipline for an Ivy League press. These publishing experiences as author and reviewer, along with my Ph.D. research in mass communications, led to this study of the role of university presses in the transmission of knowledge within a culture.

Research for this book spanned four years and relied on several methodological tools: an extended on-site study of a single university press, face-to-face interviews with directors and acquisitions editors representing more than thirty university presses, and a survey of leading university presses in the United States.

Different academic disciplines use different research methodologies. Psychologists rely on independent observations for their data. Anthropologists rely on repeated observations of a group of people engaged in their customary activities. Historians typically turn to archives for published data. Field notes are to journalists what archives are to historians— the primary sources of information without which little could be written. As a journalist, I am a historian-in-a-hurry. A journalist does not rely on the analysis of secondary data but instead creates new data through interviews and observation.

Of course, in field studies, investigators inevitably shape the source material. Field researchers have their own interests, prejudices, and ways of seeing reality. Field notes, without doubt, are tainted. But this study —flawed though it may be in its reliance on one person's information-gathering orientation—attempts to give a comprehensive overview of the decision-making processes within university presses.

This study began with a year-long, on-site observation of a middle-sized American university press. The director of the press permitted access, on a confidential basis, to peer reviewer reports, editor responses, and marketing information. The editorial committee of the press permitted attendance at its meetings on the condition that manuscripts under consideration, and the university press itself, not be identified.

Personal interviews with dozens of directors and editors, representing more than thirty university presses, followed. The interviews were on the record, with the understanding that an interviewee could request anonymity when sharing sensitive information. With few exceptions, university press personnel were extraordinarily open and frank about the way they work, and why.

The study concluded with a survey of American university press members and affiliate members of the Association of American University Presses.[1] To qualify for membership in the association, a press must have published five or more scholarly books a year for at least two preceding years and must have at least three full-time employees. A questionnaire was mailed to the seventy-four American university presses belonging to the association as of 1986. Fifty-two of the presses responded, a return rate of 70.2 percent.

The survey instrument emphasized both quantitatively provable tallies, such as the number of new titles published, and quantitatively unprovable estimates, such as the number of author queries received in a given year. In past years, research efforts to develop quantifiably provable statistics concerning aspects of the publishing process have had limited success. Fritz Machlup and Kenneth Leeson's four-volume study in the late 1970s, *Information through the Printed Word*, financed in part by the National Science Foundation and the National Endowment for the Humanities, took more than three years and at one time employed a staff of sixteen. But the authors bluntly concluded that the study remained inconclusive, due to "the intractability of the problem." Gathering data and making sense of it proved difficult. For instance, the researchers found that some publishers kept sales records by units sold, while other publishers recorded sales by dollar volume alone. Similarly, few publishers kept records of sales by discipline, and those who did defined fields of interest differently. Another disappointment to the researchers was the amount of work required to obtain primary data. When the research team tested a questionnaire designed to yield publishing lists by discipline, it took four people several days to fill out a questionnaire for only one year. As the one-time director of the Office of Scholarly Communication and Technology concluded in a review of the volumes, "One's insights are similar in reliability to those that develop through the ordinary accumulation of experience. They are tentative, and not quantitatively provable."[2]

Just as it had proved difficult to seek quantitatively provable data in the financial arena of publishing, I found it difficult to obtain quantitatively provable data regarding the acquisition practices at university presses. Few presses keep a record of every query letter they receive or a tally of manuscripts that come in "over the transom" (unsolicited), because these figures are not of operational significance to the presses. Yet rather than dismiss such information as unobtainable, my survey asked for estimates that, collectively, could help paint a portrait of the acquisition process. It should be emphasized that some data are, in the words of a responding university press director, "impressionistic estimates rather than actual counts." As a result, survey data are reported through the use of descriptive, not analytical, statistics. Data are used solely to supplement the accumulated insights of those in scholarly publishing.

Two activities separate a publisher from a printer—selection and distribution. This book concentrates on selection and, except when directly related, does not study the distribution aspect of university publishing. In addition, this study focuses on the book-publishing role of university presses and does not address the selection and distribution of knowledge through scholarly journals published by university presses, since university presses typically serve as printer and distributor of journals but not as selector of the articles published. Finally, this book focuses exclusively on university presses, not commercial scholarly publishers or specialized monograph houses. Nonprofit university presses typically operate under special economic circumstances which give them a measure of freedom from the more acute pressures to achieve profitability, which are present in commercial publishing.

In recent years, outstanding books have appeared on the sociology of publishing, prominent among them *Books: The Culture and Commerce of Publishing* (1982) by Lewis A. Coser, Charles Kadushin, and Walter W. Powell. In addition, Powell's *Getting Into Print: The Decision-Making Process in Scholarly Publishing* (1985) is an intriguing sociological study of the acquisition practices at scholarly presses, based primarily on nineteen months of field observation at two commercial houses. Excellent books also exist to help the academic author better understand publishers. For instance, Beth Luey's *Handbook for Academic Authors* (1987) discusses such topics as preparing the manuscript of a journal article, choosing a publisher for a scholarly book, and revising a textbook. In addition, other past and present editors within scholarly publishing have provided personal insights in book or journal article form.

This book differs from these past works by offering a broad journalistic overview of acquisition processes at university presses, through the words and decisions of those in the profession—not just of the large and prestigious presses, but of the smaller and less prestigious ones as well. Such a work has long been needed to assist doctoral students unfamiliar with university press practices, to guide junior scholars wanting to pursue book-length research projects, and even to help orient newly appointed university press staff or editorial committee members not already well versed in the workings of scholarly publishing.

This book is divided into seven chapters. Chapter 1 provides an overview of how university presses serve as gatekeepers of intellectual inquiry in this age of decentralized media. Of course, university presses do not serve as the only gatekeepers of scholarship. But their nonprofit status theoretically allows them to consider works purely on merit.

Chapter 2 explains how scholarly specialization in academia has led to specialization in scholarly publishing through listbuilding. Because of the continual fractionalization of knowledge, university presses have become specialists themselves, with their lists based on editorial and marketing criteria. These criteria have led university presses to publish primarily in the humanities and social sciences.

Chapter 3 outlines how the very nature of acquisitions has undergone a radical change in recent decades. No longer are editors passive recipients of suitable manuscripts; instead they actively pursue quality scholarship. Editors write to prospective authors, attend scholarly conventions, and even visit professors on campus. This shift has led to competition in the search for outstanding manuscripts.

Once the editor chooses what to pursue for publication, the surviving manuscripts are submitted to scholarly peer review. Chapter 4 explains how editors select peer reviewers and what impact these reviews have on the manuscripts under consideration. Then an editorial committee representing the university decides whether to publish the works still under consideration.

Chapter 5 details the financial dilemmas of publishing scholarly monographs—books on narrow subjects that appeal almost exclusively to specialized academic audiences. Many such monographs were doctoral dissertations in an earlier, unrevised life. University presses face the unappealing prospect of publishing the most specialized of books and attempting to sell them to the narrowest of audiences while somehow avoiding financial calamity.

As printruns (number of copies printed) of scholarly monographs decline, some university presses are seeking broader audiences. Chapter 6 outlines the expanding university press title mix—involving trade books for the nonspecialist, topical and regional books, reference works, and even original fiction and poetry.

Concluding the book, chapter 7 discusses how university presses, as a leading vehicle for intellectual intercourse, actively shape the cultural agenda. Publishing lists continually evolve as the interests and pursuits of the scholars themselves change. The final chapter analyzes this on-going evolution in listbuilding and explains how university presses continually seek to be on the emerging frontiers of knowledge.

Decision-making processes may follow certain norms, but any study must be prepared to allow for decisions to be made in individualistic rather than highly structured terms. No two university presses have identical sets of criteria for assessing manuscripts. Still, enough similarities exist to provide some standardization in the acquisition process. This book analyzes those similarities in university presses' policies and practices. In the end, however, the acquisition process remains more of an art than a science.

❦❦❦❦❦❦

1. Gatekeepers

of Intellectual

Discovery

P ublishers stand at the crossroads of intellectual discovery and the public consumption of that discovery. Rather than being neutral intermediaries in the process, publishers help determine what is "in" and what is "out" in the marketplace of ideas. By choosing to publish some works and not to publish others, they play a vital role in the transmission of knowledge within a culture. In sociologist Lewis Coser's phrase, publishers serve as "gatekeepers of ideas."[1]

In this age of decentralized media, publishing no longer occupies the near-monopolistic gatekeeping position it once enjoyed. Yet in the realm of scholarly knowledge in literate societies, publication remains the primary vehicle for intellectual discourse. Fortunately for producers and consumers of ideas alike, scholarly publishing has no single gatekeeper. Decision-making resides in a great number of autonomous firms, each with its own interests and perceptions of what is worthy of publication.

University presses serve as prominent gatekeepers in scholarly publishing because they, unlike commercial presses, can select knowledge for distribution without being wholly captives to the marketplace. The university press, after all, resides in two worlds—the scholarly community and the publishing industry.

The typical university press stands outside the regular university machinery. It is a nonprofit enterprise organizationally attached to the administration rather than to a particular school or faculty. Most presses are subsidized through the use of university buildings and services. Because a press is an integral part of the parent university, its purpose is to advance intellectual life rather than to make a profit.

Yet a book is both an idea and a commodity. Its intent is to be intellectually stimulating, but first it must be bought. Within any publishing house, some employees are more concerned with books as ideas while others are more concerned with books as commodities. The balance of power between the two is what makes university presses distinctive.[2] In commercial publishing, those who are more concerned with books as ideas report to those who are more concerned with books as commodities. In university presses, in theory at least, the balance of power is reversed.

University presses exert an influence on American publishing significantly out of proportion to their size. University press income accounts for slightly more than one percent of publishing's annual sales, yet university presses publish about 10 percent of the forty-thousand new titles in the United States each year.[3] Moreover, if National Book Awards may be taken as a measure of cultural impact, it is noteworthy that more than 20 percent of the awards and prizes made since 1950 have gone to books published by university presses.[4]

University presses serve as important catalysts for scholarly inquiry. Their role in the enrichment of intellectual life occurs, in theory, through a special process. Scholars do research. Their work is evaluated by the press' editors. Many manuscripts fall by the wayside, while those considered most promising are sent to the authors' peers for anonymous review. Still more manuscripts fall by the wayside, while others are returned to the authors for revision. In the end, an editorial committee of scholars selected from the parent institution's faculty and administration decides whether to publish a given work. Ideally, only the best works are published. These are collected and sorted in libraries, where other scholars can use them for their own research. If only the best works indeed are published, then this process becomes a cyclical flow that continually advances intellectual life.

❦ The Publishing Environment

University presses exist within a highly segmented and diverse publishing environment. While some publishers produce scholarly books designed primarily to meet the needs of an elite, highly educated clientele, other publishers produce trade books and mass-market paperbacks that are like the latest fads—they have a momentary impact, then quickly fade. Still other publishers (or divisions within the same large house) produce textbooks for the classroom, juvenile books for the young, religious books for the faithful, and specialized books that appeal to a variety of other audiences.

With the end products in each case so different from each other, it is no wonder that the processes by which works reach publication differ vastly as well. For instance, trade publishers can lure authors with monetary advances and quick publishing decisions. Based on intuition alone, a confident editor can offer a book contract over lunch. The emphasis is often on sales potential, not literary quality. After all, a trade book is a disposable commodity, soon to be replaced by the next book to reach the market. Conversely, scholarly publishers offer potential authors little, if any, financial incentive to write a book, and the decision-making process can be irritatingly slow. At some publishing houses, an editor may be unable to extend a contract offer until the manuscript has traversed the obstacle course involving peer reviews and an editorial board.

In each case, a book results. But the editorial processes differ substantially, because the purpose of publishing differs substantially. For the trade publisher, the overriding interest is making money by providing readers a product they are willing to buy. For the scholarly publisher, the overriding interest is providing a product of quality and substance. Sociologist Walter W. Powell writes:

> While scholarly publishers generally operate in a context of low risk, the high-stakes world of hardcover trade books and mass-market paperbacks is characterized by considerable risk and great uncertainty. On the other hand, the readers of scholarly books are a demanding lot, and a publisher's prestige can suffer if books of little substance are issued. In particular, the elite university presses and top scholarly houses are quite concerned with maintaining prestigious reputations. . . . Trade publishers compete for a broad mass audience and often publish outright junk with little negative consequence. Authors, agents, librarians, and others in the book-buying trade may be put off by a list of dubious quality, but the general book-buying public is not considered to be sensitive to a trade publisher's

reputation. Each trade book is regarded as an individual commodity in its own right.[5]

The extraordinary diversity in the general publishing environment does not end with these broad distinctions. Within scholarly publishing itself are two distinct types of houses—commercial and nonprofit. The commercial category includes large academic houses such as W.W. Norton and Basic Books, and specialist monograph houses such as Sage, Westview, Lexington, Jossey-Bass, and Praeger. Their nonprofit counterparts are the dozens of university presses, large and small, scattered across the nation, affiliated with institutions ranging from elite private schools to state universities.

Each type of scholarly house offers certain advantages. Irving E. Rockwood, who has been an editor at both a commercial and a university press, describes the choice as one of speed versus prestige. Within scholarly publishing, commercial publishers usually offer faster decision-making and a shorter production cycle. A number of commercial houses tend to make their own publishing decisions, consulting outside experts only when they lack confidence in their own judgment. As a result, these houses can act quickly when they find a manuscript they like. They are more willing than university presses to consider manuscripts submitted simultaneously to other presses. Commercial presses also may offer somewhat better financial terms to authors, although the amount of money involved in scholarly publishing, except for textbook publishing or the rare bestseller, is rather small. Rockwood considers commercial presses to have the early advantage for the author who wants to be published.

Nevertheless, once a contract is signed, Rockwood believes university presses have the advantage. He feels that commercial presses tend to offer less individual attention to authors because such presses operate on a volume basis—that is, they publish many titles in order to make a small profit on each one. Such a strategy puts a premium on cost control, resulting in standardized formats and designs, minimal editing, and conformist marketing procedures. Not surprisingly, writes Rockwood, "the emphasis on economy sometimes overwhelms quality, with the result that the lists involved, while often large, may be uneven in quality and unimaginatively marketed."[6]

In addition, commercial houses are subject to the Thor ruling issued by the Internal Revenue Service. In effect, the ruling requires commercial presses physically to destroy any unsold inventory on which they wish to take a tax writeoff. Slow-selling books may be declared out of print rather quickly. The rule does not apply to university presses, since they are nonprofit organizations.

While commercial presses are more approachable and much quicker, Rockwood said that most other advantages lie with university presses:

> University presses lavish considerably more personal attention on their authors than do professional and reference publishers. They are far more concerned about quality production, far more likely to provide personal editorial assistance, and far less likely to put a title out of print once published. And there is little doubt, in most disciplines at least, that a university press imprint is more 'prestigious' than that of a commercial house. . . .
>
> Suffice it to say here, however, that the choice is primarily one of speed versus prestige. If obtaining a contract—and publishing— quickly is more important than prestige, then one is best advised to approach commercial houses first. If, on the other hand, timing is less important than long-term considerations, such as prestige, then it makes sense to try university presses.[7]

Wendy Strothman, assistant director at the University of Chicago Press before becoming director of Beacon Press in 1983, makes a similar observation: "At university presses, and rightly so, time is usually sacrificed —first for quality and second for price. In trade publishing, time is first on the agenda, price follows close behind, and quality (especially of the parts of the book the consumer won't notice) is a distant third."[8]

The prestige granted university press books is based in large part on the academic recognition of the rigorous peer review system employed in the decision-making process.

🐾 Creation of University Presses

A strong association has existed through the years between universities and publishing. The invention of movable type by Johannes Gutenberg in Germany, around 1450, started a literary revolution. By giving permanence to ideas and by recording achievements, books answered a deep human need. Scholars debate whether the first university press was established at Oxford in 1478—one year after William Caxton printed the first book in the English language—or at Cambridge in 1521. Whenever the start, these early presses basically were printing houses attached to the parent universities, with London booksellers serving as the publishing agents.[9]

The first university press in the United States appeared at Cornell University in 1869. But the school's trustees were not convinced that the university needed a press, and only two pamphlets were issued before the press was declared defunct in 1883. Cornell did not reestablish its press for almost fifty years. In 1878, the Johns Hopkins University started what has become the oldest continuously operating university press in the nation. Daniel Coit Gilman, the first president of Johns Hopkins, is considered the father of American university publishing. He maintained that universities have an obligation not only to teach and to research, but also to publish. Gilman's oft-cited aphorism of 1878 has become a motto for university presses: "It is one of the noblest duties of a university to advance knowledge, and to diffuse it not merely among those who can attend the daily lectures—but far and wide."

In the United States, as in Europe, the publication of graduate school theses was compulsory in the nineteenth century. Graduate students paid for the printing of their doctoral theses, and the universities assumed responsibility for distributing the scholarly work. But as the number of graduate students increased, and their output was combined with that of faculty members, it became clear that regular publishing channels would be inadequate. Thus arose the need for the university press. Robert Frederick Lane, in a doctoral dissertation at the University of Chicago in 1939, wrote:

> There can be little doubt that many university presses, especially those with manufacturing plants, were often established in order to do the institutional printing. Allied with this was the argument that students in Journalism required a printing laboratory. The theory that a university press was a means for publishing the product of research, that it would enhance the reputations of scholars and institutions, developed relatively late in American university press history.[10]

The university press movement grew slowly and erratically in the late 1800s and early 1900s, then began to expand in the 1920s and 1930s. Early in the twentieth century, university presses in the United States were confined primarily to privately endowed universities. Even some of these schools came to question the presence of a press. In 1943, President James B. Conant of Harvard University wanted to dispose of the Harvard press, viewing it as a business enterprise with no academic virtue. In a spirited defense of the press, Harvard professor Ralph Barton Perry outlined its merits:

> The university . . . holds in its hands and can apply a seal of scholarly honesty and accuracy. Its name is a certificate of quality. In their capacity as scholars, its members write not what they think they can sell, but the conclusions they have reached as a result of thorough and expert inquiry. They are not obliged to cater to appetites and purchasing power. The public, therefore, has confidence in the university's disinterestedness and good faith.[11]

The continued existence of the Harvard press was made secure the following year.

University presses, however, remained an insignificant part of American publishing until after World War II. Chester Kerr, former director of the Yale University Press, reported that university presses until this time were run by amateurs such as printers, or scholars near retirement, or professors with no future in their chosen fields of scholarship. With few exceptions, the publishing lists consisted primarily of doctoral dissertations, some regional titles, and other publications that likely would have been called "vanity books" had their authors not been connected with respectable institutions.[12]

Many university presses served more as printers than as publishers, often wielding little editorial authority. In 1948, in his first year as director of the Johns Hopkins University Press, Harold Ingle was surprised upon being presented a book bearing the press's imprint by a professor who had taken his manuscript directly to the printer.[13] That doesn't happen anymore. One measure of the strength of university presses today—be they large or small, public or private—is their undisputed ability to exercise editorial control.

In the decades following World War II, university presses experienced unprecedented growth. In the 1950s and 1960s, they expanded with the help of foundation funding and in conjunction with the government-supported library prosperity of those years. Then came the inflation years of the 1970s. Book sales declined. Book prices went up. Library budgets were cut. Universities experiencing budgetary problems began expecting their presses to break even financially. A few university presses even went out of business. Publication was seen as increasingly difficult for young scholars. This led to a widespread belief that something was seriously wrong with the system of scholarly communication in the United States. The phrase "crisis in scholarly publishing" was used often during the decade, leading to the creation of a National Enquiry into Scholarly Communication. This panel of publishers, librarians, and scholars issued its report in book form in 1979, treating complex topics ranging from government policies to the needs of research libraries.[14] But scholarly publishing proved resilient. Today the word "crisis" seldom is applied to scholarly publishing. University presses are expanding in the latter twentieth century, with a renewed sense of their gatekeeping function in society.

❧ Gatekeeping as Knowledge Control

The term "gatekeeper" was coined in 1947 by sociologist Kurt Lewin, who contended that social forces flow along channels and pass through gates that are governed by impartial rules or by gatekeepers who make the necessary decisions on what passes through. The power group or individual makes the decision for "in" or "out." Noting that food comes to the family table through certain channels with "gates" that permit the progress of some items and exclude others, Lewin theorized, "The passing or not passing of the unit through the whole channel depends to a high degree upon what happens in the gate region. This holds not only for food channels but also for the traveling of a news item through certain communications channels in a group."[15]

The term "gatekeeper" came into the communications field in 1950 when David Manning White applied Lewin's thesis to the daily newspaper.[16] White studied in detail the behavior of a single telegraph editor, whom he dubbed "Mr. Gates," in an effort to discover the factors that influenced Gates' selection of stories for the paper. White wanted to know the factors that led the editor to reject nine-tenths of the copy he saw each day and to print one-tenth. The study revealed a number of reasons for the selection—the most obvious being space, although no paper, regardless of size, would desire to print everything available. White's study revealed the subjectivity with which the editor handled his job.

Bruce Westley and Malcolm MacLean included the gatekeeper in their conceptual model for communications research.[17] These theorists saw the gatekeeper as the agent of the audience, rather than as the originator of information or the communicator for the sender. Viewing gatekeeping as "uncertainty theory," John Dimmick contended that gatekeepers are uncertain what to select and thus depend on opinion leaders, reference groups, consensus of editorial staffs, and timeliness to make selection decisions. Dimmick concluded that a combination of these factors, in the end, may be responsible for the decision to accept or reject.[18]

All social organizations depend to some extent on the use and control of information. Gatekeeping is a form of information, or knowledge, control. In selecting which books to publish and which to reject, book publishers engage in a form of knowledge control. Gordon Neavill considered this to be an essential function of scholarly publishing:

> It is crucial to the dissemination of knowledge that all manuscripts submitted to publishers should not be accepted. If all manuscripts were assured of publication, the channels of dissemination would be glutted with works possessing neither intrinsic merit nor commercial potential, and works for which an audience did exist would sink beneath their weight. . . .
>
> It is, of course, also crucial to the dissemination of knowledge that works which merit publication on the basis of their content not be rejected.[19]

One view is that publishers serve as censors—exercising censorship each time they decline to publish a manuscript submitted to them. In fact, censorship is the deletion of objectionable material, a process quite different from selection. If publishers did not have the right of selection, they would, in effect, become clerks, publishing everything that entered the gate.

Ideally, then, the manuscript selection process is based on quality of intellect and importance of topic. The director emeritus of the University of California Press, August Frugé, has praised the standards that hold sway in university press publishing:

> The bars are reasonably high, the channels clear; the mediocre do not swamp the excellent. If this be elitism, that mortal sin of an egalitarian world, it is the elitism of excellence. Without it we might as well count pages.
>
> Thus, all scholarly publishers together have performed a social and cultural role that is not always apprehended or appreciated. . . . From the great mass of written manuscripts, and those proposed to be written, they have chosen a fraction—the best, the most useful— for making public.[20]

In book publishing, as in other forms of mass media, the gatekeepers who decide what to let in and what to keep out do not operate in a vacuum. Theirs is but a choice among available options. Authors determine the subjects they write about, and the available sources frequently determine the extent of the study. Each participant in the trip from source to reader offers particular interests, preferences, prejudices, concepts of the extent of knowledge offered, what its importance is, and to whom it is important.

Of course, in the end, all that a publisher can do is make the knowledge available. The final decision-maker is the consuming public. The public may choose not to be informed on a specific topic, regardless of previous gatekeeping decisions on its behalf. A publisher influences the dissemination of knowledge but cannot ensure its consumption. The scholarly publisher can make certain kinds of books available, but cannot make consumers buy books they do not want or make them read books that do not interest them.

❦❦❦❦❦❦

2. Specialization

Through Listbuilding

I n academia today, the specialist has replaced the generalist. University presses and other scholarly publishers have played a significant role in this process, by serving as an outlet for the fruits of academic specialization.

Scholarly specialization is the product of an educational revolution that has occurred in the twentieth century. Higher education, once confined to an elite minority, has become an egalitarian ideal. In 1900, American colleges and universities granted fewer than 30,000 degrees, of which 382 were doctorates. In 1980, more than 30,000 doctoral degrees alone were awarded in the United States.[1]

In the process of meeting societal needs, higher education became more professionally oriented and more specialized. The standardized core curriculum of the 1800s gave way to a greatly expanded academic curriculum that included new subjects of study. In an age that seriously questioned what an educated person should know, a rigid curriculum was no longer considered acceptable, and it became apparent that no student could master more than a small fraction of human knowledge. As a consequence, academic departments were created, and the practice of majoring in a specific subject became common. The transformation of colleges into universities also created, on the graduate level, an orientation toward research as well as teaching. Graduate education became devoted primarily to the increase, rather than simply the transmission, of knowledge. These changes inevitably resulted in a splintering of formal learning into ever smaller segments, which led in turn to even narrower scholarly specialization. John Higham, professor of history at the Johns Hopkins University, wrote:

> Because specialization narrows the competence of each individual
> and makes him more dependent on others, a democratic society must

either resist specialization or welcome it indiscriminately. When modernization made the advance of specialization inevitable, Americans set out to give everyone an opportunity to become an expert in some area. . . . Not only did the Americans narrow and intensify the work required for the Ph.D., so that it became a certificate of specialization, they also created a system in which every Ph.D. could aspire to his own independent sphere of influence. This was done by organizing university faculties into departments. In a department, a number of autonomous Ph.D.s divided responsibility for a field of knowledge. Every one of those Ph.D.s could have unchallenged control of his little portion of the field.[2]

Curtis Benjamin compared the continual fractionalization of knowledge to the growth of a mighty tree. As scholars become more specialized, the books that result from their research become more specialized. For Benjamin, the subjects of specialized books represent twigs on the tree of knowledge.[3] The number of specialized monographs—Benjamin's "twig books"—multiplies as the tree grows, but the twigs themselves are no larger or more important.

Scholarly publishing has struggled to accommodate the explosion of knowledge that it has played a role in creating. Since World War II, in particular, the exponential growth of academic specialization has strained the scholarly publishing environment. The National Enquiry into Scholarly Communication said of this strain: "In this kind of situation, many organisms (or writings) cannot survive, and evolution takes place more rapidly. There is intense competition for survival; thus it can be said that publication is too difficult. There is also more published than the system (or the mind of a scholar) can absorb or sustain; thus it can equally be said that publication is too easy."[4]

Some compare the publication of specialized monographs to the fitting together of a jigsaw puzzle or the gradual building of a great cathedral. But August Frugé, director emeritus of the University of California Press, believes that although scholars at times may indeed stand on the shoulders of other scholars, scholarship itself is not a huge cooperative structure, with thousands of little gaps to be filled in by diligent workers. He wrote facetiously:

When an editorial committee is considering a competent but un-exciting work on a subject of no great importance, someone is sure to announce that Professor X has filled a gap. When the ribald laughter has died down, we can understand that he has fitted a piece into the great puzzle or has fashioned a minor building block, and if we will only put it into place by publication, then other workers can make other blocks and put them in place on top or around it. And so upward and outward to the eventual glory of human knowledge.[5]

This approach is a teleological view of scholarship. The puzzle parts are not important individually, but are important in completing the puzzle. Frugé, however, believes each work, to deserve publication, must make a major contribution of its own.

Morris Philipson, director of the University of Chicago Press, said that university presses often are caricatured as publishing hard-core pedantry. He wrote:

> This is as true, let's say, as the caricature of academics as deter-mined to learn more and more about less and less. These are un-sympathetic descriptions of the value of specialization. Without an interest in the intellectual study of literature, what can one do but laugh at the appearance of a scholarly monograph on the role of the confidante in six novels by Henry James? Without an interest in history, what can one do but sneer at the appearance of a 600-page book . . . on the influence of Roman law on the government of the Holy Roman Empire? Without an interest in sociology, or psy-chology, or political science, nothing published by scholars working in those disciplines of thought will appear of any value. But then, the person without these interests is unsympathetic, because he is outside looking in.[6]

Philipson also pointed out that publishers face a dilemma in making spe-cialized knowledge known to nonspecialists:

> Somewhere beyond the ordinary layman making fun of arcane studies and the American ideal of egalitarianism, somewhere be-tween those two positions is a vague assumption that knowledge ought to be common, available to everyone. . . . How do you talk with

a layman about particle physics, or field and ring theory in mathematics, or debates over the nature of evolution in biology, or even over differences of points of view in literary theory? There are different languages being spoken, and unless you learn the language you cannot really understand what a thing says.

There is an enormous effort that takes place in this country in an attempt to bridge the gap between specialized knowledge being developed in academic institutions and what the layman can understand. Even Sunday supplement newspaper journalism feeds on that, more often than not making the mistake of trying to be sensational. But it's a very difficult row to hoe, because you're trying to engage the attention of someone who has no known interest in a given field of thought.[7]

❦ The Advantages of Listbuilding

The scholars who write most of the books published by university presses are specialists, be it in Tudor England, micro-economics, or the antebellum South. To be successfully published, scholars must recognize this truth: just as scholars now specialize, so do university presses. Some presses publish books on Tudor England; others shun the topic. A micro-economics manuscript would interest the MIT Press but would not interest the Louisiana State University Press. Conversely, LSU would express interest in a work on the antebellum South, while MIT would not.

The reason for this specialization is the acknowledgement among scholarly publishers that few presses can publish successfully in all fields. The tree of knowledge has grown too big. Academe has grown too specialized. The audience has grown too diverse.

Today, few university presses invite manuscript submissions in all disciplines. Instead, most scholarly presses specialize in selected subject fields, as an aid to both editorial and marketing functions. Each seeks to establish its own distinctive identity in scholarly publishing by specifying areas of specialty. This is called listbuilding. The "list" (of books in print) represents the areas in which a press chooses to publish programmatically.

Listbuilding has numerous editorial advantages. Because of the increasing fractionalization of knowledge, no editor can keep abreast of the latest developments in all disciplines. The puzzle has too many pieces; the cathedral has too many building blocks. By concentrating on limited areas, an editor can become more knowledgeable concerning developments in designated interest areas. This expertise in turn makes the editor more effective in cultivating and nurturing personal acquaintances with scholars in these areas. The editor can, at least superficially, stay abreast of the literature in the assigned areas, can attend a few annual meetings of relevant learned societies, and avoid fretting about other society meetings.

Another advantage of listbuilding is that editors can deal summarily with unsolicited manuscripts that fall outside the press's list. "If this doesn't seem a whopping big time-saving advantage, just ask any over-taxed acquisitions editor," said J.G. Goellner, director of Johns Hopkins University Press. "The editor presumably has to say no in nine cases out of ten, and it certainly saves time to be able to say no without reading the manuscript."[8]

Finally, a press that specifies its listbuilding territory can develop a reputation as a specialist in certain disciplines. This reputation provides visibility and helps attract the best of authors in the discipline.

Listbuilding by university presses also has marketing advantages. Promotion and marketing managers agree that it is more productive and cost-efficient to promote a list that is focused in relatively few areas than one that is randomly assembled and consists largely of "orphans"—books published without other new or old ("backlist") titles to support them.

The importance of listbuilding is evident in the importance of backlist sales in university publishing. The backlist consists of all titles still in print but not on the current year's list. While some established commercial houses have strong backlist sales, most trade publishers depend on sales during the year of publication. In contrast, scholarly publishers rely on consistent sales across the years. At the University of Chicago Press, about two-thirds of the press's income from book sales comes from its backlist. At Princeton University Press, backlist sales represent more than 60 percent of total sales.[9] Many university presses depend on backlist sales to support current ("frontlist") publication.

From a marketing standpoint, then, it is crucial to have a frontlist of new titles sufficiently related to the backlist titles so that both groups can be promoted together. "Many prospective authors erroneously assume we wouldn't be interested in their projects because we've published other titles in the same or in a related field," said Barbara Hanrahan, humanities editor at the University of Wisconsin Press. Actually, the reverse is more likely to be true. Presses want to develop a list of closely related books. Publishing a book that bears little relation to the press's list, no matter how worthy that book might be, usually forces the press to expend an inordinately large percentage of the marketing budget to reach an entirely new audience.

The National Enquiry into Scholarly Communication gave presses a specific recommendation on this matter:

> No American scholarly press is large enough to publish effectively in all disciplines. A press in a large university may be under pressure from 30 or 40 departments to publish in their fields. Politically, since the press is supported by and is intended to serve the university, it is difficult to resist these pressures, especially when works of undoubted quality are offered. But the press may have the capacity to publish only 30 to 50 books per year, and if it publishes only one or two titles a year in a field, it cannot market them efficiently. Roughly, a press can have 10 specialties if it publishes 50 books a year, or six if it publishes 30. It should plan and, on the average, publish about five books per year in each field in which it specializes. The fields of specialization must be carefully chosen by the staff and the board of the press, keeping in mind the strengths of the university and the press's previous performance.[10]

Malcolm MacDonald, director of the University of Alabama Press, said that while he tries to follow those guidelines, it is difficult for a press that publishes only several dozen new titles a year. He said that acquiring five worthy titles in each area of specialty is "easy to do if you're a Harvard or Yale, but not that easy for an Alabama. On our list are some very, very fine books that are orphans. Still, the National Enquiry's recommendation is sound, and it undergirds our thinking."

Proper listbuilding, then, means having to say "no" to manuscripts that fall outside the designated list. Editors, of course, may make an exception for an extraordinary manuscript. In general, however, most university presses do not consider manuscripts outside their lists. "Unless a press is willing to decide that there are a number of academic disciplines in which it will not publish, it will by default continue to publish whatever meritorious book comes its way regardless of the subject," Goellner said. "That's what most presses have done for most of the history of university publishing in America. It has been the easiest thing to do. It might no longer be the best." [11]

Goellner noted that listbuilding still has room for opportunism: "One of the glories of listbuilding is the opportunity to be eclectic—to a point. In my view, a press should focus its listbuilding, but it should also be open to that unexpected and wonderful book that doesn't really fit the list but is too good to pass over. The press must simply be sure that the book really is that good; and if it chooses to publish, it should do so knowing exactly what it is doing."

Fred Woodward of the University Press of Kansas has succeeded in focusing the press's list since becoming director in 1981. "The press published all over the map," he said. "It was eclectic. Yet there was almost no political science publishing." That was unusual, since the cornerstone of the Kansas press is a series of histories of the American presidencies. Twenty volumes had appeared through 1988. All other volumes have been commissioned except for the one covering the presidency of Ronald Reagan. Since Woodward's arrival, the Kansas press has sought to complement the series by developing a list in presidency-related titles. "It was inescapably clear to me that we had to develop specialty areas in publishing—and publish at a minimum three or four titles a year in those areas —to develop a presence in the field and to sustain a reputation for publishing good books," Woodward said. "But it's also inescapably clear to me that we cannot shut the door to manuscripts outside our areas of specialization that originate from the faculty of our six universities." He said that the press never rules out an outstanding manuscript, even when it falls outside the designated lists, particularly if written by a home author. "Yet I'm keenly aware of the disproportionate burden that 'incompatible' books place on an already overworked staff. We cannot blindly follow our specializations, but we must be convinced that publishing the odd book will have some sort of reward that offsets the considerable penalties."

Listbuilding by university presses is delightfully diverse. The University of Pennsylvania Press publishes in such disparate fields as linguistics, folklore, and economic theory. The list at the University of Illinois Press ranges from film studies to child development to working-class histories.

The University of Nebraska Press pursues studies in such unrelated areas as agriculture, psychology, and music.

The list is where a press creates its own niche in the crowded world of scholarly publishing. Iowa State University Press seeks manuscripts on aviation, Kent State University Press has a list in utopian studies, and MIT Press publishes works dealing with artificial intelligence. Columbia University Press pursues astronomy and space science studies, LSU Press has an interest in jazz manuscripts, and Indiana University Press publishes in semiotics. Considering how university presses share the common goal of intellectual inquiry, it is remarkable how diverse their lists have become.

❦ How Presses Choose Their Lists

University presses do not conspire in the development of their specialty areas. Each press develops its own list, and that list may undergo continual modification. This means overlapping and competition among presses in some scholarly areas, while other areas may be underrepresented.

The character of a list derives from four factors: the strengths of the parent university, the publishing heritage of the press, the sales potential of various fields of inquiry, and the scholarly interests of the editors themselves.

The first consideration in the formation of a list is the press's desire to reflect strengths of its parent institution. A university press, however, cannot be a full-length mirror. Scholarly research in any university is too diffuse. But a press has an obligation to reflect at least some of the particular strengths and emerging interests of the parent institution. The University Press of Virginia emphasizes U.S. colonial studies and architectural histories. The University of Hawaii Press, logically, specializes in Asian and Pacific studies. The Duke University Press list is tied closely to the academic specialties of the parent institution. Duke has a center on aging, and the press publishes books about gerontology and medical care for the poor and elderly. Duke has an institute in science and human values, and the press publishes in the field of ethics. Duke has a divinity school, and the press publishes in religion. Duke has an international studies center, and the press publishes policy studies along with Soviet and Eastern European studies.

Creating complications is the fact that some university presses have multiple parent institutions. The presses in Colorado, Florida, Kansas, Kentucky, Mississippi, Tennessee, and Virginia are among those serving state campus systems or state consortiums. As a multi-state consortium, the University Press of New England serves an unusually broad range of scholarly interests at its campuses. The nine consortium members are Brandeis University, Brown University, Clark University, University of Connecticut, Dartmouth College, University of New Hampshire, University of Rhode Island, Tufts University, and the University of Vermont. "If we serve our members, we can't be too narrow," said Thomas McFarland, director of the New England press. So its list ranges from Judaic studies, recognizing a strength of Brandeis, to Renaissance writings, recognizing a strength of Dartmouth. Acknowledging the diversity of its offerings, the University Press of New England opened one of its catalogs with this unusual message:

> "All publishers are rotten pimps and I hate every one of them, but you must accept their usefulness." That was the opinion of Louis-Ferdinand Celine, the controversial mid–twentieth century French writer who appears prominently on our Spring 1986 list as both author and subject. . . . This is outrageous and offensive; yet, as sometimes happens in Celine's writing, the slander contains a core of truth that might not otherwise be conveyed so memorably. Like most publishers, we try not to take ourselves too seriously. We are indeed middlemen. We purvey intellectual, artistic and emotional sustenance, the fruits of our authors' creations, to readers whose hungers and needs are every bit as real as the physical ones to which Celine alludes. We hope that the fine and diverse list which we present . . . will satisfy a wide variety of readers and book buyers. With such a list, we are pleased to reassert our usefulness.

The second consideration in the formation of a university press list is the publishing heritage of the press. Some presses have longstanding reputations based on their lists. Through the years, the University of North Carolina Press has been best known for southern studies. Starting in the 1930s, the press published critical studies concerning education, tenant farming, child labor, and race relations in the South. This aggressive publishing program in controversial areas brought financial support from northern foundations and praise from eminent scholars. At one point, noted historians Henry Steele Commager and Allan Nevins even declared North Carolina to be the best of the nation's university presses.[12] Today, the University of North Carolina Press continues to emphasize southern studies.

The University of Minnesota Press has developed a reputation in health sciences. The best-known Minnesota title is *The Doctors Mayo* (1941), acclaimed as one of the great medical biographies. Minnesota's health sciences list really began expanding in 1981, assisted by a $100,000 foundation grant. The health sciences list includes clinical works, medical history, and instructional books for the lay reader.[13]

Some presses are mandated to restrict their lists to certain fields. The Naval Institute Press is limited by its charter to maritime studies. All manuscripts must be water-related, be they biographies, histories, or fiction. Gallaudet University Press publishes only in deaf studies, since the parent institution is a school for the deaf. Teachers College Press publishes only in education. Catholic University of America Press publishes primarily in philosophy, theology, European history, and medieval and Renaissance literature. "We're a Catholic institution, and we publish with that in mind," said director David McGonagle.

Newer university presses have no publishing heritage, so they have more flexibility in listbuilding. The University of Arkansas Press was established in 1980. "We'll take our list where our manuscripts lead us," said Miller Williams, the press director. "Our list is still defining itself. There's a self-generating effect." In 1983, the Arkansas press published *China and the Overseas Chinese in the United States, 1868–1911*, by Shih-shan Henry Tsai. "Within a few months," Williams said, "we had received a dozen submissions in the general field of China-U.S. relations. We didn't like any of them well enough to publish. But if we had, we might well have become known as a press that publishes in China-American relations."

By publishing the China book, the press had opened the gates; the press quickly closed them. "The press would have had to print a form letter to handle the flood," Williams said. "Writers send manuscript proposals to presses that publish in what they write." Williams used as a metaphor the formation of planets: "When little masses come together into a larger mass, the gravity center becomes greater. If you publish four, you attract eight. Publish eight and you attract sixteen. The mass of the submissions grows exponentially. It's an example of snowballing. The reason I like an astronomical metaphor more than snowballing is that you're not going downhill—but you may be going in circles!"

The third consideration in the formation of a list is the sales potential of particular fields of inquiry. Libraries serve as the leading institutional buyers of university press books. But as the library sales percentage declines, publishers recognize the need to appeal to individual book buyers. Editors routinely state that American historians buy books, and so do bird lovers; poets don't, and neither do literary critics or theorists. This doesn't mean that university presses flock to bird-book writers and shun the proposals of literature professors. But in time, editors said, sales records cannot help but influence the development of a publisher's list.

For example, the University Press of Kansas still publishes literary criticism, but less of it than it once did. The press also publishes fewer books in European history and Slavic studies—two other traditional low-sales categories. In their place, the Kansas press is publishing more political science, social and political philosophy, military studies, and twentieth-century American history—scholarly fields with more active buying audiences.

Lists are not static; they are continually evolving. Texas Christian University Press was facing extinction when Keith Gregory moved from the English Department faculty to the press directorship in 1982. His first priority was to devise areas of specialization that were economically viable. The press decided to emphasize rhetoric and composition, religion, sports, young adult books, fiction, Texas and Southwest studies, and the American presidency. Gregory, who has since moved to Southern Methodist University Press as director, said that the TCU Press started a list in presidential studies because a benefactor was willing to underwrite scholarly books in that field.

Finally, the interests of the editors themselves constitute an important factor in the formation of a list. Most university press directors and senior acquisitions editors—the people most likely to influence the development of a press's list—majored in the humanities while in school. In fact, half of the directors and editors who were polled reported having academic backgrounds in English or history. That should not be surprising. Disciplines such as English and history, because of their emphases on the written word, are obvious training grounds for publishers. Other leading fields of study for directors and editors included economics, philosophy, and education. Only a few editorial personnel reported having an academic background in the natural sciences. The scholastic backgrounds of university press directors and editors do, quite naturally, influence the direction of a press's listbuilding efforts.

❦ The Humanities and Social Sciences

University presses publish primarily in the humanities and social sciences. In a 1948 study, Yale University Press director Chester Kerr found that 52 percent of the books published by university presses were in the humanities, 34 percent in the social sciences, and 14 percent in the natural sciences. Two decades later, Kerr found little change. A 1968 sampling showed the same 52 percent in the humanities, 37 percent in the social sciences, and 11 percent in the natural sciences.[14]

Such categorization would be difficult today. The category known as "the humanities" consists of such mainstays as history, literary criticism, and philosophy. The "social sciences" include political science, anthropology, sociology, and economics. Yet categorization increasingly depends on research methodology. For instance, many presses consider archaeology to be in the humanities along with classical studies. Other presses consider archaeology to be a social science because of its increasing emphasis on computer simulations. Broad categorizations, then, must be made with caution.

It certainly is safe to say that history is the most common listbuilding area among university presses. Table 2.1 shows that almost all university presses specify history as a listbuilding area. Also in the humanities, more than two out of three university presses specify literary criticism as a listbuilding area, and 60 percent list philosophy as a publishing focus.

Among the social sciences, more than two-thirds of the presses specify political science as a listbuilding area. There is also strong interest in anthropology and sociology. A smaller number of university presses seek

TABLE 2.1

Leading Listbuilding Areas of University Presses

The Humanities	No. of Presses (N=80)
History	74 (93%)
Literary Criticism	56 (70%)
Philosophy	48 (60%)

Social Sciences	(N=80)
Political Science	57 (71%)
Anthropology	54 (67%)
Sociology	46 (57%)

Natural Sciences	(N=80)
Biological Sciences	42 (52%)
Earth Sciences	20 (25%)
Physical Sciences	17 (21%)

Note: Data based on specified listbuilding areas of the 80 American university members of the Association of American University Presses, as given in the 1988–89 AAUP Directory.

manuscripts in the natural sciences, with the biological sciences a more popular listbuilding area than the physical or earth sciences.

The listbuilding designations of university presses are intended to encourage the submission of manuscripts in the named disciplines. But presses seldom strictly adhere to their lists. For instance, the fact that somewhat more than half of the presses specify sociology as a listbuilding area doesn't necessarily mean the rest would shun an outstanding sociological study, should it come to their attention. A publishing list simply announces a press's preferred areas of intellectual inquiry.

Rather than specify listbuilding areas by discipline or interest area, some university presses list the broad areas of "the humanities" or "social sciences." Some presses, such as Fordham University Press and the University of Pittsburgh Press, keep their listbuilding areas deliberately wide

TABLE 2.2

Other Listbuilding Areas of University Presses

Academic Disciplines	No. of Presses (N=80)
Art History/Criticism	41 (51%)
Religion	41 (51%)
Environment/Conservation	39 (49%)
Archaeology	38 (47%)
Architecture	38 (47%)
Film Studies	36 (45%)
Music	36 (45%)
Language	34 (42%)
Psychology	34 (42%)
Economics	33 (41%)
Classics	32 (40%)
Medicine	32 (40%)
Education	31 (39%)
Law	28 (35%)
Geography	27 (34%)
Child Development	26 (33%)
Photography	26 (33%)
Drama/Theatre	24 (30%)
Military Studies	23 (29%)
Journalism	21 (26%)
Public Health	21 (26%)
Agriculture	20 (25%)
Gerontology	20 (25%)
Business	19 (24%)
Psychiatry	19 (24%)
Demography	17 (21%)
Broadcast Media	16 (20%)
Dance	15 (19%)
Publishing	15 (19%)
Astronomy	14 (18%)
Computer Sciences	11 (14%)
Social Work	11 (14%)

TABLE 2.2
Continued

Academic Disciplines	No. of Presses (N=80)
Veterinary Sciences	10 (13%)
Engineering	8 (10%)
Mathematics	7 (9%)
Library Science	6 (8%)

in order to choose from an assortment of proposals. Others, such as the University Presses of Florida, do so because they serve a consortium of universities with a wide array of interests. Still others, such as the Harvard, Yale, and Princeton presses, publish enough titles each year that a manuscript on almost any topic would fit at least one existing list.

Table 2.2 shows other listbuilding areas by academic discipline. Roughly half of the presses list art history and criticism, religion, environment and conservation topics, archaeology, architecture, film studies, and music as publishing areas. On the bottom end, few university presses publish programmatically in such disciplines as computer science, social work, veterinary science, engineering, mathematics, and library science.

Overall, history is the most common area of scholarly publication. But history encompasses a wide spectrum of academic interests. So in order to take advantage of the editorial and marketing concepts behind specialization and listbuilding, university presses frequently specify interest areas within the broad framework of history. American history, for example, is a popular subspecialization. Some presses specify listbuilding areas even more narrowly. While the University Press of Virginia publishes U.S. colonial history, the Kent State University Press has a special interest in U.S. diplomatic history. Texas A&M University Press and the University of South Carolina Press both emphasize military history, and the University of New Mexico Press publishes American frontier history.

Another concept of listbuilding concentrates on population groups. Women's studies, in particular, has shown remarkable academic vitality in recent years. Table 2.3 shows that three out of four university presses now invite manuscripts in women's studies. Fewer than half of the presses

TABLE 2.3

Special Listbuilding Subdivisions of University Presses

Population Groups	No. of Presses (N=80)
Women's Studies	60 (75%)
Black Studies	39 (49%)
Ethnic Studies	38 (47%)
American Indian Studies	36 (45%)

Cultural Regions and Peoples	(N=80)
American Studies	57 (71%)
Latin American Studies	37 (46%)
European Studies	29 (36%)
Middle Eastern Studies	26 (33%)
Asian Studies	25 (31%)
African Studies	23 (29%)
Near Eastern Studies	21 (26%)
Pacific Studies	15 (19%)
Canadian Studies	10 (13%)

Miscellaneous Categories	(N=80)
Biography	61 (76%)
Regional Studies	58 (73%)
Urban Studies	36 (45%)
Bibliography/Reference	34 (42%)

invite submissions in black or Afro-American studies, ethnic studies, and American Indian studies. In addition, presses also develop lists related to cultural regions and peoples. The vast majority of university presses invite manuscripts in American studies. Almost half of the presses do the same in Latin American studies, with declining levels of interest in European studies, Middle Eastern studies, Asian studies, African studies, and the like. Some presses emphasize areas appropriate to the cultural history of their states or constituencies. Catholic University of America Press has a list in Irish studies, LSU Press in French studies, the University of Minnesota Press in Nordic area studies, and the University of Nevada Press in studies of the Basque peoples of Europe and the Americas.

Presses also publish books about their geographical regions. The University of Nebraska Press and the University Press of Kansas seek manuscripts on the Great Plains. The University Press of Kentucky and the University of Tennessee Press publish Appalachian studies. New York University Press invites submissions concerning New York. Generally, southern presses express automatic interest in manuscripts dealing with the South, and western presses similarly welcome Western Americana topics.

Between certain fields, it may be difficult to draw clear lines of separation. A history of blacks in southern politics certainly falls into the category of history, but also fits the listbuilding categories of black studies, political science, and southern studies. It may fit other categories as well, depending on methodology and on whether a historian, a political scientist, a sociologist, or a journalist conducted the study. Because each category represents a group of potential book buyers, a list is designed to avoid narrowing interest areas unnecessarily, while still providing books on specific topics of interest.

Another popular listbuilding area among university presses is literary criticism. Although many university presses are cutting back on new titles in literary criticism because of declining sales, only two presses—the University of Arizona Press and Utah State University Press—specifically state that submissions in literary criticism are not welcome. Other presses at least leave open the possibility of publication.

To leave open the possibility of publishing in a particular field, however, means having to deal with queries and manuscripts in that field. As a result, many presses specify areas in which manuscripts are not considered. The University of Notre Dame Press does not publish in psychology, Georgetown University Press avoids music and drama, and the University of Hawaii Press shuns Latin American studies. Syracuse University Press does not consider manuscripts in ancient history and the classics, and Texas Tech University Press does not publish in education or the social sciences. Such prohibitions free the press to deal summarily with any proposal or manuscript in these fields.

❦ Publishing the Natural Sciences

Although university presses publish primarily in the humanities and social sciences, many of them publish in some aspect of the natural sciences. Few, however, offer as broad a list in the natural sciences as they do in the humanities and social sciences.

For instance, while 42 of the 80 American university presses invite manuscripts in some aspect of the biological sciences, no single science discipline attracts that many interested presses. Botany is a listbuilding area at 30 presses, zoology at 26, marine biology at 18, genetics at 16, and microbiology and physiology at 13 each. In the earth sciences, geology is cited as a listbuilding area at 15 presses, oceanography at 13, and geochemistry at 6.

Through the years, university presses have yielded responsibility for the publication of science monographs to commercial publishers. Why?

One reason is historical. Even in the formative years of university publishing, the presses never fully mirrored the strengths of their parent institutions. The presses began with the humanities and social sciences and through the years have been sustained by them. The fields of science, medicine, law, and engineering were well served from the beginning by commercial publishers who found the areas profitable.[15]

A second reason is editorial preference. According to Michael Aronson, now a general editor at Harvard University Press: "University press directors and editors, by and large, have been educated in the humanities and have little knowledge of or interest in the natural sciences. So in 1945, when university presses entered upon their modern period of growth and the post-war boom in science began, science publishing became, by default, captive to the commercial publisher."[16]

A third reason is the marketplace. The potential readers of scholarly monographs in the humanities and social sciences are almost always found within academe. The potential readers of monographs in the natural sciences, however, are just as likely to work in a research institute or private industry as in higher education. Many university presses have not developed sophisticated marketing tools to reach such disparate audiences.

A fourth reason for the dearth of science publishing is timeliness. Scientists—far more than scholars in the humanities—build upon the work of others. Therefore, research in the natural sciences has a greater need for immediate publication. As a Canadian study noted:

In the humanities, the classic works of literature and criticism retain indefinitely, and even enhance with time, their original significance. By contrast, the original disclosure of even the most seminal discovery in science and engineering seldom retains the standing of a literary masterpiece. Moreover, the progressive development of scientific knowledge requires of its 'literature' a cumulative capacity and an austere style. The difference has been brought out succinctly by the advice of an eminent literary authority: 'In science read, by preference, the newest works; in literature, the oldest.' The vitality and the productivity of science depend, in fact, on a communication system that ensures the precise and comprehensive diffusion of research results within the shortest practical time.[17]

Tied directly to the need for fast publication is a final reason why university presses fail to publish science—a difference in preferred method of diffusion. Since the predominant form of publication in the natural sciences is the journal article, often thirty or fewer pages in length, the natural sciences are less dependent than other fields on book-length studies. Conversely, the humanities and social sciences are more analytical and interpretative in nature. A writer here can spend three hundred or more pages analyzing, say, rhetoric as social imagination or the idea of good in Platonic-Aristotelian philosophy. But a writer in the hard sciences relies more on provable theory than on unprovable logic. For instance, Albert Einstein's 1916 paper on general relativity runs about sixty pages—an enormous length for a paper of pure theory in physics.

Not only is journal publication usually faster than book publication, but, compared to journals, books also carry other burdens: higher publication costs and short printruns that lead to high retail prices.

Interestingly, Curtis Benjamin's "twig book" concept originally applied to the publication of scientific research. When a new field forms from the conjunction of two old ones, the new field naturally has fewer adherents and practitioners than either of the old ones. Thus, from organic chemistry and physical chemistry came physical organic chemistry. This trend toward increasing specialization keeps potential audiences small, creating the dilemma of expensive publishing procedures for short printruns.[18]

Books, though, laid the foundations of science. In 1869, Charles Darwin presented his investigations as evidence for a particular theory of evolution in *Origin of Species*. Other crucial works were Newton's *Principia* and Lyell's *Principles of Geology*. Nevertheless, seldom is a scientist opening up virgin territory; often he or she is filling gaps in knowledge. For the sake of one's career, research must be published quickly because others may be working on the same problem. The natural outlet, then, is the vast network of specialized learned journals.[19]

Today, since the natural method of diffusion for scientific research is the journal article, most scientific monographs are designed to integrate the findings of many researchers and so to define the consensus of knowledge in a particular area of science. Often such projects are planned as books from the beginning, usually with advance contracts signed before the author commences writing. University presses typically do not assume such publishing risks, because their editorial committees want to maintain control over the quality of books finally published.

University press editors wish that scientists would write books explaining the public implications of scientific policy. "We cannot seem to get science beyond the scientists. If concerned nonspecialists can't understand the scientific debate, so much for public policy questions," said David Holtby, editor and associate director of the University of New Mexico Press. "We are not reaching the general public as much as we are the decision-makers."

Holtby said that university press books need to make it to the second level in a two-step flow. "Our books are aimed at the first tier. We can't really make the leap from those who make the ideas to the public. If communicated, it must be filtered down. It's all very scholastical—debated like how many angels can you get on the head of a pin. It's so specialized. They end up writing papers that are so narrow [because of] their specialized training."

In the social sciences, Holtby said, there are "no hard answers—it's the logic that matters." But in the natural sciences, he believes that "scholars have become very narrow and cautious because hard answers are possible. We do have a few grand thinkers who like to think in philosophical terms. But not many."

Another problem is that scientists have trouble writing in a style accessible to the public. Holtby is looking for science writers who can do what Harvard University Press's authors did in genetics, sociobiology, and genetic engineering—produce science books that are readable and that touch the general public. "The best science writers are on newspapers," Holtby said. "But they often are such generalists that they aren't suited to write books."

❦ Symbiosis Between Editors and Authors

Biologists and historians, physicists and anthropologists—they all are members of the same intellectual communities. At different times they may function as authors, outside readers, or editorial committee members, playing different roles in different situations. Scholars are in a symbiotic relationship with one another in the publishing process. Similarly, scholars and academic editors, who control the gates of the book acquisition process, serve as partners in the process of scholarly communication.

Many university press directors are scholars themselves. In fact, the National Enquiry into Scholarly Communication found that two out of five university press directors hold academic rank simultaneously with their administrative position.[20] Directors and editors alike cited a trend to hire persons with graduate degrees to fill key vacancies. This usually means a master's degree, but an increasing number of Ph.D.s are entering scholarly publishing. Still, a large number of directors and editors have a bachelor's degree as their highest educational attainment.

At a convention of the Association of American University Presses in the 1970s, a Harvard University history professor caused a mild uproar by recommending that all university press editors acquire the Ph.D., so that faculty members might speak to them as equals. Edward Tripp, editor-at-large for Yale University Press, responded to that recommendation by writing, "This is impractical. Scholars can get along with one Ph.D.; editors would need one for each of the several disciplines that most of them deal with. No, although they may be well informed in one or two fields, they are doomed to remain essentially amateurs in a world of professionals."[21] Still, a number of university press directors and editors have come from the faculty ranks or from graduate programs. The director of Catholic University of America Press, David McGonagle, is a

Ph.D. and a faculty member in classics. Before becoming press director, he first served as executive assistant to the provost and then as university registrar. Others in university press work had intended to enter the professorate but became sidetracked at the start into scholarly publishing. Henry Tom, executive editor at Johns Hopkins University Press, in 1975 earned a Ph.D. in Renaissance history at the University of Chicago. "Many who would have taught a decade earlier went into publishing because of the tight academic market," Tom explained. This, he said, is good for scholarly publishing: "Because so many of us have advanced degrees, editors are better equipped to know where scholarship is moving because of our own personal interest in it."

One of the leading figures in scholarly publishing today is Morris Philipson, director of the University of Chicago Press. Following a Fulbright fellowship in Munich, he received the Ph.D. degree from Columbia University in 1959. He was a lecturer in philosophy at New York's Hunter College when the city ran into difficulty preparing its school budget. During that time of limbo, Alfred A. Knopf asked Philipson to join his company as editor of the new Vintage line. Philipson later worked for Random House and then for Basic Books, founded by Arthur Rosenthal, now director of Harvard University Press. Eight years after entering publishing, Philipson had become director of the University of Chicago Press, where he now directs a staff of more than two hundred. Philipson has won praise not only as a publisher of other people's books but also as an author himself. His scholarly work on Jungian aesthetics, stemming from his doctoral dissertation, is only one of his several published nonfiction books. He has also written a biography of Leo Tolstoy for teenagers and five novels—the latest an award-winner for Simon and Schuster. His writing career had a familiar beginning, though. His first novel was rejected by twenty-two U.S. publishers before it was published overseas.

Fred Woodward, director of the University Press of Kansas, said, "Like most people, I backed into scholarly publishing." Woodward was pursuing a Ph.D. degree in English at Tulane but never started the dissertation because he decided that he didn't want to teach. "I was married and had started a family. It had come time for gainful employment," Woodward said with a smile. An aunt actually planted in his mind the idea of working for a scholarly press. He went to the library, copied names and addresses from the latest *Literary Market Place*, and sent out blind letters. The University of South Carolina Press responded favorably. Woodward's first assignment was to edit *Jacob Eckhard's Choirmaster's Book of 1809*. He spent eleven years at the South Carolina press—first as a manuscript editor, then as marketing director—before becoming director of the Kansas press in 1981.

Other directors came to university presses with commercial publishing experience. Matthew Hodgson of the University of North Carolina Press worked for Houghton Mifflin and for the University Press of Kentucky before returning to his alma mater. Dick Rowson, after serving as president of three commercial houses, was hired from his consulting business to revitalize Duke University Press. Thomas McFarland worked at the University of California Press, Johns Hopkins University Press, and a small textbook publisher before becoming director of the University Press of New England.

David Gilbert, director of Cornell University Press, found some interesting trends when he conducted a survey of the backgrounds of sixty university press directors.[22] Half of those who became directors before 1970 entered the world of publishing through a university press, and a quarter of them entered through commercial publishing. The ratio evened out, half and half, for directors appointed between 1970 and 1975. But among directors appointed after 1975, almost two of three started in commercial publishing. Similarly, the first job in publishing for longtime directors tended to be an editorial position. Among more recent directors, the first job in publishing tended to be in marketing. Gilbert's study found that more than 90 percent of the directors were male, about a quarter had teaching experience, and almost half had worked in commercial publishing at some point.

The typical career paths of acquisitions editors are similar. One senior editor completed doctoral coursework but not the dissertation and worked in the college division of a commercial publisher before joining a prestigious university press. Another editor completed an M.A. degree in creative writing and went straight into university publishing. Salaries range from the low $20s to the $40s and higher for acquisitions editors, depending on the person's educational background and publishing experience and depending on the press' overall salary structure.

Being an editor offers both satisfactions and frustrations. James Twiggs spent fourteen years as an editor at Cornell University Press and now is acquisitions editor at the University of Arkansas Press. Twiggs said the life of an editor is attractive because "editing is a safe profession, like being a therapist or a midwife. You're not having the baby yourself." But the safety of the profession can be a frustration, because, although editors may be on the frontiers of scholarship, they are there as observers rather than as creators of scholarship. One editor wrote, "There are satisfactions . . . for the intellectually omnivorous. At a university press, the editor is at the growing point of many intellectual disciplines. On the other hand, he must resign himself to being only a dilettante of these disciplines, at once a Casanova doomed to a life of flirtations and a midwife to other people's children."[23]

The goal of scholarly editors is to attract for publication the best works possible. Without exception, editors said senior scholars make the greatest contributions to intellectual life, because they bring to a manuscript a deeper understanding of a discipline and a freedom in their writing. Still, many books published by university presses are by junior scholars.

In a polling of fifty-two university press directors, a third estimated that first-time authors write half or more of the books they publish. Another third, however, estimated that first-time authors write fewer than a quarter of the books they publish, with the remaining third in-between. Presses do not maintain such information, since it is not of operational significance to them, so these are only estimates. But with much of the frontlist obviously claimed by experienced authors, it is no wonder that first-time authors may feel hard pressed to get published.

Naomi Pascal, editor-in-chief at the University of Washington Press, enjoys finding and publishing the first-time author. "Part of our function is to identify and encourage promising young scholars," Pascal said. "But the authors who are easiest to deal with are often the most distinguished senior scholars. They have had experience in working with publishers, and they understand the proper division of responsibilities in the author/publisher relationship. Young scholars are more likely to feel that their careers are at stake, and their insecurity may make them either arrogant or unduly subservient." Senior scholars seldom have as much invested in their latest work, unless they consider it their *magnum opus*. They aren't initiating a reputation or facing the tenure gun. They are already at the full professor rank.

James Twiggs has dealt with hundreds of faculty members during his two decades with the Cornell and Arkansas presses. "I know how overbearing some assistant professors can be," Twiggs said with a chuckle. The author-editor relationship undergoes a transformation as the junior scholar evolves into a senior scholar. For the first-time author, Twiggs said, "the editor is the one doing the favors. He may praise the young scholar, but it's still the publisher with the upper hand. Along the way, the relationship switches—often after the first book. Then you try to get the scholar to sign an advance contract. You suddenly start going to dinner with him. The professor then has the upper hand—in most cases, I'm glad to say, for the betterment of everyone concerned."

❦ Reputations, Affiliations, and Tenure

Scholars in particular disciplines have reputations among editors. Almost all editors place historians at the top of their list of best writers. Editors favor the older historians with a finely developed sense of style. English professors also are judged to be writers of readable books. Political scientists, sociologists, and anthropologists tend to be ranked on the lower end of the readability spectrum.

Editors preferred anonymity for comments on this point—for good reason. "Anthropologists write with their toes," one editor from a western press said bluntly. "If you have a scale of one to ten, anthropologists will be around zero. They are by far the worst. People trained in English departments are good. Journalists are delightful. What journalists do best is take snapshots of the moment." Added an editor from a southern press, "History professors are the best writers. English professors are okay. Political scientists write confusingly. They use too much lingo. Linguists are the worst. Their writing is very muddled."

The institutional affiliation of an author once played a huge role in publishing. Editors agreed that those days may not be over, but they certainly are on the decline. One editor recalled once being an apprentice to an individual who placed great emphasis on the author's affiliation. "I used to get annoyed sometimes," the editor recalled. "But the individual grew up in an era when good people ended up at Harvard or Yale. If she got a manuscript from Mississippi State or from a community college, she started with a bias against the manuscript. But today, good people are ending up at small schools." As a result, a number of editors said they now seldom look at a vita at the beginning. Said one: "I'm becoming less impressed with academic credentials. The 'ivory tower' has a clay foundation."

Editors agreed that a letter from a Harvard or a Yale still carries prestige. "I always pay attention to a letter from the elite institutions," said Thomas McFarland, director of the University Press of New England, located on the Dartmouth campus. "But I don't toss aside a letterhead from Slippery Rock College. I see outstanding people who don't get tenure at Dartmouth. It's foolish to say there aren't good people at the smaller schools."

Another editor said that the scholar's institutional affiliation began to decline in importance during the 1970s. "Good people were ending up in Montana or at East Tennessee State," he said. "I won't say we don't look at letterheads, but we started using more of our own judgment, as we should have been doing all along."

Henry Tom, executive editor at Johns Hopkins University Press, added that where a scholar got his training once also was a telling fact. "You have very good mentors these days at small colleges and at state universities. People realized in the seventies that you don't have to be at an Ivy League institution to lead the good life. You could be at Williams or at Oberlin." Tom said that part of the challenge in scholarly publishing is to discover where the creative, original work is taking place. In history, the editor said, some of the best work is being done within such state systems as California, Michigan, and Wisconsin. He concluded, "The days of judging whether we're interested in a manuscript on the basis of academic affiliation—if the author is from so-and-so, it must be good—are disappearing."

Added editor-in-chief Naomi Pascal of the Washington press, "I don't think editors are as much influenced by an author's academic affiliation as they used to be. I have no prejudice against the Ivy League, but I know there are also fine scholars at state universities as well as at other, less well-known institutions. It's the quality of the manuscript that counts."

While the scholar's institutional home is receding somewhat in importance, several editors said that a bias still exists concerning academic qualifications. "If one doesn't have a doctorate, there is a certain amount of discrimination, I think," a southern editor said. "In the last year, I've seen a couple of manuscripts go down the river because of the lack of credentials, even though the manuscripts had good [outside] reviews." Other editors made similar observations.

Scholarly publishing increasingly plays an integral role in an institution's determination to grant tenure or promotion. The university press, because of its rigorous peer review process similar to that of refereed journals, has come to be viewed as an adjunct to the tenure and promotion system. Scholars are expected not only to engage in research but to engage in research judged worthy of dissemination.

Editors work to keep the publishing process separate from the tenure process, although authors and even tenure committees often want to merge the two. Almost every editor has a story to tell about an assistant professor who needed a quick decision on a manuscript because a book was needed as leverage in the tenure review process. Suzanne Comer, senior editor at Southern Methodist University Press, said she wishes she could remain ignorant of the consequences of a manuscript rejection. "I wish they [assistant professors] didn't tell you they were facing tenure," she said. "It's like students who tell you at the start of a semester that they need a certain grade to graduate. In the past, I know I have sometimes given special consideration to those who told me they were up for tenure. I kept seeing myself, when I came out of graduate school, in those pained faces. But it's risky getting too deep into this practice. We forget our purpose."

Editors may find themselves as advisors to tenure committees as well. Malcolm MacDonald, director of the University of Alabama Press, remembered getting two telephone calls just minutes apart from members of a promotion committee at the University of California at Irvine. Both wanted to know what the outside peer reviewers had said about a colleague's manuscript accepted but not yet published by the press. "I told the first caller that our readers were very complimentary, and I also told him that—to [the author's] credit—he never mentioned to me the promotion thing going on. Twenty minutes later, I got a call from another committee member. I was more harsh with him. I told him the author's scholarship was sound and told him I'm not in the business of advising promotion committees."

Dick Rowson, director of Duke University Press, said that university presses often operate in a highly charged internal and external political environment. He cited a time when one of his authors was rejected for tenure on the basis of an off-campus critic's evaluation of the scholarship as "specious." That made Rowson angry: "Their comments reflected on our board's editorial decision."

Cynthia Maude-Gembler of Syracuse University Press said that she occasionally realizes the power that she, in her role as acquisitions editor, may hold over careers. "Some days I'm more aware of it than others, like when someone is coming up for tenure," she said. "But I can't judge one's work on personal considerations. I can't endorse something that isn't good."

Another result of the tenure and promotion system in higher education can be a hurried manuscript. "An assistant professor facing tenure rushes into publication prematurely, so that he or she can at least say that something is under consideration if not under contract," one editor said. Academic tenure and promotion timetables can work to the advantage of scholarship by prodding scholars to engage in productive research. Yet the same timetables may work to the disadvantage of scholarship by encouraging premature publication.

James Langford, director of the University of Notre Dame Press, said that it is essential for university press books to maintain high standards of scholarship. Describing his publishing mission, Langford said:

> We are interested in good writing, in people with something to say, in new approaches to old questions—in other words, in intellectual vitality—not in professional jargon, quaint obfuscation, or in manuscripts that offer neither light nor heat.
>
> Many books should not have been published as books, but as an article or two in a specialized journal. Think how many trees would still be standing and how many warehouses would not now be jammed with books that served an author's ego and tenure quest or a publisher's desire to seem elite by publishing the quaint. I think all university presses know this today, and that's a good trend.

3. The Process
of Manuscript
Acquisition

Editors used to sit in their offices and wait each day for the mail to bring them manuscripts worth publishing. Today, a few manuscripts still come in over the transom. But far more are actively acquired by editors scouring university campuses, going to scholarly conventions, browsing through academic journals, and writing letters of solicitation to prospective authors.

The times are gone when a university press could be passive, expend little energy, yet still publish a quality list. "As every publisher knows, good books don't walk in the front door unless they see good books already there," said August Frugé, director emeritus of the University of California Press. The California press was one of the first university presses to set up a staff of specialized editors whose job was to prowl the academic halls at home and away, to locate the best authors and bid for their manuscripts. "In our early innocence," Frugé wrote, "we proposed to call them soliciting or procuring editors; after being told that we were stealing the terminology of another profession, we named them sponsoring editors, and encouraged each one to think of his/her books as a list within the larger list." [1]

The acquisition process is the heart of publishing. The other publishing functions—copyediting, book design, marketing, and distribution—can be delegated on a contractual basis. The one function that cannot be delegated is the decision of what to publish.

For university presses, acquisition is a three-stage process.

First, editors act partly as filter and partly as recruiter. They filter all queries or manuscripts that arrive at the publishing house uninvited, winnowing out those offerings deemed unworthy or inappropriate for the list. As recruiters, they go out and do some inviting of their own. Manuscripts that rank as possibilities for publication advance to the second stage, peer review. Scholars with expertise in the field serve as judges of manuscripts, ruling on their scholarly merit. Manuscripts judged worthy by scholars in the field then advance to the third and final stage, review by the editorial committee. A group of home-campus faculty members and administrators serves as the final authority in determining whether to publish a work. The editorial committee members rely on the peer reviews and editor recommendations, and sometimes on their own readings of the work. To be published, a manuscript must proceed through all three stages successfully.

Without good manuscripts brought in by editors, peer reviewers and editorial committees would have little of quality to consider. So the first stage of the acquisition process is crucial to the creation of a good list. This first stage used to be a guarded secret. Now, editors talk rather freely of the way they work.

For instance, Doug Mitchell is a University of Chicago Press editor who acquires books in sociology and history. He handles unsolicited manuscripts and letters and telephone calls of inquiry. He attends the scholarly conventions of sociologists and historians. He reads the academic journals in his assigned disciplines in order to stay abreast of current thought. He creates and nurtures networks of contacts in these disciplines, with the purpose of bringing the best possible manuscripts in the social sciences to the University of Chicago Press. He says of his job:

> Two myths seem to persist about the job of book editor. One, the glamorous, romantic image, has us spending our time squiring authors to expensive lunches. Author lunches are in fact enormously important—I liken them to the mating process or courtship. However, these lunches are apt to be a club sandwich at a hotel coffee shop, not at Le Francais. The other image, of the solitary editor, has us ambling into the office, putting our feet on the desk, and passively reading manuscripts all day. Actually, my search for book projects is an active one that leaves little time for reading between nine and five. I invariably stuff my briefcase with manuscripts and scholarly

journals at the end of the day, hoping I can read them at home that night. . . .

I have about one hundred book project possibilities in the works right now. At the same time that I am seeking out new book ideas, I am inundated by more than one thousand manuscripts and proposals annually. I keep up in my fields so I can recognize a fresh approach. If a project surprises me, that's a good indication that it has potential.[2]

Mitchell, like all editors, has acquired manuscripts in a variety of ways. One day while going through some old files, Mitchell became fascinated by a one-paragraph sketch for a book about how precision in language can cause relationship problems ranging from interpersonal to international, and how understanding that words do have multiple meanings actually fosters communication. Mitchell telephoned the professor— Donald Levine of the University of Chicago sociology department—and the manuscript evolved chapter by chapter over six or seven years. Mitchell predicts that Levine's *The Flight from Ambiguity* slowly will influence the academic community and eventually affect the language of people on the street.

Another book, *American Sociology and Pragmatism: Mead, Chicago Sociology, and Symbolic Interaction,* by J. David Lewis and Richard L. Smith, was published after someone—Mitchell never knew who—sent him a copy of the University of Notre Dame sociology department's newsletter, in which the work of the authors was discussed. Mitchell liked the topic and contacted one of the authors.

Still another time, Mitchell spotted an interesting topic in a convention program, wrote to the young scholar who had just finished his dissertation, and they had lunch while at the San Francisco convention. "The minute I read his one-page proposal, I thought we were onto something hot," he said. Mitchell's initiative led to publication of John D'Emilio's *Sexual Politics, Sexual Communities: The Making of a Homosexual Minority in the United States, 1940–1970.*

At another academic meeting, a Chicago press author introduced Mitchell to Robin Wagner-Pacifici, a young professor at Swarthmore. Later, at a luncheon, two professors from other universities started talking in Mitchell's presence about Wagner-Pacifici's research on how the mass media form the public's sense of reality, especially with regard to acts of terrorism. "This combination of events naturally fueled my enthusiasm," the editor said. *The Moro Morality Play*—about the assassination of Italian Prime Minister Aldo Moro—was published in 1986. "I would say that I discover many manuscripts in a serendipitous way, except that it happens too frequently to fit the definition of chance," he said.

Mitchell has found publishable manuscripts under the most unlikely of circumstances. One day, an unemployed Ph.D. asked to see the press's records for sociologists of the 1920s and 1930s. On meeting researcher James Bennett for the first time, Mitchell learned that the press previously had rejected Bennett's manuscript as "brilliant but off-the-wall." Mitchell liked the topic and asked Bennett to revise and resubmit the manuscript. It was published under the title *Oral History and Delinquency: The Rhetoric of Criminology*. Said Mitchell, "Every editor and gatekeeper dreams of discovering some lonely genius who had an important project to offer. And it does happen. Rarely, but it does."

Manuscripts come to the attention of editors in a variety of ways. But they all share a common characteristic—someone has to make the initial overture that leads to publication. The various methods of manuscript acquisition can be placed in three categories.

1. *Author-Initiated.* The author takes the initiative in establishing contact with the press. Some do this by sending an unsolicited manuscript. Others send a written query, call an editor, or approach the editor at a convention. Whatever the method of contact, the manuscript comes to the press's attention through the initiative of the author.

2. *Editor-Initiated.* The editor takes the initiative in establishing contact with the author. The editor may read a journal article, like the topic, and write to the scholar inquiring whether a book manuscript is planned. Or the editor may solicit a manuscript at a scholarly convention or while visiting campuses on manuscript-search trips. Whatever the method of contact, the manuscript comes to the press through the initiative of an editor.

3. *Prior Association.* The author and the editor already have established an association. The author may have been published previously by

the press or may have served as an outside referee. Or the editor and author may have become friends on an earlier occasion. Whatever their prior association, neither had to make a blind inquiry of the other. They already knew each other.

Determining the initiator in a publishing decision can be complex, because the three categories are not always mutually exclusive. For example, imagine this not-unusual scenario at an academic convention. A scholar who has published with a particular press introduces a colleague to an editor of the press. The three go for a cup of coffee. The editor mentions the press's desire to build its list in a certain field. The colleague replies that he or she happens to be working on a manuscript in that very field. The editor asks to see the manuscript. Eventually, the manuscript is published by the press.

Who was the initiator? The editor had attended the scholarly convention with hopes of attracting outstanding manuscripts and, in fact, specifically invited the author to send the manuscript to the press. Yet the author had come to the convention with a specific intent to identify a press that would be interested in the manuscript and, in fact, had succeeded in doing so by mentioning the manuscript at the appropriate time. Then, again, the editor and author might never have sat drinking coffee together had an intermediary not existed. This middleman, with a prior association with the press, played a key role in this particular manuscript's eventual publication by this particular press.

In scholarly publishing, such middlemen often are vital for both editors and junior scholars. They act as brokers and as confidantes. Authors may contact a press on the recommendation of someone already associated with the press. Editors, in turn, may contact an author on the recommendation of a trusted scholar. Nevertheless, either the editor or the author still must initiate contact with the other.

Table 3.1 shows that responding presses collectively estimated that one of every three new titles published in the year surveyed was author-initiated. Whether by query or sending an unsolicited manuscript, the author established that first contact with the press which eventually led to publication. Another one of three titles was editor-initiated. One of every four titles was based on a prior association between the press and the author. In the "other" category, university presses listed such acquisition

TABLE 3.1
Estimate of How Published Manuscripts Were Acquired

Method of Acquisition	No. of Published Manuscripts
Unsolicited Manuscript Came over the Transom	183 (8%)
Author Initiated Contact with Press via Query	608 (26%)
Press Initiated Contact with Author	845 (37%)
Press and Author Had a Prior Association	568 (25%)
Other	104 (4%)
	2,308

Note: Data based on a survey of the 74 American university press members and affiliates of the Association of American University Presses as of 1986. The 52 responding presses reported publishing 2,346 new titles in the preceding year. Two presses did not specify how the manuscripts came to their press, hence the 2,308 total.

mechanisms as literary agents, lecture series, yearbooks, copublishing and foreign projects, and poetry and short fiction contests where judges make the selections.

❦ The Dreaded Unsolicited Manuscript

Senders of unsolicited manuscripts should not be too encouraged by the fact that some over-the-transom submissions eventually are published. Table 3.2 shows that the responding presses collectively estimated that more than nine out of ten unsolicited manuscripts were returned to the authors without ever entering the publishing stream. An estimated 9 percent of unsolicited submissions were accepted to the extent that an outside referee was asked to judge the manuscript's merits. Once an unsolicited manuscript entered the publishing stream, odds for eventual publication improved to about 21 percent. Overall, responding presses collectively estimated that about 2 percent of the unsolicited manuscripts they received eventually were published.

Eight of the fifty-two responding presses said they did not send out a single unsolicited manuscript for review during the year. Twenty-one

TABLE 3.2

Estimate of Success Rate for Unsolicited Manuscripts

Manuscript Status	No. of Manuscripts	Success Rates
Unsolicited Manuscripts Received	9,610	
		9%
Number Sent for Outside Review	860	2%
		21%
Unsolicited Manuscripts Published	183	

Note: Two university presses did not give estimates of unsolicited manuscripts received. Concerning the number sent for outside review, one said "very few" and the other "less than 10." These two responses were omitted from the table. A few other presses gave ranges, and the midpoints of those ranges were used.

presses—40 percent of the responses—said that they did not publish an unsolicited manuscript during the survey year.

In scholarly communication, a striking difference exists between the selection processes of academic journals and scholarly books. While manuscripts generally come to journal editors unsolicited, this is not the norm in book publishing. Finding a publisher is more like finding an employer. Morris Philipson, director of the University of Chicago Press, proposed the following analogy:

> No publisher can bring out every single manuscript that is submitted to him, any more than a publisher can hire every person who applies for a job. You might want to work at the Oxford University Press, but it makes more sense to send a letter of inquiry describing your qualifications and asking whether there is a position available, rather than to get on a plane and fly to England to present yourself physically and ask to be hired. It is a kindness to both parties.[3]

Many uninvited manuscripts, though, continue to arrive at university presses. In using this tactic, authors promptly identify themselves as publishing novices. The manuscript will be accorded more respect if the cover letter at least suggests some type of tie-in ("One of your authors, Professor So-and-So, suggested I send you this" or "I noticed you recently published such-and-such book, and I believe this would complement your list in that area"). The cover letter also must make a case for the importance and distinctiveness of the manuscript. If an editor has to turn to the manuscript itself to find out what it is about, the cover letter needs to be rewritten.

If an author gives no compelling reason to consider the unsolicited manuscript, acquisitions editors say they can dismiss an over-the-transom submission in twenty seconds or less. What an author may have spent years writing may be rejected via form letter in the time it takes an editor to read perhaps only a few sentences. Because of the expense of handling unwanted and uninvited manuscripts, commercial publishers usually discard them unceremoniously. But university presses, as the more genteel members of the publishing family, typically return unsolicited manuscripts at their own expense.

New presses most often bear the brunt of the manuscript onslaught. The appearance of a new press means the dusting off of hundreds of unpublished manuscripts. "A new press is announced and the manuscripts flow in," said one university press director, speaking from experience. "A disproportionate number of them are bad, because they've already been tried everywhere else."

All editors have a favorite unsolicited-manuscript recollection. One recalls receiving an eighty-six-page master's thesis on John F. Kennedy. Another remembers a manuscript of similar size billed by its author as a comprehensive study of child sexual abuse. Another editor said: "I have a corner in my office designated for unsolicited manuscripts that begin with 'Dear Editor.'" The editor glances at them on slow days.

Yet editors must sift through the stacks of mail, cognizant that, on this particular day, the stacks may contain a gem. The University of Washington Press once received a package from an author without academic credentials, whose stationery was plain and whose address was a rural mail route. Inside was something called "Pictorial Anatomy of the Fetal Pig." The editors were spellbound. The drawings were meticulous in their accuracy and clarity. The text was skillfully integrated. The pig book was published, and it proved so popular that the author was asked to do the same for the frog, the cat, the dogfish, the necturus (mud puppy), and other animals worthy of close anatomical scrutiny. The press later added an atlas that enabled readers to compare the anatomical structure of the baboon, the chimpanzee, and man.

In another example of the full manuscript's selling itself, the University of Nebraska Press once received an unsolicited manuscript in a field foreign to the press—European World War II history. It was a first-person account, translated into English. It did not fit Nebraska's list at all. "Had he sent us a letter of query, we would have said, 'No thanks,'" said David Gilbert, then director at Nebraska and now director at Cornell University Press. "But an editor got it and said, 'Gee, this is fascinating.' That's a case where our editor read it and couldn't put it down."

But it is pointless for authors to proceed in this way, unless a query cannot adequately convey the purpose or style of the manuscript.

❦ Queries: The Writer's Overture

Unsolicited manuscripts may be unwanted, but query letters from authors are an accepted part of scholarly publishing. Publishers are in business to publish, and a writer cannot insult a publishing house by offering it a manuscript appropriate to its list.

A query letter tells an editor something about the writer's status. A query suggests that the author probably has not published a book before and therefore is not yet a member of any scholarly publishing network. Senior scholars seldom have to send a query. Editors pursue them, not vice versa. Still, queries carry no stigma. Editors read them with interest and will ask to see sample chapters or even a completed manuscript if the topic and approach interest them. A prospective author, then, shouldn't hesitate to approach a publisher directly.

Editors are accustomed to having query letters in each day's mail, with the number depending on the size and reputation of the press. A few editors said they enjoy the time set aside each day to peruse the queries and answer them. Others view it as a tedious but necessary chore. "I don't anticipate any great discoveries, but there is an occasional gem," one press director said. For instance, the University Press of Mississippi acquired *The Lost Colony of the Confederacy*, now in its second printing, via a query letter. The author, Eugene Harter, sent queries to several presses

TABLE 3.3
Estimate of Success Rate for Author Queries Received

Manuscript Status	No. of Manuscripts	Success Rates
Author Queries Received	32,450	
Manuscripts Requested on Basis of Author Queries	3,360	10% 2%
Manuscripts Published Originating from Queries	608	18%

Note: Three responding presses did not give estimates of author queries received, so their responses on manuscripts requested and eventually published on the basis of author queries were omitted.

to determine interest in his work on the return to the United States of descendants of southerners who had emigrated to Brazil after the Civil War. Several presses responded favorably. Harter gave the Mississippi press right of first refusal because its response was the most enthusiastic.

Yet for every manuscript eventually published following an author's query, another fifty are not published. Table 3.3 shows that responding university presses collectively estimated that roughly one of every ten queries results in an editor's request to see the complete manuscript. Of those reaching this intermediate stage, an estimated 18 percent actually proceed through editor review, outside peer evaluation, and editorial committee approval. Overall, then, responding presses collectively estimated that about 2 percent of author queries eventually result in a published book—identical to the percentage of unsolicited manuscripts eventually published.

Many university presses emphasized that no records were kept of such figures because the number of queries flowing into the press was not of operational significance to them. But a few presses were able to give specific figures. For instance, the University of Hawaii Press kept records on incoming mail in 1985 and reported that it received 520 query letters and, in turn, invited sixty of the authors to send completed manuscripts for consideration. Others made estimates based on daily intake. The University of Michigan Press said it received an average of ten query letters per weekday. From the roughly 2,500 queries a year, the Michigan press invited seventy-five authors to submit completed manuscripts. As a newer scholarly publisher, the University of Arkansas Press was inundated with submissions. Director Miller Williams said the press received two thousand unsolicited manuscripts and another 3,500 queries in 1987. That year, the Arkansas press published fifteen new titles. "Look what your chances are," Williams said, turning to a biblical analogy: "It's true: Many are called but few are chosen. Many knock on the door but few come in."

One reason for so many query rejections is that a large number of queries are aimed at inappropriate outlets. Authors need to recognize that not all presses publish in all fields. Mismatches can be prevented if authors do their homework. They should look at the books on their office shelves to see who published them and note which publishers are listed most often in their own manuscript's bibliography. The uninitiated also should look through *Literary Market Place* or the annual directory of the Association of American University Presses. These publications list each press's publishing areas and the number of titles published per year. If a press seems appropriate, the author should call the press and ask for the name of the editor in a particular discipline, so as to send a query letter to the right individual. It is even acceptable to call the editor and ask if the press might be interested in the topic. "We all field calls like that and are happy to help," one editor said. "Of course, some days we're happier than others." Editors acknowledge that a phone call can be an effective first step but said they prefer to deal on paper. It is easier for them to say "no" to a piece of paper than to a human voice.

The query letter, then, must be well crafted. Editors said it should state why the book is important, name other books on the subject, explain how this one is different, justify why the writer is the one to write this book, and then link the work to the press's publishing list. All of this should be communicated in one page, or two at most. Editors advised prospective authors against writing long, chatty, or whimsical letters. Query letters should be matter-of-fact and straightforward. Yet they must have some life; if an editor yawns while reading a two-page query letter, he or she may wonder about the three-hundred-page manuscript to follow. Editors said that they look first at query letters that begin interestingly or that make a reference to a recognizable name who had suggested that the author write to this particular press.

Since scholarly publishing exists in a close relationship with academia, unaffiliated scholars who lack a network of contacts or even a job are at a disadvantage. Even the absence of such a taken-for-granted item as an institutional letterhead can influence an editor's first impression of a query letter. Institutional letterheads signify at a glance that the writer is at least an active member of the academy served by university presses. Some authors become paranoid about that fact. Suzanne Comer, now senior editor at Southern Methodist University Press, remembers getting a query letter while at the University of Texas Press from an unaffiliated scholar who devoted the first two pages to an impassioned plea not to turn his proposal down simply because he was an unaffiliated scholar. She didn't. "We turned it down because it didn't fit our list," Comer said. "If it had been within our areas of specialization and looked promising, we would have given it the same consideration as a manuscript by an affiliated scholar."

But the unaffiliated scholar is in a difficult position. "University presses are integral parts of their respective academic communities," said Barbara Hanrahan of the University of Wisconsin Press. "The review process— that essential component of scholarly publishing—assumes that academic affiliations are significant. In addition, press boards or oversight committees, charged with safeguarding the reputation of the university as well as the imprint of the press, do pay attention to such things. On the positive side, though, editors know that decisions should be made on the merits of the projects, and I don't believe that any of us would turn away a promising manuscript solely because the author was unaffiliated."

Unaffiliated scholars do have success stories, as shown by the University of Chicago Press's publication of a book written by an unemployed scholar. "These souls are often creative people who can't get a job," said editor Doug Mitchell. "His [employment status] didn't bother me or the board. Maybe it was reverse snobbishness."

No matter what the status of the writer, some editors want to receive more than a query letter in that initial contact. Some want a vita. Others prefer to see a table of contents. Still others would like to receive a short abstract. "No processes are cut-and-dry," one press director said. "You might even send a sample chapter with the query." Several editors, in fact, said they prefer to receive a sample chapter or two with the query.

Editors may have differing beliefs about what belongs in that first mailing, but they agree on two points. First, a vita, if sent, should be a short biographical sketch. "Leave off the names of every committee you've served on and the names and numbers of every course you've taught," one editor commented. Second, authors should enclose a self-addressed, stamped envelope (SASE). Almost all university presses go ahead and respond to queries sent without a SASE. But not all. The director of one scholarly press said, "All university presses are poor, and we probably get ten query letters a day without a SASE. That's $2.20 in postage alone each day, besides the time and paper. In one hundred days, that's $220. That's about $750 a year. We can't afford it. An author may say, 'Wow, how chintzy!' But we just throw it in a wastebasket if it doesn't interest us."

Some university presses have a standard form they send as a followup to queries. It's a way to collect a lot of disparate information at one time. These "Author and Manuscript Inquiry" forms typically ask for such information as a list of competing books in the field, the target audience of the manuscript, the length of the manuscript, and the background of the author. The form also may ask whether the manuscript is a revised version of a dissertation, whether it is presently being considered for publication by another house, whether any scholars in the field already have read the manuscript, and whether a word processor was used in the preparation of the manuscript.

A decision on whether to invite the author to send part or all of a manuscript for consideration typically is made by one person—the acquisitions editor responsible for the subject area. Table 3.4 shows that half of the responding university presses said that one editor makes the decision on the typical query. Given the opportunity for an open-ended answer, more than 20 percent answered "one or two" editors. The remainder said two or more. Several respondents wrote that one editor typically makes the decision, and a second one is consulted if there is uncertainty.

University press directors and editors said they occasionally ask faculty members at their home universities to look at an abstract to determine whether the complete manuscript is worth pursuing. Some editors periodically take queries to editorial committee members in the same disci-

TABLE 3.4
Number of Editors Involved in Decision-Making on a Query

Number of Editors	No. of Presses (N=51)
One Editor	26 (51%)
One or Two Editors	11 (22%)
Two Editors	12 (23%)
Three or More Editors	2 (4%)

TABLE 3.5
Length of Time It Takes to Respond to a Query

Response Time	No. of Presses (N=51)
One Week or Less	24 (47%)
One to Two Weeks	4 (8%)
Two Weeks	11 (21%)
Three Weeks	3 (6%)
Four or More Weeks	5 (10%)
Highly Variable (1–6 Weeks)	4 (8%)

pline for advice. Authors, then, should not wait until they have written a complete manuscript before beginning the process of finding a publisher. The acquisition process can begin with the germ of an idea and an outline of the concept.

Table 3.5 shows that university presses respond relatively quickly to queries. Almost half reported in open-ended answers that they respond to a typical query in one week or less. Three out of four said they respond within two weeks. Only one in ten said it typically takes a month or longer to respond.

Several responding presses said they try to respond to queries on a day-by-day basis. One press said that queries which are photocopied letters are not answered at all. Another said that those proposals which are clearly outside the press's list are answered in one day, usually with a form letter, while those of interest require more deliberation.

A query has only one purpose—to get a manuscript into the publishing stream. Before a manuscript can advance to peer review, it first must interest an editor. Before a manuscript can interest an editor, it must get into the editor's hands. A query is successful, then, if it eventually gets a complete manuscript into the editor's hands. Some authors take a shortcut by sending the complete manuscript unsolicited. But that approach appears only to add to the author's expense without adding to the chances of success. A query is the preferred method of author-initiated contact.

❦ The Editor as Initiator

Although many scholarly books originate with author queries, university presses do not rely on the mail to bring them a full complement of suitable manuscripts. They do not wait for an author to take the initiative. Instead, university presses aggressively seek manuscripts that fit their listbuilding areas.

"We hustle," said Gregory McNamee, editor-in-chief at the University of Arizona Press. "University press editors no longer sit still and wait for manuscripts to come over the transom." Dick Rowson, director of Duke University Press, added, "We go to a lot of meetings. We are a genuine seeker of manuscripts. We are an aggressive seeker of the very best we can find." Networking is essential. James Langford, director of the University of Notre Dame Press, said, "Many of our best authors like what we do and act as 'scouts' for us among their peers."

With more than one of every three university press titles now being editor-initiated, scholarly publishers have become active seekers rather than passive receivers of manuscripts. Table 3.6 shows that the responding presses collectively estimated that authors whose manuscripts were

TABLE 3.6
Estimate of Success Rate for Active Acquisitions

Manuscript Status	No. of Manuscripts	Success Rate
Manuscripts Actively Acquired by Editors	3,880	
Acquired Manuscripts Eventually Published	845	22%

actively solicited had a 22 percent chance of having their manuscripts accepted by the editor, endorsed by outside readers, and then approved for publication by the editorial committee. This rate compares to 2 percent for unsolicited manuscripts and 18 percent for manuscripts requested by an editor following the author's query. The greater the initiating role of the editor, the greater appear the chances of publication.

Acquisitions editors often are on the go. They travel to university campuses to visit scholars in their offices. They attend academic conventions to pursue the authors of papers selected for delivery. They seek to develop a network of senior scholars to help the press attract quality manuscripts.

At home, their days are spent in administrative detail—writing letters, fielding phone calls, securing outside readers, handling inquisitive authors, and preparing paperwork for editorial committees. They court the eminent scholars of the parent institution and cultivate the rising stars. They write to professors who received prestigious research grants. They read specialty journals in search of topics worthy of book-length treatment.

Charles Grench, executive editor at Yale University Press, sees about 100 to 125 manuscripts a year. He takes home a couple of manuscripts each week to scan or to read. He also puts the journals that come into the office each week into his backpack and carries them home. In all, he reads about thirty journals or publications a month, ranging from *The New Yorker* to the *Journal of Asian Studies* and the *Wilson Quarterly*.

If Grench sees a well-conceived and well-written article that lends itself to larger treatment, he contacts the author. Sometimes the tactic leads to a publishable manuscript; at other times, he is too late. While reading the *Journal of American History*, Grench was intrigued by an article on bare-knuckle prizefighting. Grench contacted the author but discovered the book already was committed to another university press. "If you don't catch people early on, you may never publish their work," Grench said. "In a sense, we see ourselves as talent scouts. We have an obligation to get the best work."

Mercer University Press added eminent religion scholar William Mc-Loughlin to its list of authors by actively pursuing him. An editor wrote McLoughlin at Brown University after reading an article of his in the *Journal of Church History*. The editor asked if the topic was going to be a book. McLoughlin responded by letter that the book Mercer wanted already was at the Yale University Press, but that he had a series of essays not yet committed for publication. They exchanged a few more letters and a phone call or two and eventually reached agreement to publish the essays as a book titled *The Cherokee Ghost Dance*. McLoughlin's name adds prestige to this newer press's religion list.

Without editors actively acquiring scholarly manuscripts of high quality, a university press would be unable to build an excellent list. "Toward this end it is absolutely necessary to hire highly intelligent, and thoroughly motivated, acquiring editors who travel to the universities and get to know scholars first-hand and who develop and invite manuscripts that contribute to scholarship," said Chris Kentera, director of Penn State University Press. "If a press does not have an active acquisitions program for scholarly books, via qualified editors, there is not much chance it will publish much worthwhile material. They frequently become little more than vanity presses for their own faculty."

❦ Publishing the Home Faculty

The university press once existed almost exclusively as a service agency, publishing the work of the home faculty and little else. This role has undergone a dramatic transformation in the latter half of the twentieth century. All university presses, of course, still publish works by their own faculties, but that role no longer predominates.

In a 1948 study, Yale University Press director Chester Kerr found that 60 percent of the manuscripts published by the thirty-five university presses then in existence were written by scholars at the presses' parent institutions. In a 1968 followup, Kerr found that the percentage had dropped to 40 percent.[4] That percentage evidently has dropped even more in the past two decades. In a 1986 polling of fifty-two university press directors, only six said that the works of scholars at the parent institution constitute 40 percent or more of their frontlists. More than half of the respondents said home authors write fewer than 20 percent of their new titles. This means university presses increasingly are publishing books written by persons not affiliated with the parent institution. The acquisition process is not a closed system.

Publishers believe that scholarship would suffer if the university press were viewed as a service agency or auxiliary enterprise akin to the bookstore or student housing. August Frugé, director emeritus of the University of California Press, has written of the irony that a press must succeed elsewhere in order to succeed at home:

> No university is great enough and large enough to support a distinguished press—as opposed to a service agency—with home products only. There are not enough good things at home even if one could get all of them, and one never can. And in every university there are always too many middle level things, adequate but not excellent. These are suitable to a service agency, but if a press fills its list with them, the best scholars at home will soon go elsewhere to prove themselves where the standards are higher. Or they will say, and sometimes within earshot, if you publish the stuff Professor X turns out, you won't publish me.[5]

Yet a university press is, after all, the press of the home university. The quest to be a publisher of distinction can be carried to the extreme, if it alienates the parent institution. Frugé said that a proper balance between service agency and publisher of distinction is required. Turning to a personal example from the 1970s, he wrote:

> If the press is part of the university, it had better not be too rigid about what one of our editors calls the Berkeley Problem, referring to medium quality manuscripts from one of our campuses. In partial contradiction to some remarks above, I think we have to accept the need for a double standard—while never allowing it to get too double. For even with the finest of reputations, a press had better not stray too far from the parent university.[6]

Ideally, a university press list should complement some of the academic strengths of the parent institution. So it would be expected that some home faculty manuscripts would be published. Also, by building a distinguished list in a field, such as military history or linguistics or Renaissance religion, a press can become a kind of intellectual presence roughly comparable to the presence of a good academic department.

Special considerations do exist for home authors at many presses. For instance, no University of Chicago Press editor can reject outright the work of a member of the University of Chicago faculty. Rejection can only follow a negative report from an outside reader. Press editors have the freedom to reject other manuscripts on their own authority. Currently, about 15 percent of the press's authors are University of Chicago faculty or staff.

Several university press directors pointed out that, with the creation of state campus systems and consortiums, their "home" authors now come from several campuses rather than just the main campus at which the press is located. The University Press of Kansas is located on the University of Kansas campus but also serves Kansas State University, Wichita State University, and three others in the state regents system. "All things being equal, a manuscript is more likely to be published if it's from our own faculty," said Fred Woodward, director of the Kansas press. About 20 percent of its frontlist comes from faculty at the six regents universities.

The University Press of New England, which serves nine eastern institutions, publishes about forty-five new titles a year. The acquisitions editors regularly scour consortium campuses for worthy manuscripts, and about two-thirds of the new titles are published for Brandeis, Brown, Clark, Connecticut, Dartmouth, New Hampshire, Rhode Island, Tufts, and Vermont. "On our member campuses, we have the endowed and the less-endowed," said press director Thomas McFarland. "We have Brown and we have Rhode Island. There is always the potential for conflict, but it's a congenial group." In addition, acquisitions editors also look elsewhere for one-third of the press-owned titles carrying only the University Press of New England imprint.

University press editors know the importance of maintaining a close relationship with scholars at the parent institution. But they also recognize the need to create an awareness of the press—and to acquire outstanding manuscripts—at other campuses. One way of doing this is to go to other campuses and knock on professors' doors. Professors like having their work and their opinions sought, especially when the visiting editor has a pure acquisition mission and not a sales mission as well.

When in Atlanta on business, director Malcolm MacDonald of the University of Alabama Press set aside a couple of hours to go to Emory University, where he visited with professors in history, political science, anthropology, and English. Later, a professor—himself published twice by the University of Georgia Press and once by Harvard University Press —notified MacDonald when Emory University purchased a collection of H.L. Mencken letters and a colleague began editing them. The Alabama press published the letters in 1986. On another occasion, the English department chairman called MacDonald about a student's dissertation on the poetry of Emily Dickinson. The press eventually published that one, too.

"It's networking," MacDonald said. "Most senior people already have their publishing connections. They know that, and I know that. Sometimes contacts you initiate that way don't result in a manuscript for seven or eight years. It's a continuous process. You want to plug into as many networks as possible. I call on senior faculty and ask who their best young people are."

Many editors complained of the time required for campus visits and of the tendency for professors not to be in their offices unless a visit is scheduled in advance. As a result, many editors don't make campus visits, but one such editor from a prestigious press said, "I don't knock it. It's good PR."

In 1977, editors from the Temple University Press decided to take the money allocated for sales visits to bookstores and spend it on acquisition visits to campuses nationwide. Such visits were something of a novelty at the time, and the experiment paid dividends. "The appearance of a Temple editor at the University of California, Berkeley, is a sure way to attract attention," wrote Kenneth Arnold, then director of the Temple press in Philadelphia and now director of Rutgers University Press. "The novelty is a sufficient draw, and getting attention is half the battle. The scholar is likely to think, 'If these guys have come all this way to see me, they must be good.'" That first California trip resulted in Temple's publishing two books it otherwise would not have obtained.[7]

Other presses have immediate name recognition, yet still make campus visits. An acquisitions editor at an Ivy League press said that the faculty at Harvard, Yale, and Princeton prefer being visited by New York trade publishers, while he prefers making campus visits in California where the Ivy League presence is less expected. "Being from a big-name press, there's never a door closed to me—because of the name," he said. "No-one ever says, 'I don't have the time,' and my colleagues at less prestigious university presses say that happens to them."

An editor for a western university press added, "You could go to a campus and easily collect twenty-five manuscripts from junior scholars, and some of them would be good. But that's not what the big presses want. They want the senior scholars."

❦ Personal Contact at Conventions

Chain-smoking and animated, executive editor Beverly Jarrett of the Louisiana State University Press stood at her exhibit booth, chatting with one of her authors. The scholar had stopped by to tell Jarrett that he wanted her to meet someone. The scholar provided a thumbnail sketch of the person and the person's work. Jarrett made some comments in her notepad and, after the scholar left, remarked, "His recommendation means a lot to me." Later in the convention, Jarrett had a thirty-minute visit with the person recommended. "You talk about more than the manuscript. You get to know each other as humans," Jarrett said. "And I did ask to see his manuscript immediately."

Down the aisle, then editor-in-chief Don Haymes prowled in front of his Mercer University Press booth, eager to talk with scholars as they walked by. The Mercer press had reserved exhibit space early in the year, thereby landing a choice location next to the main hallway. The table and nearby shelves were packed with Mercer titles. If one of them sold, fine. But the books were there mostly for show. The Mercer press was displaying its books in hopes that others would want their manuscripts to join such a list. A professor specializing in pre–Civil War American history stopped by the booth. Haymes asked if he was working on anything Mercer might be interested in publishing. "Only long-term. Nothing I'm ready to talk about yet," the professor replied, with his head cocked to one side as he scanned the titles and authors on the Mercer shelves. This was a fact-gathering mission for the professor, and he picked up a free copy of Mercer's catalog of titles.

At breakfast one morning, Charles Grench of Yale University Press visited with a junior scholar wanting to find a publisher for his revised dissertation. The author had initiated contact by sending Grench a query letter. Grench liked the topic and wrote back, asking to see some sample chapters. "You can tell from that whether a person can write," Grench said. This person could write, so Grench arranged a breakfast meeting at the academic convention they both would be attending.

Jarrett of LSU, Haymes of Mercer, and Grench of Yale, along with editors from twenty-eight other university presses and from just as many commercial presses, attended the 1986 convention of the Organization of American Historians. It was a happy hunting ground for scholarship. Thousands of historians poured into a New York City hotel for a four-day convention featuring the readings of more than two hundred papers on topics ranging from "Black Anti-Semitism" to "Fraternal Orders in Victorian America" and "The Military Legacy of the Vietnam War." The editors, though, were not at the convention to hear papers delivered. They had come to see and be seen. Here they could develop and maintain networks of informants, at last connect a face with that name on a query letter, greet old acquaintances, and meet new ones. Here they could associate in a personal way with the lifeblood of scholarly communication—the writers themselves.

It is to an author's advantage to get on the convention program. Like most acquisitions editors, Cynthia Maude-Gembler of the University of Tennessee Press prepared for the convention by skimming the 205-page program for topics suitable for the press's list. Weeks before the convention, she wrote 150 to 200 letters to program participants and others, expressing interest in their topics and inviting them to come by the Tennessee exhibit booth for a visit. At one or another point during the four-day convention, many of them did. By being on the program, then, an author may enjoy having an editor make that initial contact. The author becomes the pursued rather than the pursuer. The practice of writing to program participants is a standard one, except that Tennessee writes to more people than some presses do. Other editors mentioned sending 20 to 50 letters per convention. "That's how we do it to get traffic," Maude-Gembler said. "A press our size has to do it; a Harvard doesn't."

Editors want a lot of traffic at their exhibit booths. They want senior scholars to recommend the work of their best students or their friends. "We've gotten a lot of recommendations this way," an editor at a middle-sized press said. "You pick their brains for ideas. A Vann Woodward or a Peter Gay—they wouldn't dream of publishing with us. But they've been lovely." Without being present at scholarly conventions, a press would miss this type of referral.

Editors want the writers they have under contract to drop by and give progress reports on their manuscript revisions. In 1981, senior historian John Hope Franklin put an editor in touch with a young scholar who was completing his dissertation. Outside readers called the manuscript worthwhile but asked for revisions. For the next few years, the editor received progress reports from the young scholar twice a year at history conventions they both attended.

Editors want their authors, past and present, to drop by just to stay in contact. During the day it is not unusual to see the hotel coffee shop dotted with twosomes—one an editor, the other a scholar. But editors consider the exhibit booth their home base. Charles Grench of Yale University Press camps at his booth. "I see a lot of people that way. They're looking for me at the booth," he said. Many are scholars who have published with Yale; Grench said they just want to say hello and stay in touch.

Editors want prospective authors to drop by as well. Although no quantitative evidence exists, editors believe that prospective authors have a better chance of being published when the initial contact is a face-to-face encounter rather than a faceless query. "There's a distinct advantage to a one-on-one conference," one editor said. "If I've met you and talked with you about your manuscript, that is much better than a query letter and a written response. We can sit and talk about the work at some length, and begin to know each other as individuals as well."

Editors have quietly discouraged scholars from bringing complete manuscripts with them to conventions. Now, prospective authors bring two- to five-page proposals to give to editors. Most proposals delivered at conventions are from unpublished authors, often those wanting to revise their dissertations into books.

"Most people who have published before have learned how to identify the most appropriate publisher for their current work," said Barbara Hanrahan, humanities editor at the University of Wisconsin Press. "The less experienced authors tend to be the ones who come into exhibit booths with inquiries. The person who comes up and asks, 'Are you the acquisitions editor?' usually has a manuscript to offer. Only a small percentage of them will interest us."

But some do. A visitor at Hanrahan's convention booth one year was a young English teacher at a private college. Hanrahan invited her to send the complete manuscript, and it received favorite readers' reports and was published to good reviews.

"Wonderful books come from many sources—friends of friends, query letters, at conventions," one editor said. "People who say they don't get editors all that interested at conventions and people who say that routine letters of query don't pan out, that's true. But there are exceptions. The most satisfying experience is taking an author who has a first book and watching the book and the author's career take off. That's very satisfying."

An Ivy League editor said he collects several proposals at almost every convention he attends. "I'm too polite to say 'I won't even look at your three-page proposal,' so I accept them," he said. At a recent convention, he accepted a manuscript proposal concerning gender roles in the New England area. The editor was interested. Another manuscript proposal concerned relief efforts and the New Deal. The editor wasn't interested. He had talked with the author and was not impressed.

In a single day at a convention, an editor may visit individually with dozens of people. Conversations begin to run together in the editor's mind. Following each conversation at the historian's convention, LSU's Beverly Jarrett scribbled notes to herself between cigarettes. Because she visited with so many people in such a short time, she didn't want to forget any promises she had made or forget any names that had been dropped. Each evening, Jarrett pulled out her notepad and wrote letters to persons she had talked with that day or to persons referred to her. "After I've spent eight hours smiling and seeing people, I like to isolate myself, make a pot of coffee, and write letters," she said. "Then it's done—while it's fresh on my mind." Jarrett, now the director of the University of Missouri Press, has since given up smoking, but not her pot of coffee.

Editors who are normally tied to the office because of the glut of correspondence usually enjoy going to conventions. Budget permitting, university presses send representatives and a multitude of books to the conventions that dovetail with their listbuilding efforts.

Copies of the presses' books are occasionally sold at professional meetings. But the sales income realized at a convention rarely pays the cost of exhibiting. "It's not sales but manuscripts we're after," one director said. "It's to show the flag, to have a presence. You can't quantify that. It's not like you get a shipment of lawnmowers, you put an ad out, and the next day you sell ten lawnmowers. It's not that easy. It's impossible to quantify the results of any academic meeting. It's a crazy business. I'm here primarily because the other presses are here."

Convention-going has become an increasingly vital acquisition mechanism. For instance, the University of Alabama Press staff went to sixteen scholarly conventions in 1986—double the number of the preceding year. "It's all part of an effort for increased visibility," the director said. Since anthropology and archaeology are listbuilding areas for the press, the editors have added several meetings a year in those fields to their agenda.

Among editors, the Modern Language Association (MLA) convention ranks as an essential one to attend. The MLA annually attracts about ten-thousand people. In the field of history, the American Historical Association and the Organization of American Historians conventions are essential. Other prominent conventions are sponsored by such diverse groups as the American Philosophical Association, the National Women's Studies Association, the American Political Science Association, and the Association for Asian Studies. University press editors also attend narrow-specialty conventions and regional meetings.

Editors never quite know the repercussions of attending—or skipping—a convention. Sometimes an editor's presence at a convention can have an unexpected ripple effect in other areas. For instance, the University Press of Kansas acquired *The Radical Politics of Thomas Jefferson* because the director went to a Shakespearean meeting in Minneapolis. A Jefferson manuscript at a Shakespearean meeting? "It was really an odd situation," press director Fred Woodward said. "I shared a cab with a Shakespearean scholar from Lafayette College. He wasn't working on anything I was interested in. But when he got back, he told a colleague in political science who was working on the Jefferson manuscript. That's how it came to our attention." The book fit the press's list in presidential studies.

The acquisition process involves a number of serendipitous encounters. But writers always are looking for guidance as to how to get their manuscripts published, as if it were a science. Convention planners have learned in recent years that some of the most popular sessions deal not with aspects of specialty scholarship, but with insights into scholarly publishing. The interest in these sessions comes primarily from junior scholars and doctoral students seeking to learn the signposts in publishing. In fact, many go to conventions as much for the opportunity to visit with editors as to hear their colleagues present papers.

The historian's convention in New York City featured two sessions on scholarly publishing. Both sessions packed their meeting rooms—the first one so full that people were turned away at the door. Those in attendance included:

— A Ph.D. candidate in history at a Massachusetts university who had written a dissertation on French-Indian relations. He had not talked with any editors at the booths yet; he first wanted to get a feel for the publishing process.

— A history professor at a Tennessee university who had approached five scholarly presses in the state of New York about his manuscript dealing with an aspect of New York history. None had been interested. He wanted to know where he was going wrong.

— A teacher at an Oklahoma university who had an unrevised dissertation concerning American newspapers during the Revolutionary War. She, too, had yet to talk with any editors.

— A nonaffiliated scholar who had earned a Ph.D. in American studies. At an earlier convention, she had visited with several acquisitions editors, and one university press had expressed interest in her historical biography. She sent it to the press half-finished, and it went to one outside reader for an evaluation. The report was negative. "It was a bone-headed report," she said without humor. The unaffiliated scholar went ahead and finished the biography and now was ready to pursue publication again. She had initiated conversations with acquisitions editors of several university presses by stopping at their exhibit booths. She said that three presses had expressed varying degrees of interest, and she planned to send the manuscript to the press showing the greatest enthusiasm.

While some junior scholars wish they could create some interest in their work, others become the objects of competition. At the New York

City convention, at least three university presses actively courted a junior scholar who presented a paper titled "Civilizing Missions: Afro-Americans, Christianity, and Colonialism." She was in the process of writing a book on the subject—her first book. The acquisitions editors of the three presses had sent letters of interest to her beforehand, and at least one of them had talked with a religion professor at Princeton University who was serving as a respondent to her convention paper. He had called her work excellent.

Two of the wooing presses wanted the book because they have lists in both religion and black studies; one book would fit two lists. The third press was starting a new Afro-American series. The editors from all three presses visited with her at the convention, and all knew of the attention she was receiving from the others. "She's in the driver's seat, even though this is her first book," commented one of the editors. The junior scholar was in the position to choose to give one of the presses an exclusive option, or she could seek an advance contract, or she could submit the manuscript to all three presses on a simultaneous submission basis.

"Scholarly publishing has become a lot more competitive," one of the competing editors said. "You're slitting your own throat if you ignore that fact."

❦ Competition in Scholarly Publishing

The only real competition in scholarly publishing is the quest for manuscripts. As one editor put it, "The competition between university presses is for the superior manuscript. We can all get the average ones." This competition is not an outright rivalry as much as it is "quiet diplomatic seeking"—a term used by Edward King, assistant director of the University of North Carolina Press. Editors win some and lose some. But they say that competition helps keep their standards high. Competition is viewed as an essential component within an aggressive publishing program.

In the polling of fifty-two university press directors, two-thirds said that competition for manuscripts is increasing among university presses, and the remaining third believe that the level of competition remains unchanged. No respondent believes that competition is decreasing. The director of a "Big Ten" press responded, "The larger presses feed on the author pool in the Big Ten where they can shove aside the smaller local university presses." A southern press director commented, "Competition is keen, and increasing." The director of an eastern press added, "Increasing—but for fewer manuscripts." Even those directors indicating that competition is static suggest that competition already is considerable. The director of a northeastern university press said, "Staying the same. There is always stiff competition for the best manuscripts."

Example: Anthropologist Jon Christopher Crocker of the University of Virginia spent extensive time with the Bororo Indians in South America and acquired a familiarity with them deep enough to get an inside view of their culture. Editor-in-chief Gregory McNamee of the University of Arizona Press heard about his work while attending an American Anthropological Association convention. Arizona has a broad list in anthropology. "The author already had submitted the manuscript to a couple of presses," McNamee said. "I won the manuscript through speed of reading. I told reviewers we were in competition for this manuscript— please hurry along." Arizona published Crocker's *Vital Souls: Bororo Cosmology, Natural Symbolism and Shamanism* in 1985. "It's inevitable you'll be competing for the best authors in a discipline," McNamee said.

Not all presses compete in all areas, however. Competition, after all, is dependent on listbuilding. Two-thirds of the university presses specifically solicit manuscripts in anthropology; others likely wouldn't have been interested in the Bororo shamanism study, had Crocker offered it to them. Stanford University Press, which publishes in law, need not worry about competition from Indiana University Press, which doesn't solicit manuscripts in law. But Indiana and Stanford both offer strong lists in women's studies, and they may compete vigorously for the same authors in that field. Tiers of competition exist, and editors know who their prime competitors are, both within university publishing and in commercial scholarly publishing.

Overall, editors consider the best university presses to be—in alphabetical order—California, Chicago, Harvard, and Yale. These four large presses were most frequently named by editors as having lists of distinction in a broad range of disciplines. In addition, Princeton often is called a model university press because it hasn't become a heavy trade book publisher.

Given the choice of publishing with Harvard University Press, say, or with "State University Press," most authors gleefully will go with Harvard. The name offers prestige. Smaller presses do not have Harvard's ability to engage in large-scale marketing. A Harvard or Yale imprint sells copies. But editors outside the Ivy League believe that the gap is closing. The quality of Ivy League presses is not declining; the quality of university presses in other regions of the nation is improving. A midwest press director said, "There are good presses all across the nation. They are no longer concentrated in the Ivy League or the snob schools." For instance, the LSU, Indiana, and North Carolina presses have national reputations in selected disciplines.

The reputation of a university press is tied closely to the academic reputation of the parent institution. One press director at a football powerhouse school in the Southwest even commented without amusement, "The image of our press seems to follow the fortunes of the football team."

The smaller presses have learned to recognize their standing within scholarly publishing. "When I first started, I thought that when a manuscript was rejected by one press, it was not worth publishing. I've found out that that's not true," said Seetha Srinivasan, associate director of the University Press of Mississippi. In one instance, the Mississippi press published a book previously rejected by the LSU and South Carolina presses. The book became a History Book Club selection. "We're new. Authors sometimes will start at more established presses," she said. "But at first, I was very indignant having to consider a manuscript rejected elsewhere."

Another southern press wooed an eminent historian who had twice published with Harvard. The historian had expected Harvard to pass on his third manuscript, but Harvard had the right of first refusal and instead claimed it. "I try long shots," the acquisitions editor for this less prestigious press said. "Smaller presses must be seen as competitive with the larger presses. Word gets around."

Some established authors prefer smaller presses because they are more personal. The University Press of New England publishes just a third as many new titles as Harvard and one-fourth as many as Yale. "We're not hesitant to go after authors who would go to Harvard or Yale," said Thomas McFarland, director of the New England press. "We've had

TABLE 3.7

Willingness to Consider Simultaneously Submitted Manuscripts

Simultaneous Submission Policy	No. of Presses (N=52)
Accept Simultaneous Submissions	19 (37%)
Refuse Simultaneous Submissions	6 (11%)
Typically Refuse But Make Exceptions	27 (52%)

authors turn down a competitive offer from a larger press, preferring the intimacy of working with a smaller publisher. If an author calls me with a question, I can answer it. They're not dealing with dozens of people, and we work on tighter schedules than most larger presses."

Some editors describe themselves as acquisition activists but not as competitors since, as one put it, "There's not enough money involved for it to matter much." Competitive acquisition methods include allowing multiple submissions and offering advance contracts, monetary advances, and similar inducements designed to attract an author to a press.

Scholarly publishers prefer to consider manuscripts within a context of exclusivity. Each prefers being the only publisher evaluating a particular manuscript at a particular time. Yet Table 3.7 shows that few university presses absolutely refuse to consider a manuscript simultaneously submitted to other presses. More than one of every three responding presses is openly willing to consider a manuscript submitted elsewhere at the same time. The majority still prefer not to but make exceptions now and then.

The appropriateness of exclusivity in manuscript review is a matter of perspective. Time is important to scholars, especially those facing tenure or promotion decisions. From the author's perspective, it seems that a single-submission policy could drag the publishing process out for years. An author can hardly be faulted for attempting all possibilities to ensure rapid publication of a manuscript. But time is important to editors, too. They don't want to waste time in evaluating a manuscript, finding outside reviewers, paying the reviewers to evaluate the work, and having an editorial committee consider the work—only to learn that another press was in the shadows all along and will publish the manuscript.

The answer, from the editors' point of view, is for authors to spend more time studying the lists of presses and send query letters to those presses deemed most appropriate. If more than one press expresses interest, the author should select the most enthusiastic or prestigious one and let it have the manuscript on an exclusive basis for a designated amount of time, such as six to nine weeks.

One acquisitions editor said she seldom considers multiple submissions simply because her time is at a premium, outside readers must be paid more in exchange for a quick review, and failure to win the simultaneously submitted manuscript means no direct dividends for the time and money expended. "There's a lot of wealth to be shared," another editor said. "To compete takes a lot of time with the whole review rigamarole. If six presses are going through this, five books are not going to be pursued and five books won't be published."

Editors, though, are growing more accustomed to simultaneous submissions. But they insist on one thing: being told. "We accept multiple submissions since scholars often can't wait for successive single submissions, but we must be informed," said Jeannette Hopkins, director of Wesleyan University Press. "It's discourteous not to tell a publisher. By the time it is ready for board discussion, but not before, we require that an author tell us whether a Wesleyan contract offer will be accepted."

Some university presses, at the very beginning, insist on the right of first refusal—in writing. "We do not assume single submission unless our authors have said it," one editor said. "We ask for rights of first refusal, and we do not proceed with external review until they've been given. If we happen to learn that another press is also reviewing a project—and we've not been told this and agreed to it up front—we immediately withdraw from further consideration of the project. And we don't forget that author's name."

Of course, deception can occur. One western editor recalled that his press once had accepted a revised dissertation for publication, given it an editing plan, and devoted some twenty hours in-house editing to it already, only to learn that the author had signed a contract with another press. "It was carefully disguised," the editor said. "We had asked him, and he said no."

If the author is candid and if more than one press has a sufficient interest in the topic and agrees to a multiple submission, then competition can become keen. One editor divides manuscripts into four priority piles. Top priority goes to multiple submissions, since those involve immediate competition. Next are the obviously good manuscripts. Third priority are those manuscripts the editor asked the author to submit, based on a query letter or a conversation. The bottom-priority manuscripts are all others.

In a simultaneous-submission case, editors act quickly to find readers, readers are asked to give expeditious reviews, and the author can expect a speedy decision, possibly along with other inducements such as design, production, printrun, and marketing concessions. One editor, though, warned, "The fever of the auction room in this artificial atmosphere can lead to unrealistic expectations on the part of the sellers and excessive offers on the part of the buyers. The excitement and tension of the horse race can tempt competitors to cut corners or bend rules."

Another signpost of competitiveness is a press's willingness to offer advance contracts for traditional monographs. An advance contract is a commitment to publish, offered before a manuscript has been completed. Almost all presses offer advance contracts, although a number of presses do so rarely. First-time authors seldom are offered advance contracts; this form of inducement tends to be reserved for established authors with proven publishing records. Sanford Thatcher, editor-in-chief of Princeton University Press, wrote:

> My main objection to the proliferating use of advance contracts, from the publisher's side, is that they can too easily lead to the subtle erosion of scholarly procedures and standards at university presses. Procedures are undermined whenever in the haste to beat a competitor a press director decides, if he can, to do without external reviews or to bypass his editorial board or both, as some have the authority to do. These more neutral sources of advice and perspective can help check misguided enthusiasms: anyone who has worked with readers and an editorial board knows how many mistakes they have prevented him from making.[8]

Advance contracts may give an author security, but they are inherently unequal. An advance contract commits the author to publish with a particular press, but the press has an escape clause in the event a manuscript is not what was expected. Still, an advance contract makes sense in certain situations. It is valuable when close cooperation between press and author is needed for a major project, such as a reference work or the start of a series. Such a contract may be necessary in commissioning a book translation or in convincing a scientist to write a book. Monetary advances frequently accompany advance contracts. These advances tend to be in the $1,000 to $10,000 range, usually on the lower side. The advance is recouped by the press through withholding author royalties on the first printing.

Overall, competition is viewed positively by editors. The desire to acquire the best manuscripts possible, even when this requires competitive practices, is considered essential to keeping publishing standards high. But Thatcher cautioned that too much of a competitive spirit can undermine scholarly publishing's strengths. He wrote:

> Competition is not an unalloyed good. We are all aware of its dark and seamy side in the history of capitalism generally. What we may not recognize is the harm that competition, a relatively recent phenomenon in scholarly publishing, can do to our business specifically. At the heart of university press publishing is a very special process of review, which validates the imprint of a press: because of it, the imprint guarantees the proven scholarly merit of a work. Anything that tends to undermine or interfere with the rigor of that process is a potentially serious threat to the integrity and uniqueness of university press publishing.[9]

Ironically, while university presses compete in acquisitions, they may be cooperating in other endeavors such as editorial and design work, marketing, warehousing, and sales. For example, in its first five years of existence, the fledgling University of Arkansas Press did its own acquisitions, and the University of Missouri Press initially handled all other publishing functions on a contractual basis, with Arkansas taking over one department's responsibilities each year. Columbia University Press acts as publishing agent for New York University Press. Order fulfillment for the University of Tennessee Press and others is handled by Cornell University Press. Many presses have formed cooperative groups for domestic and foreign sales representation. Most presses freely swap information about design, manufacturing, fulfillment, and computer work. Acquisitions editors even have been known to refer authors to other presses, if a proffered manuscript was not appropriate for the editors' lists. Editors do not view such referrals as part of their job descriptions, but they may make them if the manuscript impresses them and they know of another press that publishes in the field.

❦ The Editor's Decision Time

Whether the manuscripts are invited in response to a query letter, solicited in the course of visiting college campuses, or located by attending scholarly conventions, whether right of first refusal is obtained by agreeing to multiple submissions or by offering advance contracts, acquisitions editors are rated on the strength of what they "bring in."

Once a manuscript is in the house, though, the editor must decide whether the manuscript is worthy of entering the second stage of the scholarly publishing process. The editor must decide at this point whether to proceed to the peer review stage or regretfully to return the manuscript to the author. An editor, after all, does not want to spend months gathering peer reviews and working on author revisions on a manuscript that clearly falls short of the press's standards. An editor makes this decision by reading, or at least glancing at, the manuscript. An editor must be able at this stage to say "no"—even to a manuscript the editor may have aggressively pursued. Beverly Jarrett, when with the LSU Press, wrote:

> The word 'no' is probably the only word more important than 'yes' in an editor's vocabulary. The value of acquisitions editors knowing when to stop reading, when to disengage from a manuscript that is not going to work, cannot be overestimated. As slowly and carefully as editors read—or should read—it is wasteful to keep reading long into a manuscript after a first sense that it is going to prove unacceptable. The sooner an editor can get to the page on which he or she is confident in saying no, the sooner that editor can get on to the next manuscript—and the author can get on to the next press.[10]

Jarrett reads the entire manuscript when she says "yes." Other editors, however, said they rarely read a complete manuscript. Sometimes they read a chapter or two with care; at other times they merely skim it. They are evaluating, not necessarily reading.

An editor at a prestigious university press said he doesn't have time to read each manuscript that comes in—even those that interest him. He glances at the table of contents, the preface or introduction, and reads bits and pieces of the middle chapters. "It's an art," he said, smiling. "I'm able to talk about reorganizing the book or whatever. Most authors, I think, believe I've actually sat down and read the entire manuscript. Of course, I don't tell them differently."

In contrast, one Ivy League press editor reads a good chunk of each manuscript before deciding to "sponsor" it—push for its publication. This editor, who sponsors twenty to thirty manuscripts a year, believes in reading a lot of each manuscript before sending it out for review, so that negative feedback in an outside review won't come as a complete surprise. On agreeing to sponsor a manuscript, the editor becomes an unabashed advocate of the work throughout its passage toward publication. Editors commented that once a press sends a manuscript out for review, the press has made a tacit agreement with the author to publish the manuscript if the reviews are favorable.

Throughout this stage, editors try to do their business with authors on paper—not on the phone or in person, unless there can be a prompt follow-up letter summarizing what was said. Jarrett said that editors need clearly to acknowledge at the outset any limitations on what is being promised, in order to avoid surprise or anger on the part of authors later on, should the manuscript not fare well in the remaining two stages of the editorial process. "By limitations, I mean that the imprint of the press is not under my exclusive control," she said.

No matter how much I like the author or believe in the project or want my press to publish it, I am not able to decide independently that LSU Press will publish a particular book. Much as an author may fall for, or win over, an editor—and want to believe that publication with that press is a cinch—we are obliged not to forget the limitations on our power and not to let our prospective authors forget them. It is obligatory, in my judgment, that an editor say in writing that his or her own commitment to publication must be endorsed by external peer review and confirmed by the press's faculty board.

🍎🍎🍎🍎🍎🍎

4. Validation

Through Academic

Peer Review

No matter how enthusiastic an editor may be, each manuscript must meet the test of peer review before it can be published. This is an evaluation of a manuscript by the author's peers—referees outside the publishing house.

Since scholars serve as the primary audience for university press books, it is only natural to have scholars evaluate a manuscript's contribution to a discipline before the publishing decision is made. This tradition of scholarly refereeing was born in the journals and now is the norm in scholarly book publishing as well. Leading scholars in a discipline are considered the natural gatekeeping advisees for that discipline.

This mandatory process of scholarly peer review serves as a double-sided insurance policy. For the press, peer review provides confirmation that a manuscript is worthy of being on its list. For the author, peer review can help catch errors and improve the work.

"It's easy to understand why authors often view the review process as an obstacle course," said Barbara Hanrahan, humanities editor at the University of Wisconsin Press. "It's very difficult for any author to deal with the fact that the completion of a manuscript isn't the end, but really just the beginning of quite a long process. The author may believe the manuscript is finished, but the editor and the readers don't believe anything of the kind."

The review process is unpredictable, which makes publishing itself an unpredictable business. "If the review process were predictable," Hanrahan said, "it could be conducted by machines instead of people. Each project is unique, and the review process is different each time. Editors constantly make choices and decisions. The situation is further complicated by the fact that the review process is also a balancing act. Ideally, it must serve both the press's interests and the author's at the same time. That is often difficult to accomplish. No matter how long you've been an editor, you always worry that you'll make the wrong decisions, the wrong choices, during the course of a review process and have to turn down a manuscript you want to publish because you obtained a negative reading from an inappropriate reviewer."

To minimize that possibility, the norm in university publishing is to obtain two outside readings. With at least two peer reviews as guidance, editors reduce the fear that a good manuscript will be rejected or a bad one published on the basis of a single misguided critique. Table 4.1 shows that almost nine of ten responding university presses typically send a manuscript to two readers for evaluation.

Depending on the editor's enthusiasm for a manuscript or the need for speed, a university press may send multiple copies of the manuscript to readers simultaneously or send the manuscript to one reader at a time. In the latter case, obviously, the first review carries great weight. Several responding university presses stipulated in the survey that a second reading frequently is dependent on a neutral or favorable first reading. If the first one is highly negative, the manuscript may be returned to the author at that point.

Presses seldom seek more than two outside reviews if both are positive. When a press seeks a third, fourth, or fifth review, it indicates that the editor is an advocate of the manuscript but one of the first two reviews was less than positive. A New York editor said his press had used as many as five readers on a manuscript, but added that a press probably should decline to publish the manuscript if it takes that many readings to arrive at a publishing decision.

"When you get a strong negative, it takes a lot to overcome it," said an acquisitions editor at a midwestern university press. "Once, we had a negative report from an anthropologist, but we thought it was a good work. We ended up getting five positive reports on the manuscript." The manuscript was published. This was a case in which an editor believed so strongly in the worth of a manuscript that a single negative review was

TABLE 4.1

Number of Outside Readers Who Typically Evaluate a Manuscript

Number of Readers	No. of Presses (N=51)
One	2 (4%)
Two	44 (86%)
Three or More	3 (6%)
Variable Number	2 (4%)

Note: The "variable number" category includes a midwestern press which responded that it uses one or two readers, depending on the manuscript, and an eastern press which replied, "two to ten."

considered an obstacle worth overcoming. In other cases, when the editor may not believe so strongly in a manuscript, an early negative review may end the decision-making process.

A few presses responded that a manuscript may go to the editorial committee with only one review, if the reviewer is a top scholar and gives a strongly favorable recommendation. But this is not general practice. The quality-control mechanism of peer review allows a press to reject a manuscript on the basis of a single negative review more often than it would publish a manuscript on the basis of a single positive review.

❦ Selection of Outside Readers

The network of outside readers that a press builds and maintains plays a large role in establishing the reputation of an imprint. One reason that acquisitions editors are given academic territories of listbuilding rather than serving at large is to allow them to become knowledgeable enough to identify the outstanding scholars in a discipline.

Editors find reviewers as they find authors. They chat with scholars at conventions, visit college campuses, and draw on friendships. Editors keep a file of potential reviewers, by discipline. "We have a file on computer," a southern editor said. "If we get a book in pre–Civil War intellectual history, we can go to our list of reviewers in that field."

Stephen Cox, director of the University of Arizona Press, compares a university press editor to a person seeking medical advice. Cox wrote, "Just as there are many kinds of doctors to treat many kinds of symptoms but relatively few doctors expert in any particular syndrome, there are a great many academics generally qualified to evaluate a particular manuscript but only a few who are truly expert."[1]

In search of an expert on Shakespearean studies, an editor could turn to a multitude of scholars for advice. That would not be the case for a manuscript on literary life in postwar Poland. The narrower a manuscript, the fewer the specialist scholars who would be recognized as expert enough to pass judgment on the manuscript.

The best scholars in each discipline usually are swamped with manuscripts to review. In narrow fields, in fact, presses may turn to the same experts. An editor at one university press told of publishing a book previously rejected by a university press in a neighboring state. The editor first learned of the previous rejection when she called a scholar to ask if he would review it. The scholar responded that he already had read the manuscript for another press. She asked which one, and then called the press to ask why the manuscript had been turned down. She discovered that the rejection had been based on listbuilding considerations, not on the quality of scholarship. She was satisfied. "Sometimes a manuscript rejected by one press is just right for another," the editor said.

The selection of expert readers for interdisciplinary manuscripts is more complex. A reader must have both the interest and the intellect to evaluate a broadly synthetic work.

Many other hazards exist in finding the right readers for a manuscript. A manuscript that uses a new methodology or theoretical framework can be doomed if an editor turns solely to mainstream traditionalists within a discipline. The politics of readers also can be important. "You don't want a neo-Marxist reading a particular manuscript—it would kill it," one editor said. Added another, "A Marxist will hate a Durkheimian approach."

In addition, editors must avoid intellectual schisms. They must be cognizant of diverse schools of thought that may exist in a particular discipline. Editors seek to be familiar enough with a discipline to recognize that some experts would be inappropriate as readers for a manuscript because of conceptual differences.

The University Press of Mississippi publishes a lot about native son William Faulkner. The press's associate director, Seetha Srinivasan, knows that distinct camps of scholars exist in Faulkner studies. "If I get a manuscript from a member of 'A school of Faulkner' and send it for a review to a member of 'B school of Faulkner,' it will come back with a guarded review," she said. "We have to be very careful not to get someone belonging to a particular school. You have to be familiar enough with the subject and then find persons in the field who will be knowledgeable about the subject and at the same time be objective about the manuscript."

The advocates of one school consider Faulkner the precursor of the southern renaissance. As a result, they write in the tradition of southern letters. *The Heart of Yoknapatawpha* is a University Press of Mississippi example of this approach. Another school emphasizes a psychological reading of Faulkner's work. This approach is influenced by European critics and stems from the popularity of Faulkner translations in Europe and the Soviet Union. An example of a nontraditional approach is *Intertextuality in Faulkner*, which came out of a 1982 Paris conference and was published by the Mississippi press. The press publishes both types of works. "It doesn't really matter to me which school they're in," Srinivasan said. "What is significant to us is, is the scholarship sound?"

Certain informal rules apply in the selection of outside readers. They cannot be in the same department as the author, or even on the same campus. Editors try to avoid readers who might be influenced by considerations such as friendship, animosity, or even second-generation disputes in which scholars cling to the grudges of their mentors.

Authors often are asked to supply recommendations for peer reviewers. "We just got a book on the history of lumbering," said the director at a smaller university press. "I have no idea who would know about that. I asked the author for a list of scholars in the field. I'll probably call those and ask them for others. That way, I find experts the author doesn't know."

This technique also is a good way to note an author's knowledge of those best qualified to judge their work. "If they name two people in their department and their dissertation adviser, there's good reason to be leery," said Kate Torrey, editor-in-chief at the University Press of Kansas. Editors also may ask authors to name those they do not want to serve as outside readers, and why. This way, a press can avoid the coincidence of asking an author's bitterest critic to be a manuscript judge.

In such an imperfect system, the potential for abuse exists. But editors said that few authors attempt to rig readers' reports by recommending cronies or by attempting to dodge the most demanding scholars in their field. Editors who feel strongly about a particular manuscript or feel a loyalty to a particular author could themselves rig the system by selecting outside readers they believe would judge a manuscript favorably. But editors said they don't do it. A bias already is built into the system, because the editor is making the initial selection of manuscripts that will make it to the peer review stage. "You don't want to build a second bias into the system in the selection of referees," one editor said. "The process offers a tempering of enthusiasm." The review process, when conducted fairly, becomes a system of checks and balances for the publishing house.

As a byproduct, the selection of readers can pay dividends later in terms of acquired manuscripts. A press wants the best readers it can find, not only because they can give a manuscript the best critique, but also because, at a later point, readers can become authors for the same press. Editors said that they routinely ask reviewers what they are working on. "Sometimes we ask someone in a field to review just to establish a contact, because we want something that person is working on," a western press editor said. Editors told of occasions in which a scholar first served as a reader for a press and later published a book with the same press.

❦ Why Scholars Agree to be Readers

Few scholarly activities bring so little public glory as serving as a manuscript reader. Only an editor may ever know that the scholar plodded through five-hundred pages of typescript and prepared a six-page, single-spaced critique chronicling a manuscript's strengths and weaknesses. The manuscript itself, if the report is negative, may never make it into print. The scholar, in such a case, never will be able to hold a published book in hand and say that the hours spent on the product were worth it.

The scholar also certainly doesn't do it for the money. Readers' fees provide only slight financial compensation for the time and effort involved. University presses generally offer fees ranging from $75 to $150, depending on the length and complexity of the manuscript. In lieu of money, most university presses offer an equivalent value in books at discounted prices. Sometimes readers will request a book or two, with the discounted prices subtracted from the stipulated fee. Usually, though, readers take the money in full.

In no way does the reader's fee cover what the expert does. So why do scholars agree to serve as manuscript readers? One reason is that manuscript refereeing is regarded as part of the job description of a scholar. "The money is secondary. It's an honorarium," one editor said. "Think about it. That's less than minimum wage. They do it for protection, to ensure that material in the discipline stays high. Also, it's a way to keep up, to see new trends before they become generally known."

A major inducement for scholars to spend their time reading and evaluating a manuscript is their own interest in the subject. New manuscripts include new information that, if of any value at all to a scholar in the particular field, will have to be read anyway when eventually published. To read it in manuscript form, then, is not necessarily wasted effort. Another reason is that scholars enjoy getting to know editors who, in the future, might want to sponsor their own work.

Once the press decides that a manuscript is worth consideration, the editor must identify and contact appropriate outside readers. The editor's overtures to the appropriate outside readers is a delicate editorial skill. Some editors write letters; some send telegrams. Most said they use the telephone because it is faster and more direct and because it results in a higher acceptance rate.

"Seldom am I turned down," one editor said. "You have to do your homework first. I let them know I'm not calling them out of the blue." Added another, "If you get turned down repeatedly, you start wondering about the manuscript. After all, if we can't *pay* people to review this manuscript, how are we going to get people to pay to read it?"

This step of finding and contacting the appropriate readers can take from a couple of days to a couple of weeks, depending on the urgency of the situation and on the fervor the editor may have for the manuscript under consideration. For authors, time can be important. Some may be

TABLE 4.2

Average Length of Time a Reader Takes to Evaluate a Manuscript

Length of Time	No. of Presses (N=51)
One to Three Weeks	2 (4%)
Four to Five Weeks	21 (41%)
Six to Eight Weeks	25 (49%)
More than Eight Weeks	3 (6%)

Note: These ranges were not specified in the questionnaire. The open-ended responses—several of which contained such ranges—have been grouped in these categories for ease of comparison.

facing tenure or promotion decisions at a specified time. The time factor is exacerbated by the tendency among university presses to discourage multiple submission of manuscripts. Even after an author has interested a press in the manuscript, the publishing machinery moves slowly. It can take months or even years from the point of manuscript submission to the point of published book. So an important factor in the publishing process is the length of time it takes outside readers to evaluate a manuscript.

Table 4.2 shows that about half of the responding presses estimated that outside readers typically report back in six to eight weeks. Most of the other presses estimated the average response time to be four or five weeks. Of course, not all manuscripts are typical, and not all readers respond within a typical time frame. An eastern press director said, "Anything from one week to six months. Those who take six months are swiftly dropped from our stable of reviewers." Another editor noted that some readers put the manuscript on a corner of their desk, where it gets covered with other papers. "We've had readers who have even forgotten they have the manuscripts," the editor said. "I've had readers who went on vacation without sending in their review or returning the manuscript. Academics are not the most efficient!"

Some scholars realize, upon receipt of a manuscript, that they do not have a real interest in its topic. An Oxford University Press editor said that she once had a scholar return a manuscript without critiquing it, saying in appropriate British terminology, "It's not my cup of tea." Kate Wittenberg, executive editor of Columbia University Press, said that reviewers are instructed to let the editor know immediately if they realize they can't get to a manuscript sent to them. Still, editors said, some manuscripts get pushed aside.

University presses tend to send manuscripts to the busiest scholars and are, in a sense, asking a favor of them. There really is no way around this imposition, however, short of staying away from busy people who are busy precisely because they are the experts in a field.

A universal fear of young scholars whose manuscripts have at last reached this stage is that the busy scholar who agreed to evaluate a manuscript is swamped with manuscripts and will sit on it for two semesters. But editors routinely specify a deadline for a reader's report to be submitted. The University of Iowa Press, for example, asks its readers to report within four weeks. Others give six or eight weeks. Or the deadline may be negotiated individually with a reader. "If they're late, you nag," replied an acquisitions editor.

❦ What Readers Say about Manuscripts

Some university presses simply ask readers to examine the manuscript and comment in narrative form on its suitability for publication; other presses provide a questionnaire for reviewers to fill out, to ensure that all aspects are covered.

Each press has its own list of questions. Readers may be asked to state the principal theme or thesis of the manuscript and to address various questions: Is the scholarship sound? Is it accurate, balanced, thorough? Does the manuscript represent a contribution to knowledge? Is the author's style readable? Should any portions of the manuscript be rewritten or jettisoned? Would the reviewer recommend the work to colleagues? Finally, does the reviewer recommend publishing it as is, only after revision, or not at all? Readers are asked to write all comments on the form or in a letter. They are requested not to write on the manuscript itself, since it either will go to another reviewer or be returned to the author.

Readers repeatedly are encouraged to take a position on a manuscript's scholarly worth. An Ivy League acquisitions editor said that the "nebulous middle" is common ground for reviewers. Editors don't like it. They want the experts in a field to tell them whether the manuscript should be published as a book. "We tell reviewers to move off center," said the director of a university press in the Southwest. "A lukewarm review—well, it doesn't really help us. We ask them to get off dead center. We school our readers to say yes or no. We tell them they won't kill the book by listing some reservations."

The reports recommending a manuscript for publication don't have to be totally favorable. Few are. One reader wrote, in effect, "In my opinion, the author is working his way down a blind alley. But he is exploring it so interestingly and with such valuable insights that I think his work ought to be published."[2] Another editor recalled one reviewer who responded, "I don't agree with the author's perspective, but is the literature there? Yes. Is he fair? Yes." The reviewer recommended publication.

At this stage of the scholarly publishing process, many manuscripts that looked promising to editors—and perhaps even were solicited by them—lose their appeal. The number of manuscripts that receive unqualified endorsement in the outside review process is a distinct minority. Table 4.3 shows a clear tilt toward a low manuscript acceptance rate and a high manuscript rejection rate by outside peer readers.

Specifically, fourteen responding presses said that their outside readers collectively recommended publication, with little or no revision necessary, for fewer than 20 percent of the manuscripts evaluated. Another eighteen presses said their outside readers recommended outright publication for between 20 and 29 percent of the manuscripts considered. Yet nine presses estimated that their outside readers recommended outright publication at least half of the time. Seventeen presses estimated that outside readers recommended against publication at least half of the time, while only three presses said that this happened less than 20 percent of the time.

Although a trend appears clear (counseling guarded optimism on the part of an author who does reach this stage in the decision-making process), the variability from press to press suggests that each press has its own philosophy about the outside peer review process. Some presses rather freely send manuscripts out for review. Others are considerably

TABLE 4.3

Estimate of Responses by Outside Readers

	By No. of Presses (N=52)				
	Under 20%	20–29%	30–39%	40–49%	50% up
Recommend Publishing with Little or No Revision	14	18	9	2	9
Recommend Substantial Revision before Publishing	7	11	11	8	15
Recommend Not Publishing	3	12	15	5	17

Note: These ranges were not specified in the questionnaire. The open-ended responses have been grouped for ease of comparison.

more selective, not sending a manuscript out for review unless the editors are fairly sure that it will get positive recommendations. Ironically, the higher percentages of favorable recommendations often were reported by the more prestigious presses, which publish a large number of books by senior scholars whose works are unlikely to receive anything but a favorable recommendation. Many of the lower percentages of favorable recommendations were reported by smaller, less prestigious presses which typically deal with junior scholars. In search of the best works possible, these presses may send a lot of less-than-best works to outside readers for evaluation.

Converting the individual percentage estimates into actual numbers of titles and then compiling an overall average, we see that responding presses collectively estimated that about 29 percent of outside reader responses recommended publication with little or no revision necessary, 36 percent of the responses recommended substantial revision before publication, and 35 percent of the responses recommended against publication of the manuscript in any form.

Editors said that a recommendation for substantial revision is tantamount to a rejection. Often the editors will keep the project alive if the author is willing to revise the manuscript heavily, but once revised, it is treated much like a new project in that it goes again for outside reviews. The toughest reviewer on the first round of reviews may be asked to evaluate the revised version, or a fresh reviewer may be enlisted.

Malcolm MacDonald, director of the University of Alabama Press, said:

> Administratively, even in those cases in which we return a manuscript to an author with great encouragement to revise on the basis of one or two readers' reports, we consider our communication to be a rejection, and we consider the manuscript anew when it arrives revised for consideration. We do this because the author continues to have freedom to choose another course of action for his manuscript than the one we offer. We make certain he realizes that he has that freedom, precisely because we do not want to be put into the position of having offered encouragement, only to be forced to reject the manuscript again.

Editors said that senior scholars who receive outside reviews calling for substantial revision may turn to another press at that point, if they believe their original work is publishable and need not be rewritten. First-time authors, though, seldom want to abandon a press that has encouraged resubmission.

Not only do acquisitions editors determine which manuscripts enter the publishing "gate" and then select the readers they consider most appropriate, but also editors must know how to interpret the outside reviews upon receipt. A former director of the Wesleyan University Press offered this example:

> I recall seeking the advice of a scholar whom I consider to be the oracle in a particular field, and he suggested two readers for a specific script, people whom he knew and whose judgment he respected. 'But you must know how to read their reports,' he warned. 'A is a kindly man who finds something to praise in everyone and everything he encounters. Pay no attention to his praise of the manuscript, but be alert for any reservations he expresses, even by implication. B, on

the other hand, prides himself on being tough and is a congenital fault-finder. Pay no attention to his inevitable list of flaws—but if he says anything good, however begrudgingly, note it well.'[3]

The selection of readers is one skill, then, and the ability to interpret their reports is another. Thomas McFarland, director of the University Press of New England, said, "We can tell the difference between a good report and sniping. There's a lot of instinct in this, but there's some science to the selection process, too." Editors say that they can spot the negative reviews that are animated by personal or nonobjective criteria. The nonobjective review may not be disregarded, but other reviews are sought for balance.

One way to lessen the impact of unfair evaluations is to give the author the chance to see, and refute if possible, criticism of the author's work. Authors may take exception to the accuracy or appropriateness of readers' suggestions. This response by the author goes to the sponsoring editor, not to the outside reader. Unless there is good reason to start a third-party correspondence service between author and outside reader, presses avoid it. Presses want to protect outside readers from the darts of the scorned. After all, from the press's point of view, the reader performs a time-consuming service that provides no glory and little money. No scholar agreeing to serve as an outside reader wants to acquire an irate pen-pal in the process.

The key method of protecting outside readers is assuring them anonymity. Without this protection, many readers might refuse the task or might not respond with candor concerning the worth of a manuscript. With this protection, anonymous readers also avoid becoming continual advisors to aspiring authors whose work falls in the "nebulous middle."

Another guarantee of objectivity is proposed from time to time. This proposal suggests mutual anonymity—that when a manuscript is sent to a reader, the name of the author be omitted as well. No hard data exist on whether readers are greatly influenced by the fame or obscurity of the author. But editors said that a psychological element indeed may exist. They point to the appearance in readers' reports of such prior-influence phrases as "the author is a senior scholar" and "the author is recognized in the field." But mutual anonymity would prevent editors from assuring an objective review. Editors said that they need to share the name of the author to avoid arranging outside reviews from good friends, former colleagues, or sworn enemies who might know the work was in progress.

Are authors entitled to learn the contents of the readers' reports that have served as the basis for rejection? Does the author have a *right* to know? Several editors said that a publisher does not have an obligation to say anything other than yes or no. But none recalled ever holding back a critique from an author. It would be a waste to have scholars in a field critique a manuscript, particularly if the outcome is negative, and then not share the specifics with the author. Such sharing can result in the author's improving the work and having it published elsewhere as a contribution to scholarship. Even when the outside reviews are primarily positive, readers typically offer suggestions for revision. An author should either make the revisions along the lines suggested, or offer good reasons not to do so. It is not necessary for the author to make every change suggested, but it is essential to reply to the editor in a reasoned manner.

For example, a scholar reviewing a historical study called the manuscript significant in its revisionist work, but criticized the author for delighting too much in attacking the views of other historians. The reader's report said, "While other historians may require modification of their interpretations, it is somewhat ungracious to discount them all as worthless. An author is certainly permitted to press his own interpretation vigorously, especially when it is original, but he might well do so with . . . moderation." The reviewer noted that his own article on this subject had not been cited, adding: "Perhaps that is just as well; the article and its theme would probably have been dismissed with all the other historians whom [the author] relegates to the junk pile of historiography." The author, on seeing this critique of his work, responded to the press that he would be happy to make the suggested changes in his manuscript, adding, "I never meant to imply that every historian who wrote on the subject was inept. What is required is more graceful phrasing."

In the peer-review process, scholars have no obligation to find something nice to say about a manuscript. They can be blunt and even harsh. One peer reviewer wrote of a manuscript:

I am sorry that I could not find more nice things to say about it, but honestly I am rather depressed to find him wasting his time like this. The book has a thrown-together, dictated-but-not-read quality, and in my opinion could not be made into a serious work of scholarship or even a "good read," however much time were spent on revisions. . . .

I tried manfully to keep from scribbling on the manuscript, as you requested, but toward the end succumbed to natural indignation. It is disheartening to see one's own work cited by someone who has either not mastered it or, worse, has not even read it. I hope, however, that you will not put my negative report down to wounded professionalism; I would have written a favorable report if it were at all possible. . . .

The style in which this manuscript is written ranges from cute to embarrassingly bad. The adjectives I would use are personal, whimsical, clumsy, gauche, dull, and sententious. Some of the chapters begin like sermons by a young preacher who was wounded by a course in sociology.

The reviewer chastised the author for sending a manuscript to a publisher without first having other scholars read and critique it. He said no senior scholar would think of launching a manuscript without first having picked as many brains as conveniently possible.

The author was shown this and a second negative review, and he replied in a letter to the press's director:

I want to apologize for the two wretched reviews of my manuscript you ended up paying for; they were by light years the two worst I have ever received for anything. . . . I am in the process of tearing the book down and incorporating many of [the second reader's] suggestions.

Upon revision, the press sent the manuscript back to the second reviewer for a new evaluation. The first reviewer had been so negative that it was not considered worthwhile to send him the revised version. The second reader gave the revised version a positive recommendation, and the author responded: "I was pleased to see that my reader has changed his evaluation of the manuscript and actually had some good things to say about it this time. It is not the most effusive report I have ever seen but the distance from his first one is gratifying." The press then involved a third reader, who called it a manuscript worth publishing as written.

What makes this a heartwarming case study is that the revised manuscript was published, it received good reviews, and it did well in sales. The review process had served to make the manuscript better.

Not all peer reviews are critical or call for a rewriting. One reviewer wrote: "I've read quite a few manuscripts over the last several months—for colleagues and friends and university presses. Being something of a perfectionist, I have invariably found things to criticize and changes to recommend, even in the works of distinguished historians. But, frankly, [this manuscript] is a fine piece of work which ought to be published essentially as it stands." The reader paid the manuscript the supreme compliment of saying it superseded his own monograph on the topic.

Throughout the process of gathering and interpreting evaluations, editors are weighing the positives of the manuscript against the negatives, deciding whether the manuscript should go to the next stage of the decision-making process. Malcolm MacDonald of Alabama said:

> At every stage of the manuscript consideration process, we are presented with only two choices. Initially, for example, the inquiry stimulates the choice to invite or not. When a manuscript arrives, the choice is whether or not to seek an external review. When the review is completed, the choice is whether or not to obtain a second review. Finally, with two supportive readings in hand, the choice is whether or not to recommend the manuscript to our Press Committee for acceptance. Often these choices are not clear-cut and demand a great amount of discussion among colleagues. But the press's response cannot be ambiguous, for that is unfair to the author.

🐝 Committee Control of the Imprint

At university presses, editors may have in their possession a manuscript that they like and even one that outside readers admire as a contribution to scholarship, but the ultimate decision to publish still rests in the hands of a committee comprised primarily of university faculty members.

This committee of academicians plays no role in the publishing process until the very end. Salaried professionals—the acquisitions editors—decide which manuscripts the editorial committee gets to consider. The editorial committee does not consider any work that has not already passed through the acquisitions filter. After the editorial committee makes its decisions, all future publishing functions—editing, design, production, and distribution—will be handled by more salaried professionals.

Yet sandwiched between those to whom publishing is a profession is this committee of book-publishing novices. This assortment of practicing scholars operates with a different bottom line than the publishing professionals. Rather than considering an author's prestige or a manuscript's sales potential, they are to consider only the quality of scholarship.

Jack Miles, now with the *Los Angeles Times*, recalled his amazement upon attending his first university press editorial committee meeting: "While I was an editor at Doubleday and still just a candidate for a position with the University of California Press, I attended a meeting of the California editorial committee. The meeting astonished me. None of the faculty members asked whether the books under consideration would sell, and the faculty members did all the talking. The only question considered was whether a book was any good."[4]

The committee's function is to control "the imprint"—a term that many in scholarly publishing pronounce as if it began with capital letters. Only upon formal committee action can any book appear bearing the official title of the university press which is publishing the work.

Being named to the editorial committee of a university press may be the most popular committee assignment on campus. After all, this is a committee that actually produces something. It does not meet to *prevent* something—empire-building, the autocracy of deans, or a new idea that would merely increase the workload. The committee has the wholly positive purpose of awarding "the imprint" to deserving manuscripts. Within months of a decision, the committee members get to admire the physical product of that decision. This generally happy cycle lends an air of congeniality to the group. Factions seldom form, and members view themselves as colleagues in an interdisciplinary scholarly enterprise. Even more delightful, they get to make their decisions with minimal consideration to financial constraints. Although presses do not operate in a budgetary vacuum, it is not their committees' money or even its members' departments' money that is at stake.

The editorial committee is a group normally ranging in number from seven to fifteen, who represent major areas of study within the parent university. The composition of these editorial committees is diverse, consisting exclusively of faculty members at some presses and featuring a mixture of faculty and administrators at other presses. In 1989, the editorial board at Syracuse University Press had eleven members—one each from engineering, political science, drama, physics, history, philosophy, human development, religion, sociology, English, and library science. The committee on publications at Yale University Press consisted of the press's director and eight faculty members—two from history and one each from political science, law, classics, sociology, child studies, and the natural sciences. The editorial committee at the University Press of New England has one scholar from each of the nine member schools, and each campus has its own committee that serves as a prescreening mechanism. The University Press of Kansas has an editorial committee consisting of two members from each of the six regents institutions. There is no mandate to appoint members to complement the press's listbuilding areas. "Some of our most valuable editorial committee members come from the hard sciences—not an area we publish in," the director said.

Committee members are appointed for rotating terms ranging from two to five years. Selection of board members typically is made by the chief academic officer of the university. At some universities, the press director negotiates with the chief academic officer on the selection. "We study the makeup of our board very carefully," one director said. "As much as possible, we try to fit our listbuilding areas. We also look for well-read, conscientious individuals." Added an editor at another press: "We check out prospective board members over lunch. We go after those who are scholars in our listbuilding areas. Once, we wanted a junior faculty member who was not tenured. Our recommendation was turned down." Tenure often is a requirement for appointment to editorial committees. A byproduct of this policy is that most committees tend to be predominantly white and male. Editors cited this as a problem, particularly if the press publishes in women's studies or black studies. But the pool of female and minority faculty members who are tenured is rather small, and they are in demand on other committees needing female or minority representation.

Editorial committee members receive some "perks." Typically, smaller university presses give board members a copy of each book produced during their service on the board. Larger presses may limit the number to five free books a year, to be selected by the board member. Members of the Yale committee on publications receive an honorarium, but a paid

TABLE 4.4
Estimate of Editorial Committee Rejections

Rejection Rates	No. of Presses (N=51)
No Manuscripts Rejected	20 (39%)
1–5 Percent Rejected	21 (41%)
6–10 Percent Rejected	7 (14%)
More than 10 Percent Rejected	3 (6%)

Note: These ranges were not specified in the questionnaire. The open-ended responses have been grouped for ease of comparison.

committee appointment is rare. Responded one director: "We give them a free lunch every month. That's it."

Although "editorial committee" is a common term for this group, it is by no means the only term. These committees go by a variety of names. Wisconsin has a Committee on the University Press, Tennessee an Editorial Board, Harvard a Board of Syndics, Princeton a Board of Trustees, Johns Hopkins a Faculty Editorial Board, and Chicago a Board of University Publications. Whatever the name, their missions are identical—to approve the manuscripts that ultimately will bear the university's imprint.

Table 4.4 shows that if a manuscript makes it to the editorial committee stage, its chances of publication are exceptionally good. Twenty responding university presses reported that their editorial committees rejected no manuscripts in the survey year. Another twenty-one presses estimated the rejection rate to be 5 percent or below, meaning that at least nineteen of every twenty manuscripts presented for approval eventually are awarded the imprint. Seven presses reported that their editorial committees rejected 6 to 10 percent of submissions, and three gave a rejection rate of more than 10 percent. Of those three, one estimated a 15 percent rejection rate and another a 20 percent rejection rate. The third, with an editorial board rejection rate of 50 percent, explained that the editorial committee formally rejects all unsolicited manuscripts deemed unworthy to be sent for outside review.

Several acquisitions editors said privately that sometimes they submit a manuscript that received lukewarm outside reviews to the editorial committee for consideration. The manuscript might get through and, if it doesn't, the author will be angry at a faceless committee rather than at the editor for not pursuing publication to the very end. Some editors said that their committees like to say "no" now and then, so a few borderline projects become sacrificial lambs.

By converting the individual percentage estimates into actual numbers of titles and then compiling an overall average, we estimate that, for the responding presses collectively, about 3 percent of all manuscripts brought before editorial committees ultimately are denied the imprint.

University press directors and editors say the approval rate of editorial committees is high because, by the time a manuscript reaches the committee, it has proven its quality both to the editors and to academic peers. "We do not take to the board any unpromising projects," a University of Minnesota Press editor said. Added Miller Williams, director of the University of Arkansas Press, "It's a pretty damn good book by the time we go from 1,000 manuscripts and 3,000 query letters to eight published books a year."

❦ Powerful and "Pussycat" Committees

The editorial committees at university presses all may have the same mission, but some have evolved into powerful boards while others serve basically to approve the editors' choices. An acquisitions editor at a southern university press called his editorial committee "a pussycat." The committee is comprised primarily of business professors and others who know little about the press's list areas. The editor said that the committee gives blanket approval to all editorial suggestions. At a midwestern university press, the editorial committee has never said no to a proposal, and only two "no" votes have been cast by any individual members in the past decade. "I've never taken a project to them without my strong recommendation," the director said. "If I am held accountable for how the press does, then I need a lot of leeway in what the press publishes." An editor at an eastern press agreed, saying the editorial staff serves as the decision-maker and the press's editorial board then approves 99 percent of the manuscripts brought to it.

At some university presses, however, editorial committees have developed reputations for unpredictable independence. An editor at a northern press commented about her press's editorial board, "They don't want to be a rubber stamp. Projects you are sure will sail through will run into problems. Others you think are safe will get caught in the funniest arguments." While at another press, this editor sponsored a manuscript on deconstruction and theology. Deconstruction is a development in contemporary critical theory that, when applied to theology, challenges a lot of traditional notions about the timelessness of God. Members on the editorial committee balked at granting publication to such a work. She finally told the committee, "I don't think you should refuse to publish a book because it takes a field in a new direction." She won the board battle by one vote. "I was desperate. I couldn't imagine going back to the author and saying I couldn't win a fight for his book."

Editors do develop a loyalty to the manuscripts they choose to sponsor. Once they have obtained positive outside reviews from the scholar's peers, an editor expects the editorial committee to say yes. If the manuscript is threatened in an editorial committee discussion, then the editor often becomes a crusader.

The relationship between editors and editorial committees, then, at times is one of camaraderie and at other times can become adversarial. A potential for strain exists because editorial committees rely completely on editors to bring manuscripts to the publishing house. Yet editorial committees have the power to decide not to publish a work after an editor may have spent months acquiring the manuscript, obtaining positive outside reviews, and working with the author on the necessary revisions— and committees occasionally use that power. A. Bartlett Giamatti, once a member of the Yale University Press publications committee, wrote:

> I believe a university press is intellectually healthy when a spirit of affectionate antagonism exists between the editorial committee and the house editors. . . . Editors, after all, control the process in a fundamental way; they decide what will and will not enter the system. Editors are also charged with soliciting readers' reports, encouraging projects, dealing with authors. Editors create the agenda for the editorial committee in every sense.[5]

Objecting to the term "affectionate antagonism," Yale editor-at-large Edward Tripp replied:

> It is true that the role of a final arbiter can be crucial, if not necessarily central, to the successful operation of any process of selection. But a faculty editorial committee holds only one of the many keys with which a press tries to lock out mediocrity and lock in quality. That this is the last key to be turned lends the acts of the committee an impressive finality—but their effectiveness depends on what has happened beforehand. The problem is that the committee, unlike the editors, has not been hanging around the barn. When it finally locks the door, how can it be sure the horse is still inside?[6]

Tripp said that editors are human and thus suffer from blind spots, too great an empathy with authors, and unreasoned dislikes that may cloud their judgment. "At such moments," he wrote, "unworthy manuscripts may storm their defenses or good ones slip away. In the latter case, the committee will never hear of them. In the former there is, theoretically, a second line of defense." Tripp added:

> The truth is that as much quality as the committee will see has already been identified or it would not be seeing it. The committee's role is, in fact, to identify the *absence* of quality—to pluck the remaining weeds out of the bouquet that the editors bring to each meeting. This is a purely negative function, in that, if the committee did not exist, the best manuscripts chosen by the editors would be published anyhow—along with some less good ones.[7]

In the early 1980s, the editorial committee at Princeton University Press routinely pitted manuscripts against one another. Professor Robert Darnton said that during his years on the board, a dozen or so manuscripts would be selected for publication each month from a field of fifteen to nineteen manuscripts, all of which had passed the previous tests. "There is no ironclad quota, but there are always losers—and more of them each year as the competition gets stiffer," Darnton wrote.[8]

At the 1985 convention of southern university presses, while awaiting a talk by Alex Haley, several university press directors and editors began talking about Princeton's acquisition methods and its editorial board.

"Young scholars are excited to get a letter from Princeton," one director said, "but they solicit far too many manuscripts." Since only two-thirds of the manuscripts that met outside reader approval were accepted by the board during this time, it meant that a considerable number of scholars were encouraged, and then, at the last step, their manuscripts were rejected. "I'm not saying their [the authors'] lives have been ruined," one editor said, "but they have been traumatized for awhile." The Princeton board traditionally did not carry over any manuscripts from one meeting to the next. If a manuscript did not receive approval on first presentation, it was out. "It's really traumatic," another editor said. "They're playing with their lives. They encourage them, get them all excited, and then the board dumps the manuscript." Some of the Princeton editors felt so guilty about this, another southern editor said, that she occasionally received a call from a Princeton editor trying to place one of the turned-down manuscripts at another press. One director told of publishing a Princeton board reject. "Too late for him. He was denied tenure. I'm not saying it ruined his life—he's now in the movie business in California—but that wasn't what he originally wanted to do," this director said.

An acquisitions editor for Princeton University Press confirmed that the Princeton editorial board in the early 1980s did turn down a large number of manuscripts. "It was a difficult situation for editors," she said. But she added that the board-editor relationship at the Princeton press had become more reciprocal in recent years.

The Princeton situation was not typical. Usually, an editorial committee faces no quota, but decides which manuscripts to publish based on the scholarly merits of each. An editor for Yale University Press said that the Yale board is not used as a mechanism to say "no" to manuscripts. If found worthy, all manuscripts brought before the board could be approved for publication. A quota system, so to speak, is employed by presses at an earlier stage. Press personnel know how many new titles they can publish in a given year and still stay within their budget and staffing limitations, so they use past experience to determine how many manuscripts they need to have under consideration at any one time.

The membership of editorial committees, of course, continually changes. Some presses, though, have developed reputations for having maverick boards. The editorial board at one prominent West Coast university press has the reputation of being "a wild card," as one editor put it. One established scholar related how it took this press five years to publish his manuscript on psychoanalysis, a work which involved the medical profession. He had made substantial revisions based on a set of readers' reports, he said, only to have an editorial committee member demand, "What right does a non-M.D. have to write a book like this?" The board ordered the editor to select a new chief reviewer—this time, a practicing medical doctor was mandated. On this second round, more than eighteen months passed before the manuscript reached the board again. This time, the manuscript was approved for publication. The author praised his sponsoring editor, calling him "a gladiator in the ring for my manuscript." But the author said that he was bitter that he had been forced to delete some of the more penetrating psychoanalytic insights in order to make the manuscript acceptable to the editorial committee. "A lot of the edge, a lot of the pungency was taken out. I don't disavow the book, but it's not the book I originally wrote," this author said. "Now, I love a good editor, but I'm talking here about intellectual censorship. If the cream-of-the-crop press is putting pressure like this on authors, what about the little press? They can't be as daring."

❦ Presenting Manuscripts for a Vote

Depending on the size of the press and the activist nature of the board, editorial committee meetings range from once each month to only three times a year. This is a time for faculty members serving on the committee to clear their calendars for at least half a day.

A few presses—primarily the small ones—encourage editorial committee members to read at least parts of all manuscripts under consideration. At the larger presses, that is all but impossible, since so many manuscripts are considered. One committee member often is designated to report on a particular manuscript. When no-one on the committee is particularly suited to review a given manuscript, the editor may be designated to make the presentation. "For a project on medieval literature, I would present that project myself because there's no-one on the editorial board with expertise in the field," one acquisitions editor explained. At the largest university presses, which publish an average of one new title per work day, the editorial committee cannot even divide the workload. Editors present all projects under consideration.

At this late stage in the acquisition process, editors worry that extraneous factors may enter the picture. For that reason, some editors prefer—although this is seldom spoken aloud—that faculty members on the board who are outside a manuscript's scholarly field *not* read the manuscript beforehand. An acquisitions editor at a university press in the southwest related an example in which an extraneous factor harmed the scholarly process. "One board member took a book not in his field home with him," the editor said. "His wife, who was tangentially related to the field, criticized it. The editor, as a result, had to get another series of reports. If someone on the board is an expert in the field, then of course they should read it. Otherwise, we'd just as soon they not."

No matter who makes the presentation, each editorial committee member has in hand a dossier on each manuscript—readers' reports, author's responses, sometimes part or all of the manuscript itself. When the appointed time comes, the committee member or editor makes a report. All committee members have in front of them photocopies of the same correspondence, which they may or may not have waded through themselves in preparation for the meeting. If the committee member goes on at length without focus, another committee member likely will cut through the verbiage with a direct question such as "Should we publish this book?"

One of the rewards of a professor's committee service is becoming familiar with scholarship that he or she otherwise might not read. Professor Hugh Kenner fondly recalled experiences during his six years on the University of California board:

> In theory, manuscripts went to committee members already expert in the subject field, but so broad and continuous is the spectrum of submissions that Omniscience itself couldn't select that knowledgeable a committee, not even from California's nine-campus faculty. So sponsoring editors grow expert at spotting unlikely zones of responsiveness in committee members. For years all our film manuscripts were presented by a man whose certified competence, French literature, was rarely called on, and everything pertaining to music by a biologist. Another biologist was our Swahili expert. If you want ran-

dom wide-ranging expertise, you seem to strengthen your chances by stacking the deck with biologists. Things were never so lively as in the days when by some miscalculations there were five of them on the committee at once.[9]

At Kenner's first-ever editorial committee meeting, one manuscript under consideration was a fiercely detailed account of the taxonomy and habits of the Tasmanian Bandicoot. The committee member assigned this manuscript had become captivated by photographs of the Bandicoot. As Kenner told the story:

> He set out to sell us not on the monograph but on a higher theme: the Bandicoot. He passed around photos. He rhapsodized on their sharp little eyes. He sketched impassioned sagas of their ways with one another in the night. After five minutes he had us panting to emigrate to Tasmania. After five more, his trajectory terminated, he turned around twice out of sheer undissipated rapture, and sat down. In the silence that followed, we voted to publish the monograph. I never heard how it did, except that it wasn't a bestseller. . . . But the members of the Editorial Committee who filed out for lunch that day were lifelong Bandicoot-lovers to a man.[10]

This is not to say that editorial committees take their task lightly. Vigorous debates about the scholarly worth of a manuscript can break out among committee members. The committee may express concern about the listbuilding directions of the press. The committee may negate months of work by an acquisitions editor by concluding that a work fails to meet the standards of the "imprint." But amid these deliberations, scholars enjoy the give-and-take with scholars in other disciplines in an endeavor that actually has results.

🍎🍎🍎🍎🍎🍎

5. Finding and Financing Scholarly Monographs

University presses are best known as publishers of scholarly monographs—books on narrow subjects that appeal to specialized audiences. These are the books that serve as a butt of jokes among those uninitiated to scholarly publishing. After all, a person without an interest in the intellectual study of a particular discipline naturally would find books in that discipline to be of little, if any, value.

For instance, without an interest in financial history, one might view a 712-page book with the title *Money and Banking in Medieval and Renaissance Venice* (Johns Hopkins University Press) as a tedious exercise in minutiae. Without an interest in cultural anthropology, one might consider a book with the title *Asiwinarong: Ethos, Image, and Social Power Among the Usen Barok of New Ireland* (Princeton University Press) intellectually unapproachable. Without an interest in the labor movement, a book with the title *Rebuilding the Pulp and Paper Workers' Union, 1933–1941* (University of Tennessee Press) might seem proof that scholars are determined to learn more and more about less and less. And without a specialized interest in literature, one might question the need for a book such as *Hero, Captain, and Stranger: Male Friendship, Social Critique, and Literary Form in the Sea Novels of Herman Melville* (University of North Carolina Press), which contends that Melville was homosexually oriented but could realize his desires only in the world of the ship.

Scholarly monographs seldom have an appeal outside academic circles. Monographs are not stacked on bookstore shelves; there is little walk-in customer demand for a book on the Usen Barok of New Ireland. Bestseller lists are not packed with monographs; there is slight general reader interest in a 712-page book that explains banking and finance in medieval Venice. Monographs are not the talk of the party; with the possible exception of those at a lumbermen's reunion, revelers have little desire to chat about the Pulp and Paper Workers' Union of fifty years ago. Monographs are written not to secure popular appeal and general readership, but to contribute to the intellectual inquiry of a small corps of scholars within a particular discipline.

For instance, one of the latest developments in archaeology is the use of computer simulation. Archaeological data are examined by fitting sets of conceptions into computerized models that imitate the real world and simulate the operations of past cultures. Models are based on such discoveries as the number of pot shards found at a site. How many people used them? What foods did they eat? Did they carry their water by hand? Like a lawyer in court, the archaeologist, in determining settlement patterns, builds a case. In trying to explain the past, the study of archaeology has evolved from random data collection to cultural description, proceeding through chronological ordering to interest in processes, and now to systems construction. "For archaeologists, computer simulation is the leading edge of the field," said David Holtby, associate director and editor at the University of New Mexico Press. "The best of the graduate students are realizing they need to study it. The best of the faculty members are realizing it, too." In the early 1980s, the New Mexico press published *Simulations in Archaeology*, edited by Jeremy Sabloff. The book is part of the School of American Research Advanced Seminar Series.

If a person on the street were asked to name a university press book, Holtby said the person likely would select a title such as *Simulations in Archaeology*. "That's the way it ought to be," Holtby said. "But we ought not to overlook clear writing. These are going to be tough books because of the methodology, no question. But there will be generalists interested in this. Publishers and authors must not forget those readers."

Although a monograph is written as a contribution to the intellectual understanding of a specialized audience, authors and university presses alike always hope that a given book will have an impact beyond scholarly circles. Morris Philipson, director of the University of Chicago Press, said:

Scholars who are concerned with moving forward with a line of development in their given discipline are always involved in what they hope will be original contributions to their line of study. That applies to all the books we publish. Their developments, their discoveries, their innovative arguments matter a great deal to a small number of people. For these developments to matter to a large number of people is always unpredictable.[1]

Sometimes a scholarly book does assume an importance within the culture as a whole. A case in point is Stanley Elkins's *Slavery: A Problem in American Institutional and Intellectual Life* (1959). The University of Chicago Press had an initial printrun of 1,200 copies. The book sold almost 200,000 copies and was instrumental in the emergence of black studies as an academic discipline. Philipson said that the monograph was written in a highly scholarly style intended for American historians. But the times were ripe for a study of slavery. The civil rights movement and a consciousness of race relations created demand.

Other scholarly books have reached broader audiences through the years:[2]

— In 1943, the University of Oklahoma Press published *Plowman's Folly* by Edward Faulkner, a county agricultural agent. He argued that farmers were ruining the soil by overturning it with the traditional moldboard plow. He suggested loosening the soil with the disk harrow. The book sold more than a quarter of a million copies. A former director of the press said, "His thesis was not only controversial but heretical, yet it has since changed the face of American agriculture."

— In 1950, Yale University Press cautiously published two-thousand copies of a book by a sociologist, then watched in astonishment as David Riesman's *The Lonely Crowd* made its way through American culture. The book is an analysis of American middle-class character. Yale licensed paperback rights to Doubleday, and the book since has sold more than one million copies.

— In the mid 1950s, Princeton University Press published *I Ching*, a book of ancient Chinese divination and cosmology edited by Hellmut Wilhelm. The "flower children" discovered the volume in the late

1960s; Bob Dylan said that he always consulted it. It has since sold more than a quarter of a million copies.

— Thomas S. Kuhn's *The Structure of Scientific Revolutions* is considered one of the most influential books ever published by the University of Chicago Press. Kuhn's book argues that science proceeds not by the steady, cumulative acquisition of knowledge, but by a series of peaceful interludes punctuated by intellectually violent revolutions. Hailed as a landmark in intellectual history, the book was conceived while Kuhn was a graduate student in theoretical physics. It has influenced sociologists, economists, historians, and philosophers. Since publication in 1962, it has sold more than 600,000 copies.

University presses have a rich heritage of publishing influential works. The University of Chicago Press published John Dewey's *The School and Society* in 1899 and still sells about two-thousand copies a year. Columbia University Press published Woodrow Wilson's *Constitutional Government in the United States* in 1908. Princeton University Press published Albert Einstein's *The Meaning of Relativity* in 1922. More recently, university presses have published such influential books as Norman O. Brown's *Life Against Death* (Wesleyan University Press), Herman Kahn's *On Thermonuclear War* (Princeton University Press), and Marshall McLuhan's *Gutenberg Galaxy* (University of Toronto Press). In the 1960s, the phrase "the battered child" was introduced into the language via a university press book that carried it as a title.

A more recent example of a scholarly work that reached a public much larger than the one to which it was directed is John Boswell's *Christianity, Social Tolerance and Homosexuality*, published by the University of Chicago Press in 1980. Boswell, a historian at Yale, argued that the Christian condemnation of homosexuality did not exist before the time of Thomas Aquinas. "The book was in no way written for the general public," Philipson said. "It was written with all the scholarly apparatus of the genuine work of scholarship." The footnotes alone contained phrases in English, Greek, Latin, Aramaic, Arabic, French, German, Spanish, Italian, and Old Icelandic. Boswell received a National Book Award in history, and more than fifty-thousand copies have been sold. Philipson continued, "No commercial publisher can ever control the conditions under which a book is published; therefore, it's always a matter of accident when it hits. On the other hand, it's very easy to explain why a scholarly book has significance within its discipline, and that makes for safe and sound and happy publishing of a certain kind."[3] Acquisitions editor Doug Mitchell added that Boswell's book "almost single-handedly established gay studies as a legitimate academic enterprise."

The book came to Chicago through its academic network. Boswell first submitted the manuscript to the Yale press but withdrew it. Jaroslav Pelikan, a Yale colleague who has published with both the Yale and Chicago presses, suggested that Boswell try Chicago next.

The book was not Boswell's first. Yale previously had published his first work under the title *The Royal Treasure*—a scholarly monograph that was a revised version of Boswell's dissertation.

❦ Publishing Dissertations

A number of scholarly monographs are revised dissertations. This is not surprising, considering that a doctoral dissertation constitutes a major intellectual enterprise in the life of a scholar. It also is not surprising that university presses serve as a prime publisher of dissertations, since many of the presses were established decades ago just for that purpose.

Universities once mandated the publication of dissertations. Before a student was awarded a doctoral degree, his or her dissertation had to be published as a book, at the author's expense. Publication became the measure of scholarship.

Since the dissertation was conceived primarily as a test of a candidate's mastery of scholarly method, it tended to have a tedious scholarly apparatus with footnotes on each page, and it sometimes incorporated heavy use of quotations in original languages. Since publication was by the traditional letterpress method, the prospective doctoral candidate often faced an expensive printer's bill.

Some presses established subsidiaries to handle the glut of dissertations requiring publication. For instance, in 1940, Columbia University Press created King's Crown Press as a subsidiary to publish dissertations by offset from the author's typewritten manuscript, dispensing with the careful copyediting all manuscripts had received in the editorial department. The reason for the new imprint was to protect the Columbia press imprint from being tainted by association with books of inferior appearance and low editorial standards.

Still, the publication requirement created too much of an economic strain on the doctoral student and on university presses and libraries alike. Manufacturing costs increased for authors, while the number of manuscripts became too great and their use too little to justify institutions' binding, shelving, and cataloguing them. This change coincided with the rapid increase in number of doctoral degrees awarded in the United States, reflected in the figures for these years:[4]

1900:	382
1910:	443
1920:	560
1930:	2,071
1940:	3,276
1950:	6,519
1960:	9,732
1970:	29,479
1980:	32,615

Gradually universities emancipated doctoral students from the publication requirement; in 1947, Columbia University apparently became the last major institution to do so.[5] By that time, the dilemma of how to make dissertations available to other scholars had been solved by a plan to put American dissertations on microfilm and store them with a company in Ann Arbor, Michigan. The cost of microfilming was much less than the cost of printing. Academic libraries no longer needed to store written dissertations, except perhaps those of students who earned doctorates at the parent institution and possibly a few of special interest. Microfilm copies of others could be obtained when needed.

This advance freed university presses to publish only those works deemed to be superior and deserving of broader dissemination. The change helped to instigate a dramatic transformation of university press acquisition practices from passive to active. With the freedom to do their own listbuilding, editors became more aggressive in their efforts to locate appropriate manuscripts.

At the same time, the doctoral process itself was undergoing scrutiny.

In a speech to the Association of American University Presses, University of Chicago President Ernest Cadman Colwell criticized the dominant pattern of professional and institutional advancement in academia:

> The pattern of advancement . . . committed to memory by every serious graduate student in every American university, runs as follows: "Publication is the path to preferment and prestige. Promotion, money, and professional status are the result of scholarly publication. Scholarly publication is a contribution to knowledge. A contribution to knowledge is a Ph.D. dissertation, a monograph published by a university press, or an article in a learned journal. Professional progress is directly proportional to the length of the bibliography."
>
> The American scholar learns this creed while he is still working for his Ph.D. degree. He begins with the requirement that the dissertation constitute a contribution to knowledge and be published. He reads other dissertations, talks to his fellow students, and finds out that a contribution to knowledge may consist in the discovery of a fact that the world has gladly forgotten, a fact whose sole value is that it furnishes material for a Ph.D. dissertation. The pressure created by this definition often leads to no more significant result than making known to the faculty of a department something in which they have no interest or concern. "The grass withereth and the flower fadeth," but not as rapidly as last year's Ph.D. dissertation.[6]

Colwell said that the dissertation should be defined solely as evidence of ability to do independent work. Its value, then, exists for the university that grants the degree, and not for the world of learning as a whole. To merit publication, dissertations should meet accepted norms of excellence, he told the editors. "The university press should not have two standards for scholarly publication: one to be applied to Ph.D. dissertations; the other, to all other works," Colwell said.

The double standard no longer exists. But a sizable number of dissertations, in revised form, still are published by university presses. In the polling of fifty-two university press directors, a third estimated that 20 percent or more of their new books are revised dissertations. This figure may be low. As one director replied, often it is difficult to tell because authors are not prone to identify a manuscript as a revised dissertation. Some presses ask authors this question on manuscript submission forms;

others figure that the information does not matter, so they do not bother to find out.

The word "dissertation" is both appealing and repellant to editors. The word has a mild appeal, in that editors recognize that the eminent scholars of tomorrow are beginning their intellectual pursuits in the form of a dissertation today, and editors want to discover the brightest new minds. But the word often creates a negative reaction. Dissertations are considered to be ponderous, overdocumented, and concerned with topics of little interest or significance. One press director said that the phrase "revised dissertation" makes a manuscript less attractive to editors who would prefer books by mature scholars. A midwestern director said that he remains skeptical of revised dissertations because top scholarship requires its author to "bring the wisdom of many years of experience, which junior scholars don't have."

The problem, editors said, is that most dissertations are written without book publication in mind and without any audience in mind other than the student's dissertation committee. Because the desire is to complete a dissertation, the tendency is to choose for investigation problems that promise neat, rapid solution. Simple rather than complex problems are chosen, and research is restricted to areas that are relatively unimportant to society.

Editors complained that too many doctoral students are allowed to squander the dissertation research experience on narrow, "safe" subjects rather than choosing a topic of substance. James Langford, director of the University of Notre Dame Press, remarked, "It seems to me that a good trend would be for more dissertation committees to encourage in-depth research on real issues and allow a latitude in how the dissertation is written so that it can be aimed at a book from the outset. Too often we still see undisguised or barely disguised dissertations on the use of the comma in Doris Lessing's early works."

Editors, though, resist becoming directly involved in the dissertation process. At a 1986 scholarly convention, a professor suggested that doctoral candidates consult a publisher while in the process of picking a dissertation topic. That idea brought a swift "no" from a panel of editors. "We can't be of help in selecting a topic," replied Kate Torrey, editor-in-chief of the University Press of Kansas. "That's the purpose of the academic process." Another panelist, executive editor Henry Tom of

Johns Hopkins University Press, recalled that a professor once suggested at an Association of American University Presses meeting that a university press editor serve on dissertation committees to teach students how to go about writing a book. "You could hear the gasps from the editors," Tom said.

Editors contended that the dissertation and the book must remain separate creations, because, although not mutually exclusive, they have two distinctly separate purposes—one to earn a stamp of academic validity, the other to offer knowledge to an audience. Occasionally, the same manuscript satisfies both criteria. To do so, the topic must have an appeal beyond the dissertation committee, the research plan must have depth and rigor, and the student must have an ability to write clearly and interestingly.

Richard Wentworth, director of the University of Illinois Press, said that a good way for editors to discover excellent dissertations in progress is to keep up with top scholars and their best students. When Wentworth was director at the LSU Press, where southern history is a top priority, he learned of a doctoral student working with historian George Tindall at the University of North Carolina. The student, Dan Carter, was writing his dissertation on the Scottsboro rape case in Alabama.

"I picked up the dissertation two weeks after it was completed," Wentworth said. "I started reading it at a campsite in North Carolina. It was a hell of an exciting time, excitingly written. When I got back [to LSU], I knew I had to get it before he sent it to any others. But in university publishing, you have to have someone confirm your judgment. We did it quickly. Two weeks after picking it up, we made a good offer that included a full-page ad in the *New York Times*. We promised good handling of the manuscript in design. We promised prompt publication. I think he knew he had a hot topic. It proved to be very big." The LSU Press published the book under the title *Scottsboro: A Tragedy of the American South*. The book won a Bancroft Prize in 1970 from Columbia University and later served as the basis for a television movie. By publishing Carter's dissertation, the LSU Press established a lasting relationship with the young scholar. Since then, Carter has published twice more with the LSU Press in the field of southern history.

Wentworth said that the Scottsboro study is one of only two dissertations he has seen that could be published as written. The other was in western history, written by a young scholar who did not live to see his work in print. John D. Unruh, Jr., entered the Ph.D. program in history at the University of Kansas in 1967 and took eight years to complete his dissertation. Weeks after earning his degree, he underwent surgery for removal of a brain tumor which proved malignant. He died two days later, at the age of thirty-eight. His nine-hundred page manuscript, with its accompanying two-hundred pages of footnotes, already was in the hands of the University of Illinois Press. The manuscript was shepherded to publication by his widow and by a colleague of his at Bluffton College in Ohio, where Unruh had taught.

In 1979, the Illinois press published this book under the title *The Plains Across: The Overland Emigrants and the Trans-Mississippi West, 1840–1860.* It won seven history awards. The book corrects a multitude of popular myths about the California-Oregon Trail. For example, the image of wagon trains encircled by arrow-shooting Sioux was an exaggeration, and Unruh's reading of more than 250 overland emigrant diaries showed that Indians saved far more lives than they took, by providing directions, food, and supplies. In a front-page review in its book section, the *Washington Post* called Unruh's book a "magisterial history," adding, "Remarkably, he has accomplished this miracle in a highly unlikely medium—a doctoral dissertation—that is so rich in anecdote, so sparklingly written, and so free of academic gobbledygook that it might have come from the pen of a best-selling popularizer." [7]

Added Wentworth of the University of Illinois Press, "The chances of a nine-hundred page dissertation being published are very slim. An editor has to have a lot of optimism. A great majority of dissertations are not publishable as written. This one was. But most can be quickly returned."

🐝 Revising the Dissertation

A dissertation and a book look strikingly similar. Both have a table of contents, a preface, a text divided into chapters, footnotes or endnotes, and a bibliography at the end. But there the similarity usually ends.

A dissertation is a test of a student's ability to gather evidence and arrange it logically. The style is frequently ponderous and stilted, with abundant footnotes serving as guarantor of proper research. The early chapters of a dissertation tend to be replete with citations, digressions, and justifications, not to mention defensive maneuvers designed to deflect aggressive questioning from the dissertation committee. The author of a book is not a student seeking to prove research ability but, instead, is a scholar seeking to impart knowledge accumulated through extended research. A different mind-set is required.

A dissertation, then, must undergo revision before it can be published as a book. The word "revision" implies an effort to "re-see" a topic. To acquire that necessary "new vision," editors suggest an initial trial separation of the writer from the dissertation. They recommend setting the dissertation aside for a time, perhaps a year or more, to clear the author's mind. The author then should pick up the dissertation and read it as objectively as possible, asking the question, "Is there an idea here worthy of book treatment?"

If the answer is yes, the author should start by writing an introduction. It may not be the final version, but it will compel him or her to refine the argument at the beginning of the revision process, when it is most essential to do so. The introduction should explain in clear language what the book is about. Before sending a manuscript to a publisher, the author should make sure that the introduction is direct and clear. When it is not, an editor may suggest tactfully that the author abandon the present text. With humor, a retired university press editor suggested to fellow editors the following approach (what really is in the editor's mind is in brackets): "Please [for God's sake] review [throw away] the present Foreword [now labeled Forward] and devise [or ask a friend to write] an opening to describe [if possible] the idea [if there is one] behind your book [so-called]."[8]

The structure of the manuscript also must have a fresh "vision." Dissertations tend to have a convenient but artificial form built on the traditional model of "statement of the problem, review of the literature, research methodology, findings, and analysis." Not only can this formula create a tired sameness in dissertations, but also it can interfere with idea-oriented writing. Editors said that a book must have a sense of progression. Anything, such as a lengthy review of the literature, that does not contribute to that forward movement interferes with the structure and selectively should be integrated into a narrative style.

The writer of a book must delete all dissertation signposts. One of them is what Olive Holmes called "the trumpeter effect," in which the author of a dissertation keeps interrupting the work to refer to what already has been written or what will be available to the reader in a later chapter.[9] The apologetic introduction also must be deleted. Readers of books, unlike readers of dissertations, are not scrutinizing the manuscript for limitations, so there is no need to explain in depth what the author has not done.

A book needs to deal in ideas, not methodologies. This principle is seldom questioned in the humanities, but recently social scientists have become enamored of methodologies and systems. Methodologies are seldom of interest to readers of books; at most, they might deserve inclusion in an appendix. One editor compared a dissertation to an unfinished house: "The wiring and the plaster are showing—the skeleton that shows that a committee helped build this house." In a book, evidence of wiring and plaster must be eliminated.

Once a proper structure is in place, the author must rewrite the body of the dissertation. Some sentences may stand unchanged; others must be rewritten. The dissertation was written for a specific audience—four or five Ph.D.s serving on the author's dissertation committee. A book is written for a much broader audience. "A dissertation written by a neophyte is defensively written," said Kate Wittenberg, executive editor of Columbia University Press. "When you are writing the book, you are the expert. You are writing a definitive work."

One popular technique is to write a book for a specific reader. The writer should choose a real individual—someone unfamiliar with the work—who would want to read a book on the topic. The author should write directly to that reader, including the information this person needs to know and taking out the rest.

Miller Williams, director of the University of Arkansas Press, said that a major impediment to publication of dissertations is the language in which they are written. "Some of them are first turned in written in humanese. The author is then brow-beaten by the dissertation committee to turn it into dissertationese. It's deliberately made unpublishable," Williams said. "It is difficult to turn a dissertation back into humanese. It's like trying to balance an unbalanced martini—you just have to pour it out and start over. It's hard to go back and rehumanize a dissertation without literally starting over." Williams gave examples of dissertationese: "It was anger-provoking in him" (it made him mad) and "He was often met with mirth responses" (people laughed at him a lot).

Editors said that dissertation writers, particularly those in literary criticism, tend to engage in heavy use of the special language of their particular discipline. Authors should recognize that the more narrowly written a manuscript, the narrower the potential audience.

Editors also said that dissertations are plagued by servility to the convention which forbids the author to say anything that is not substantiated by a footnote. In addition, writers may avoid stating a forthright fact through the use of what a former university press director called "the cowardly conditional." He said that social scientists are particularly culpable: "All things else being equal, it would appear to be the case that, under given circumstances, it may not be uncommon for writers of dissertations to execute certain prose styles which those who seem to like their English straight and strong might conceivably call a perversion of the language." [10] Editors also criticized the rampant use of the passive voice, saying that its popularity is rooted in the unsubstantiated notion that assertions in the passive voice appear more objective and more scholarly than those with an active verb.

Several editors suggested that authors on the verge of revising a dissertation read such books as George Orwell's *Politics of the English Language* and E.B. White's *Elements of Style* before starting revisions. "Writing that is muddled and fuzzy," one editor said, "tells us the author's mind might be muddled and fuzzy."

Young scholars, in their haste to get a book in hand for a tenure committee, often rush their dissertations to a publishing house without giving enough thought to marketing their own work. Scholarly publishing consultants have arisen in recent years to provide manuscript marketing advice. Marjorie Sherwood and R. Miriam Brokaw, both former editors at Princeton University Press, formed a consulting service to help scholarly writers revise their dissertations for broader audiences. They also recommend the presses most appropriate for a scholar's work. "These faculty members are not being told by their advisors how they should shape their dissertations into book form," Brokaw said. "The advisors are giving students an exercise in research. That doesn't mean it can be published."

Elizabeth Shaw, formerly of the University of Arizona Press, also established an editorial consulting service. "I'm sure there are exceptions," Shaw added, "but I don't think many dissertation committees are terribly concerned with the potential interest of a dissertation beyond the committee."[11]

Editors and consultants alike advise writers never to send an unrevised dissertation to a press unless an editor specifically asks to see it. Writers should send a query letter instead, perhaps with a table of contents and a sample chapter. The first chapter often is not the best one to send. Writers are under no obligation to tell an editor that the manuscript under discussion is a dissertation. But if writers do so, then the query letter should explain what revisions have been made or are anticipated. Suzanne Comer, senior editor at Southern Methodist University Press, said:

> I've seen some really deadly query letters—ones that start like this: "I have recently completed my dissertation and I am writing to see if you would be interested in publishing it." Or "My committee has told me this is a publishable work so I am submitting it." That's a killer beginning. It shows it hasn't been revised. If you just have to put in the fact that it's a dissertation, put it in the third paragraph and mention that it has been extensively revised. Someone's dissertation could be doomed on the basis of a poor query letter.

❦ Titles and Other First Impressions

A manuscript's title contributes to that first impression which is so vital in the acquisition process. An author is expected to submit a manuscript with a working title. "You breathe a sigh of relief when a manuscript comes in with a good title," said an editor at a West Coast press.

In evaluating the appropriateness of a title, an editor asks two questions: Does it properly describe the book? And, will the title help sell the book? Many university press contracts now give the publisher final say in the matter of the book's title. One publisher wrote:

> For obvious reasons, this is not an area in which one wants to strong-arm an author, and the overwhelming majority of disagree-

ments over titles are resolved amicably by persuasion or compromise. But there remain occasional authors who seem perversely bent on giving their books cryptic or precious titles that will, by any reasonable standard, greatly diminish whatever chance the publisher might have of publicizing and marketing the book effectively. It is to prevent such disasters that the contract was worded as it was. My advice here is to compromise if you can; but if every avenue of acceptable compromise is blocked, invoke the contract and give the book a title that will not drain blood from an honest sales manager's face.[12]

A good title can sell a book. In 1956, Princeton University Press published a work with the unwieldly title *The Existence of Intangible Content in Architectonic Form Based upon the Practicality of Laotzu's Philosophy*. It sold about one-thousand copies and went out of print. Despite its unmemorable title, the book developed a small underground following, for it made connections between western culture and oriental mysticism. So Princeton reprinted the book, with the new title *The Tao of Architecture*, and sold more copies in its first four months than in its entire previous appearance.[13]

The naming of books, although serious business, can be a point of humor in scholarly publishing. Professor Robert Darnton, who served on Princeton's editorial committee, noted the tendency for authors to give their books broad titles, then stick in a colon and engage in wholesale reductionism. Darnton explained, tongue-in-cheek: "A title should operate like a funnel. Suck the reader in by announcing something grand in the main title, then squeeze him through the subtitle into a monograph."[14] Illustrative of Darnton's principle, university press books published in the mid-1980s included *Sisters and Strangers: Women in the Shanghai Cotton Mills, 1919–1949* (Stanford University Press); *Representation and Revelation: Victorian Realism from Carlyle to Yeats* (University of Missouri Press); and *Monopoly's Moment: The Organization and Regulation of Canadian Utilities, 1830–1930* (Temple University Press). The tendency toward alliteration is a popular titling technique, with Ps particularly popular: *The Politics of Provincialism: The Democratic Party in Transition, 1918–1932* (Harvard University Press); *Persuasions and Performances: The Play of Tropes in Culture* (Indiana University Press); and *Puritan Poets and Poetics: Seventeenth-Century American Poetry in Theory and Practice* (Penn State University

Press). The subtitle usually is needed to tell the reader what the manuscript is about. Without a subtitle, the reader would be forced to guess about the subject matter. Darnton remembered one manuscript received during his tenure that simply was labeled *Mostly Chaos* and another titled *Trumpets Blown in the Empty Night*. Darnton admits, though, to secret admiration for two professors who were quite direct in titling their works. The first was a physicist who called his manuscript *Lecture Notes for Astrophysical Sciences 522*, the second a biologist who called his manuscript *The Nesting Behavior of Dung Beetles*. Neither work, Darnton was sorry to say, made it into print.

Some editors rebel against main titles so literary or poetic that the reader has no idea what the book is about. One former editor did a spoof on the title *Vision and Response*, offering a set of possible subtitles:[15]

Vision and Response: A Study in Optics
Vision and Response: A Case Study in Urban Renewal
Vision and Response: The Mormon Trek Westward
Vision and Response: The Effects of Pinups on Healthy Adolescent Males.

Authors are counseled *not* to copyright a manuscript before sending it to a press. "It's offensive because it says, 'I don't want you to steal this book,'" one university press director said. "Look, publishing a book is like a marriage. We don't want to live with a person who is paranoid. It won't get stolen. If it's bad, we don't want it. If it's good, we want your next book, too. Besides, most publishers and magazines are honest anyway. So don't put a copyright on it. That'll kill you in a minute. It shouts 'Amateur!'"

Finally, the manuscript should be prepared carefully on a typewriter or letter-quality printer. Editors are not fond of the dot-matrix type, since it is more difficult to read. The manuscript needs to be attractively presented, double-spaced on nonerasable paper, with large margins for editing. Notes and bibliographies need to show care. Everything is to be double-spaced, including footnotes and the bibliography. "It won't affect your acceptance or rejection," one director said. He paused, then restarted. "We try to accept or reject a book on the importance of the manuscript to the field. Oh, the agony caused by prima donnas or ignoramuses. We can't help but be influenced by that."

❦ Financing Scholarly Monographs

A university press not only must find scholarly monographs meriting publication, but also it must finance them. A university press may be a "Non-Profit Org." in the eyes of the U.S. Postal Service, but it cannot ignore economic realities. University press directors must have the characteristics of both a book-lover and a banker. Their presses, after all, seek to serve the life of the intellect—undeniably an altruistic purpose. Yet for the intellect to be successfully served, business acumen is needed. Books are written to be read. Without a readership, books do not accomplish their purposes. So presses must sell the books they publish.

Some may consider this attention to the business function a form of commercial publishing mentality. But show a commercial publisher the last ten books published by any university press, and ask how many would have been published commercially, and the difference becomes obvious. A commercial publisher always can say "no" to a manuscript on the basis that it is not likely to be profitable. Not so a university press. The aim of nonprofit university presses is to advance knowledge, not to make a profit. If a manuscript is not accepted after an editor already has invited it for consideration, the editor must convey a conclusion—no matter how politely it is done—that the book was unacceptable on grounds other than commercial ones.[16]

In university publishing, a tension continually exists between the scholarly and the business functions. What Robert T. King, then director of the University of South Carolina Press, wrote two decades ago still applies:

> The truth is that the university publisher can usually afford to lose a *little* money on the manuscript he accepts. Knowing how much he is likely to lose, and how much he can afford to lose, has to be part of his job. This does not mean that financial considerations dominate the university publisher's decision; it means that in the decision-making process the financial considerations will be inextricably tangled with the evangelistic ones, and neither will prevail alone.[17]

The ideal of intellectual service and the reality of financial servitude are inexorably linked at university presses. "When looking at a manuscript, financial considerations are important," said Seetha Srinivasan, associate director at the University Press of Mississippi. "I ask: 'Is it appropriate

TABLE 5.1

Importance of Selected Factors in the Decision to Publish

Factors	Essential	Very Important	Somewhat Important	Not Important
Book Complements the Press's Backlist	13	31	7	0
Author a "Name" in His/Her Field	1	23	21	5
Author has Ph.D. or Terminal Degree	2	21	12	14
Book Promises to Make a Profit	4	7	29	9
Book Could Be Used as College Text	1	9	25	15
Author Previously Published a Book	0	10	25	15
Book Promises to Be Controversial	0	6	29	15
Author from Ivy League or Major School	1	3	18	28

Note: The items above were ranked by 49 to 51 presses. By assigning a "4" to essential, a "3" to very important, a "2" to somewhat important, and a "1" to not important, we may place the cumulative results in rank order of importance:

Book Complements the Press's Backlist	3.12
Author a 'Name' in His/Her Field	2.40
Author has Ph.D. or Terminal Degree	2.22
Book Promises to Make a Profit	2.12
Book Could Be Used as College Text	1.92
Author Previously Published a Book	1.90
Book Promises to Be Controversial	1.82
Author from Ivy League or Major School	1.54

for our list? Can we combine an ad/promo campaign with similar titles?' "
Her press once received a three-hundred page manuscript, accompanied
by eighty-five photographs, on native son William Faulkner. The Mississippi press publishes a lot of Faulkner studies. "It would have been
a very expensive book to produce, with a limited audience," Srinivasan
said. "But we didn't want to lose a potential gem. So we sent it to outside
reviewers. Our readers' reports were lukewarm. That clinched the decision. We rejected the manuscript." She added, "Financial considerations
play a large role when a project looks expensive. We don't want 'brown
mountains' in our warehouse."

Table 5.1 shows that responding university presses awarded some importance to the promise of financial gain in the decision to publish. But
they said that other factors play considerably larger roles. Leading factors were whether the manuscript complemented the backlist, whether
the author was a "name" in the field, and whether the author had a Ph.D.
or terminal degree. Financial reward from publication ranked fourth on a
list of eight factors submitted to university press directors. Of lesser importance to directors were whether the book could be used as a text in the
classroom, whether the author previously had published a book, whether
the book promised to be controversial, and whether the author was from
an Ivy League or major school.

Several university press officials commented that the eight aforemen-
tioned factors bear mostly on the initial decision of whether to consider a
manuscript, not on the final decision to publish, since that decision rests
with an editorial committee and is based on reader evaluations. On the
survey, one editor changed the "profit" factor to read "make back investment." Another added that his press has "complex financial requirements
not expressed in terms of a profit; they lead to an index-numbered bottom
line."

❦ The Search for Subsidies

University presses publish the most specialized of books, sell them to
the narrowest of audiences, and somehow are expected to do this
without financial calamity. Presses frequently accomplish this challenging
task by finding underwriters—institutions, foundations, or individuals

willing to provide a financial subsidy for publication of a scholarly monograph which is not expected to pay its own way. The subsidy, often called a scholarly subvention, can come from any source except one—the author. The refusal to accept author subventions is a relatively new development. The Kerr Report of 1948 found that the costs of university publishing were paid by (1) the consumer, (2) the author, (3) the university, and (4) the outside organization. The consumer paid the bulk of the bills by buying the books produced. The author subsidized scholarly publication by paying subventions and by working without remuneration. The university provided subsidies of its own, such as free office space and staff salaries. The outside organization—whether a learned society, foundation, or research institute—offered support for individual titles.

The most common source of title subsidies, until well into the 1950s, was the author. The practice of having authors help pay the cost of publication was accepted, by authors and presses alike, as an essential element of scholarly publishing. Authors considered their "return" to be anticipated salary increases, promotions or tenure, and enhanced academic standing.

The practice of inviting, or even permitting, the author to help pay the costs of producing a book was eliminated in the 1950s and 1960s. If any university press still engages in the practice, it has kept quiet about it, to avoid comparison with vanity presses. Interestingly, the Ford Foundation played a significant role in overturning this longstanding arrangement. Previous to the mid-1950s, the foundations, according to former Duke University Press director Ashbel Brice, had policies of awarding millions for research and not a penny for publication. But between 1956 and 1965, the Ford Foundation provided $2,750,000 in grants for publication. These grants, together with matching funds supplied by the recipient universities, had a string attached. To avoid the "vanity press" comparison, no money could be used to publish a book that the author had helped subsidize in any amount.[18]

By the time that the grants ended, university presses were in flush times. Thanks to federal government programs, library budgets were booming, and presses were expanding at unparalleled rates. University presses announced that they would accept financial subsidies from any source except the author. The flush times ended, however. As universities began cutting budgets in the 1970s, the idea that university presses should be self-supporting gained currency. As an effort to eliminate money-losing projects took hold, the scholarly monograph began to fall into disrepute because it was unable to pay its own way.

Since the 1970s, with publication costs high and the outlook for break-even sales low, university presses increasingly have turned to other sources for help in publishing monographs. A key source is the author's home university. A 1983 survey by a Columbia University Press editor found that 7 percent of seventy responding English and Romance language departments at selected universities said that their institutions "frequently" provided subsidies to support publication of books by home faculty. Another 49 percent "occasionally" did so. The remainder said that, to their knowledge, subsidies were not available from the home institution. Subsidies were more common among private universities than state-supported ones.[19]

Edward Berman, an education professor at the University of Louisville, served on his university's Academic Publications Committee, which has a fund available to subsidize scholarly works which have been refereed successfully but require financial assistance for publication. The committee served as Berman's introduction to the world of scholarly publishing subventions. He was shocked to learn that scholarly journals in some disciplines today will not publish an article until the author has arranged payment, from either the author's institution or the author's own pocket. Berman wrote of this pay-to-be-published policy:

> I was rather unsophisticated and reacted with incredulity on learning that some colleagues—especially those in the physical and natural sciences, mathematics, and psychology—had to pay to see the results of their research in print. It seemed outrageous that someone who had spent time and effort in undertaking decent research should be subjected to the ignominy of having to pay to share that information with professional colleagues.[20]

Berman's committee handled subvention requests for journal publication amounting to $900 on one occasion, $1,200 on another, and $1,340 on a third. He said that the message going out to scholars is that they had better publish if they want tenure and promotion. But if they publish, there is a good chance that they will have to arrange for payment, too.

Berman said that it probably is only a matter of time before journals in the "soft" sciences and humanities follow the lead of those in the "hard" and behavioral sciences and begin charging fees to publish. Berman's committee also provided a $6,000 book subsidy to one university press and an $8,500 subsidy to another, on behalf of faculty members whose book manuscripts had been accepted for publication subject to obtaining a subvention.

University press directors said that they try to be careful to separate the editorial process from the financial process. One director said that his press never asks for or accepts a subsidy prior to approval by the editorial committee. The press doesn't want it to appear that financing influences the editorial decision. An East Coast editor commented, "Beware of authors who come in talking of $3,000 subsidies from their home university. They have probably offered the same money everywhere else." A southern editor said that his press occasionally accepts a manuscript conditional on obtaining a subsidy, but added, "Our press takes the initiative of finding a subsidy because we don't want anyone thinking the author is buying us."

Presses may ask the author to be an active partner in the subsidy search, but usually they don't ask the author to be solely responsible for obtaining a subsidy. For instance, one author first learned of the need for a subsidy in a letter of manuscript acceptance from a newer university press. The letter said in part:

> Our press prefers to maintain high editorial, design and production standards while holding the line as much as possible on the price of our books. Obviously, we must have help to do this. We feel strongly that institutions with which scholars are affiliated have a stake in the survival of university press publishing. So we ask authors to investigate the possibility of securing a title subsidy from their institutions. For this book, we would like to secure a subvention of $2,500.
>
> We want to publish your book, and we will almost certainly find a way to do so, even if we have to uncover some unknown fund of our own to come up with the capital. But we rely on your good faith effort to pursue aggressively any possibilities in this regard. If we can be of any assistance—by writing letters or making phone calls

commenting on the quality of your work and/or further justifying our need for such a subsidy—please let us know.

The press went ahead and sent a signed contract a few weeks later, assuring publication regardless of the outcome of the author's search for a subsidy. Other presses, though, will delay sending a contract for a scholarly monograph until financing is secured.

Financial considerations occasionally play a role in the editorial committee's decision-making process. At one press, the business and production staffs compute a manuscript's costs and expected income, once the editors and outside reviewers agree that it is worthy of publication. That analysis goes to the committee, along with the readers' evaluations. If the committee decides that a book is too costly, it can make publication contingent on obtaining an outside subsidy.

Subsidies can come from the author's home university, a foundation, a learned society, or even an individual. "There are people I can call, if I don't call too often," said Matthew Hodgson, director of the University of North Carolina Press. "I'll do that particularly for a young person's book. I get on the phone, say, to a lawyer in a small town, who is doing well, and say, 'How are you, how's your tax situation?' Usually by then, the response is, 'How much do you want?' "[21]

Subsidies are sought for two kinds of books: those believed to have extremely limited audiences and those with extremely high production costs. University press officials are in agreement that books with extremely high production costs deserve subsidies. These include expensive series of edited personal papers or books containing a lot of photography, architectural drawings, or special design techniques. But there is amiable disagreement about the validity of seeking financial backing for traditional scholarly monographs that appeal to small, specialized audiences.

Indiana University Press director John Gallman agrees that subsidies are valid for important scientific publishing, but he questions the tendency to pursue subsidies on traditional monographs. "Many university presses, raised in an educational environment that looks for handouts for nearly everything, do tend to think subsidy too often," Gallman said. "British publishers publish scholarly books for profit. More American university presses ought to be able to publish scholarly books as a break-even proposition. The reason they don't is that they are too perfection-oriented and too bureaucratized." Gallman said that the mission of a publisher is to publish books, not to beg for money. Books that are marginal economically may well be marginal intellectually, he said, and the author perhaps should write an expanded journal article rather than a book. In the time saved by not looking for subsidies, Gallman said, editors could concentrate on looking for good books.

J.G. Goellner, director of Johns Hopkins University Press, countered by saying that the paramount reason for the university press is to advance knowledge. "Within the context of book publishing, knowledge is advanced chiefly through scholarly monographs—not through trade books, textbooks or reference books," Goellner said. "Scholarly publishing is, almost by definition, subsidized publishing." Goellner said that scholarly publishing gets support in a variety of ways, such as authors' waiving royalties, authors' submission of machine-readable manuscripts, free office space, annual operating subsidies from the parent institution, and endowment income. He said that it is not unreasonable to expect the author's home institution to help finance publication of a book not expected to recover its publishing costs.

Every university press is subsidized in one way or another. To begin with, there are reduced book rates and other government subsidies. Then the parent institution typically provides hidden subsidies—free office and warehouse space, free custodial service, free utilities—and sometimes even pays salaries. In a survey of administrators at institutions with university presses, John Corson found that forty-seven of fifty-one university presses receive some hidden subsidy.[22] The four presses that received no hidden subsidy were all at private universities. Even those few university presses which operate as independent entities still benefit from the constant availability of faculty editorial boards and other university scholars as consultants. An invisible subsidy also exists in the automatic purchase of books by many libraries.

University press officials said that there has been little change in the subsidy situation in the 1980s. A southern press director said that his university guarantees free office space and more than $250,000 in staff salaries a year. Book sales amounting to slightly more than $500,000 cover the press's operating budget. Another director said that his press generates sales to cover 68 percent of its operating budget; the rest must come through subsidies. At major presses, the financial expectations are higher.

At the University of Chicago, the press is advanced money each year for operating expenses but must pay the university back with interest.

University presses also are pursuing outside endowments to provide subventions for numerous books. Harvard University Press has an endowed fund called the Belknap Press. More presses are looking for such support outside the traditional university budgetary channels. The University of California Press received a $250,000 grant from the National Endowment for the Humanities, which must be matched on a three-to-one basis with other contributions. The Ahmanson Foundation has provided $200,000 of that matching fund to support the publication of art books. Other publishing categories for which the press has established separate endowed programs include translations, Asian studies, music, Judaica, and the classics. The California press also invites donors to help finance the publication of specific titles, and for doing so—with a subsidy of $1,000 or more—contributors will be thanked by name in the books they support.[23]

When universities face budget constraints, pressure is placed on university presses to become more self-sufficient. Datus Smith, former director of Princeton University Press, noted with displeasure:

It is one of the great ironies in university affairs that it is precisely because university presses are successful in getting other institutions and the general public to pick up a major part of their operating cost through subsidies and sales income that the administrators seem surprised and resentful about whatever remaining balance they are asked to help defray. I often wonder if university presses might not get on better with the administrators if they were more like the Department of Philosophy, say, in having no directly identifiable income of their own. The university is quite reconciled to the fact that student tuition pays only a fraction of the cost of undergraduate education, and there is no bitterness about picking up assured departmental deficits, no shaking an accusing finger at department chairmen. Yet whenever it appears that the press director may be having trouble in raising from outside sources the total amount of his press's costs, there is a great clucking of tongues and an implication that the university administration has been betrayed.

If communication is in fact an essential element in the research process, it is utterly unrealistic for a university to pretend that publication is a frill instead of a basic part of the research enterprise. And, in dealing with specific cases, it is inexcusable for a university to accept responsibility and grant funds for a scholarly project without thinking through to the end and considering how communication of the results of that research is to be financed.[24]

❦ Marketing the Scholarly Monograph

Like any business, university presses need money coming in to approximate the amount going out. Editors insist that they need not adopt the marketplace mentality of the commercial publisher. Yet scholarly publishers also cannot be completely oblivious to sales.

A few university presses have developed multi-tiered lists to categorize books based on their commercial potential. The "C" books are monographs not expected to pay their own way. The "B" books are expected to break even. The "A" books are expected to be financial successes and counterbalance the money losers. Sociologist Walter W. Powell, in his study of scholarly publishing, wrote:

> These different categories of books receive dissimilar marketing attention. Obviously, in each season a university press will have to balance its mix of books. If a list needs to be cut back, a press may postpone some of the Cs. Another way of dealing with this problem, and of avoiding postponements, is for editors to defer making final decisions on C manuscripts. The rationale behind such a move is certainly reasonable; but . . . it is incumbent on university presses to explain to their C authors—who are typically young and inexperienced—why a postponement or deferral is necessary.[25]

The market for scholarly monographs has plummeted in recent years. Sheldon Meyer, executive editor of the Oxford University Press operation in New York, said that a printrun of 3,000 copies once was common; now the typical printrun is 1,500. Others said that their first printings of monographs have dropped from the 2,000 range to 1,000. Almost all editors said that they have cut their printruns on scholarly monographs by 40 to 50 percent since the 1960s. This decline in printrun size occurred in conjunction with library budget cuts and rising production costs, particularly in the inflationary years of the 1970s. With unit sales going down, book prices went up, as presses sought to break even.

Editorial expense actually is one of the smaller costs of publishing a book. The largest cost is production. No matter how few copies are printed, publishers face significant "first costs" of production—typesetting (or desktop publishing), proofing corrections, the press run, binding, and so on. In a desire to insure the permanency of their books, scholarly presses also have gone to the more expensive acid-free paper rather than using acidic wood pulp, which turns yellow and brittle with time.

One way to keep production costs manageable is to publish camera-ready copy. This is an accepted publishing procedure in the hard sciences, particularly for books containing technical matter. These books lack elegance, but the objective in science publishing is to share information quickly before it becomes outdated. Scientists, more than scholars in the humanities and social sciences, build on the work of others. Camera-ready copy is the most inexpensive method for rapid publication, since it places the preparation burden on authors.

But camera-ready publication has yet to become a form of printing acceptable for traditional scholarly books. An Ivy League editor said that his press publishes arcane language books and a few Chinese literature books under camera-ready stipulations with authors. This keeps the list price of such books at $34 instead of $100. But he added, "I don't think American historians, for one, would be interested in this. There is a certain standard of elegance that we all demand in a book."

Determining the costs of publication is not that difficult. Standard formulas exist that manipulate the net book price, the number of the first printrun, and production costs until an acceptable balance is reached. While production costs can be specified rather clearly, it is nevertheless difficult to forecast the amount of income a book is likely to return, since that depends on how the public responds. For highly specialized books, a publisher can form a fairly accurate conception of the potential market, based on sales figures for similar monographs. The broader the intended audience, however, the more difficult it becomes to predict public response.

One set of reliable purchasers through the years has consisted of libraries. They account for more than a third of all university press sales.

Some libraries buy directly from scholarly presses, but many go through specialized wholesalers called vendors. Libraries have standing orders for university press titles on an approval basis. Each library has a "profile" on record with its vendors. A library might specify that it wants all titles available in film studies, speech communication, and Latin American history, but not titles in photography, architecture, and folklore. Theoretically, the profile fits the university's educational mission. The library at a university with a law school but no medical school might automatically order all titles dealing with the law but not those in human medicine. Or a library might specify that it does not want to receive textbooks. Vendors ship books fitting the library's profile. Librarians look through the shipments, cataloguing those they will keep and returning any titles not of interest. The result is that an academic library in Florida might retain all titles published by the University of Washington Press, except for a provincial one such as *Washington Public Shore Guide*, and a library in New Hampshire might retain all books published by the University of Pittsburgh Press except for local-oriented ones such as *Discovering Pittsburgh's Sculpture*.

Libraries use vendors for two reasons. First, vendors are more convenient than dealing individually with hundreds of presses. Vendors handle the titles not only of university presses, but of commercial publishers as well. Second, libraries receive a discount on most titles purchased through vendors. Unlike scholarly journals, which often have higher prices for libraries and institutions than for individual subscribers, scholarly books usually are offered to libraries at a discount. This discount typically is 10 to 12 percent off the net sale price available to an individual buyer.

Increasingly, titles that once would have been standard purchases for a multitude of libraries are not being bought. Library budget crises have resulted in more selectivity. Several university press directors said that they used to be able to count on selling at least eight hundred copies to U.S. libraries. Now, the figure is more like five hundred to six hundred— and dropping. Editors report that some authors of scholarly monographs typically say, "Every library will have to have a copy." But such purchases no longer are taken for granted, especially now that interlibrary loans have become more common.

University presses also have encountered a buyer's resistance among scholars who once bought books for their professional use and for private collections. Books once were considered an essential tool for scholars; for many, because prices are now so high, books have become a discretionary item. Concern about the price of university press books is pervasive. As one scholar put it, he and his colleagues are suffering from "sticker shock" at a time when faculty salaries have not kept pace with the economy.

To attract individual book buyers unwilling to pay $29.95 for a clothbound monograph, university presses are publishing more paperbacks priced at $15 or less. Scholarly paperbacks have been around since the mid-1950s, when Indiana University Press put out paperback editions of such works as Rolfe Humphries' translation of Ovid's *The Art of Love.*[26] But the 1970s and 1980s have seen a proliferation of paperback editions. Many presses now release cloth and paperback editions simultaneously —the higher-priced, more permanent cloth editions for libraries and the lower-priced paperbacks for individual buyers. The goal is to make specialized monographs affordable to scholars.

University presses also have become more aggressive in seeking potential buyers. They are advertising in publications such as the *New York Review of Books*, the *New York Times Book Review*, specialty journals, and academic convention brochures. They send promotional news releases, along with free copies of the book, to newspapers, magazines, journals, and others that might review the book. They have sales representatives who visit bookstores, offering discounts ranging up to 48 percent for bulk purchases. They send direct-mail brochures to thousands of scholars.

The grouping of related titles in direct-mail advertising has become a vital promotional component in scholarly bookselling. It is a common practice to rent mailing lists for one-time use. For instance, as of September 1988, a marketing staff could obtain the 26,766 names on the Modern Language Association's mailing list for $80 per thousand—a cost of about $2,000. The Middle Eastern Studies Association offered its mailing list of 1,592 names for $100 total, and the College Music Society's list of similar size was available for $55 per thousand names. The American Anthropological Association was one of the most expensive, charging $110 per thousand names for a mailing list of its 10,220 members.

With a direct-mail approach, brochures plugging a specialized list can be sent to those known to be interested in the field. The brochure emphasizes the latest books published in the field and names backlist titles of related interest. This is an effective way to keep the backlist titles before their intended audience. Direct mailings frequently offer discounts of 20 percent or more off the retail price. A return rate of 3 percent is considered good and more than pays for the mailing of a brochure at bulk rates to thousands of scholars. But marketing managers said that they consider themselves fortunate these days to get a 2 percent response rate. They yearn for the "good old days" before book prices became so high, when direct mail from scholarly publishers resulted in a 4 to 6 percent response rate.

"My budget is going down the drain," said Patricia Malango, direct mail manager at the University of California Press. "Costs have gone up drastically for direct mail, since associations are having to finance their new technologies for maintaining membership rosters." Malango said that "quantum leaps" in mailing-list costs increased her expenses for acquiring mailing lists from $18,000 in 1987 to roughly $30,000 in 1988. With roughly 300,000 pieces of direct mail sent each year, that averages to about $100 per thousand potential book-buyers to obtain the mailing lists.

Unlike commercial trade and mass-market paperback publishers—who print a book, expect immediate sales, and then let the book go out of print—scholarly publishers depend on continuing sales over several years. University press directors said that they plan printruns based on selling about 60 percent of a first printing in the first year, 20 percent the second year, and 10 percent the third year. Of course, if all of a first printing sells in the first year, so much the better. A second printing of the monograph likely will be ordered. But if only 30 percent of a first printing sells in the first year, the press may be looking at a long-term "brown mountain" in the warehouse. To keep the book selling that second and third year, a press uses direct-mail brochures to promote new titles and the related backlist.

University presses also have started to adopt the commercial "big sale" mentality. In 1987, a group of university presses offered a combined book bonanza to raise money, reduce inventory, and display their books to people who otherwise might not know of their existence. The presses sent catalogs to hundreds of thousands of potential customers, operated 24-hour, toll-free ordering services, and offered big discounts. Conceived by Columbia University Press, the sale featured titles at savings of up to 90 percent. Twenty-five university presses participated in the sale.

Not all university press officials, including some who occasionally run such sales, are pleased about them. "We have done them to generate cash flow when we've been strapped, but discounts demean the value of our product," said Donald Ellegood, director of the University of Washington Press. "What we do by having such sales is condition our major customers, libraries, and scholars to wait until they can get our books at discount a year or so after publication." Gayle Treadwell, marketing director at Harvard University Press, which rarely holds big book sales, expressed similar sentiments. "I've always felt you don't want to sell off your books at less than value," she said. "If you plan and print properly, you shouldn't have a lot of excess stock to sell off at large discounts."

But major presses can bring in more than a quarter of a million dollars through periodic sales. Cornell's 1983 sale grossed more than $340,000, according to Cynthia Gration, the press's advertising and promotion manager. Her 1986 sale featured more than seven hundred titles. To publicize it, Cornell sent out five hundred thousand notices to names on its own lists and on some thirty-five other lists that the press rented.[27]

Authors have a vested interest in seeing their books sell. Not only do sales disseminate their work but, through royalties, may reimburse them somewhat for the work they put into the book. The "standard" royalty rate is 10 percent of the book's selling price. But in fact, there is no standard when it comes to royalty rates offered by university presses. The figure can range from zero to 12 percent, or a press may offer a 10 percent royalty on the net hardcover price and a 5 percent royalty on the net paperback price. The higher royalty can be passed on to the libraries, which are the leading buyers of hardcover books. University presses try to keep the paperback cost low to encourage individual sales, and one way to do that is to reduce the author's royalty rate on paperbacks.

The larger university presses recognize that, in the competition for quality manuscripts by established scholars, author royalties are a contractual expectation. But many of the newer and smaller presses—and some of the large prestigious ones as well—may stipulate no royalties on the first printing, especially on monographs not expected to pay their own way. The belief remains that scholars will benefit from publication through promotion and recognition and should not expect financial remuneration as well, particularly when the press itself does not expect to make money on the publication. One senior editor said that there seems to be an increasing trend among university presses toward contracts specifying no royalties on the first printing.

Because of this low royalty structure, literary agents seldom play a role in scholarly publishing. Agents make their livings from the royalties their authors receive from books. Since books published by university presses rarely realize a significant profit, 10 percent of little or nothing is not much incentive for someone making a living as an agent. Lloyd Lyman, retired director of Texas A&M University Press, said:

> Initially, university presses were set up to work with scholars, to help the publish-or-perish syndrome. An agent doesn't and shouldn't be expected to know the academic importance of a scholar's work. University presses do, since they solicit the opinions of other noted authorities on the merit of a particular author's work. Because time isn't of the essence for us, as it might be for a trade house, we are seldom in competition with other presses. Therefore, university presses usually shy away from simultaneous submissions and the auctioning off of manuscripts. These techniques are obviously of benefit to agents since their existence depends solely on the financial end. Royalties are often negligible on the books we publish. Even though an agent may have strong feelings about a client's work, an agent can't seek tenure; an author can.[28]

Sheila Levine, sponsoring editor at the University of California Press, said that she prefers not to deal with agents, because they "up the ante" yet the author seldom gets more. "There's not a lot of money to be made on most university press books, so there's not a lot to negotiate. Why give away some of it to a third party?" Of her one hundred on-going projects, two involved agents. She said one agent initiated the acquisition process, and the other agent became involved only at the contractual stage.

Naomi Pascal, editor-in-chief at the University of Washington Press, said the involvement of an agent will not stop her from considering a manuscript on its merits. But she added, "I certainly don't prefer dealing with an agent. Almost none of the manuscripts we publish are submitted by agents, and very few of our authors are represented by agents. Since we are a scholarly press, our typical author is a professor who does not look to publication for a livelihood, but writes books for other reasons."

The scholar's motive in writing is prestige more than profit, and the publication of scholarly monographs has been the mission of university presses from the start. But editors themselves are aware of the financial consequences of a list too full of scholarly monographs on narrow topics with limited appeal. This awareness may not control the editorial process, but it certainly influences it.

An oft-cited aphorism to describe the task of finding and financing scholarly monographs was coined in 1947 by Tom Wilson, former director of Harvard University Press, who said, "The university press publisher has as his objective the publishing of the maximum number of good books this side of bankruptcy." [29]

This statement not only is clever and catchy, but also it contains much truth. Book publishing is a highly capital-intensive business.[30] Scholarly publishers pay authors' advances on royalties and the salaries or fees of copyeditors, designers, and printers; then months or even years go by before the revenue associated with those investments is realized. In addition, much more capital is tied up in inventory and accounts receivable. Such facts have made it incumbent on even the most idealistic of university press directors to pay attention to financial concerns when approving manuscripts for publication.

❦ ❦ ❦ ❦ ❦

6. Trade Books
and the
Expanding
Title Mix

Select the book published by a university press rather than by a commercial publisher or small regional house:

(a) A scholarly monograph entitled *The Romantic Sublime: Studies in the Structure and Psychology of Transcendence*

(b) A trade book written by an American military officer and called *The Army and Vietnam*

(c) A regional photography book with the name *The Lighthouses of the Chesapeake*

(d) A book of fiction with the title *Alice and the Space Telescope.*

A person who selected (a) would be correct. University presses are recognized primarily as publishers of scholarly monographs that appeal to narrow, specialized, academic audiences. As a contribution to literary criticism, *The Romantic Sublime* combines a historical study of the sublime with the concerns of psychoanalytic criticism and of structuralist and semiotic theory. It develops a model of transcendence built around a set of dialectical oppositions between the metaphorical sublime of Kant and Burke and the egotistical and metonymical sublime of Wordsworth, Keats, and Shelley. Although few persons other than literary scholars may be able to relate to the thesis, the book showed enough popularity in academic literary circles to merit new release in paperback form in 1986.

If you selected (b), however, you were also correct. Increasingly, university presses are publishing serious trade books by those both within and outside the academy. Written by a Pentagon strategist, *The Army and Vietnam* contends that the U.S. Army's failure in Vietnam lay in its incorrect assumption that it could transplant to Indochina the operational methods used successfully in World War II.

A person who selected option (c) would have been correct as well. Many university presses believe in publishing regional titles with appeal in their own geographic areas. *The Lighthouses of the Chesapeake* is an award-winning book containing 170 photographs which document all of the thirty-two lighthouses still standing along the Chesapeake Bay shoreline.

Finally, a person who selected alternative (d) would have been correct, too. A few university presses have begun publishing a type of fiction that requires an intellectual reading. For instance, *Alice and the Space Telescope* is a fantasy journey through the wonderland of modern astronomy. The novel, written by the director of the Royal Observatory in Edinburgh, Scotland, features the Lewis Carroll characters of Alice, the Mad Hatter, and the Cheshire Cat. The book is based on the most extraordinary "looking glass" ever designed—the Hubble Space Telescope, to be deployed on a future space-shuttle flight. By scanning the cosmos from above the distorting effects of Earth's atmosphere, astronomers will be able to see seven times farther than at present. Half of the book is an adventure story, and the other half is an explanation of astronomy for the lay reader.

What makes the answers to our multiple-choice question particularly fascinating is that all four of these titles were published by the same press —Johns Hopkins University Press, which is the oldest continuously operating university press in the United States. Furthermore, all four titles were prominently featured in the same catalog.

Johns Hopkins University Press, best known for publishing in medicine, is not unusual in having such a broad mixture of titles. Deviations from the purest scholarship—the traditional scholarly monograph—have become more conspicuous in university press listbuilding in recent years. Presses are widening their title mix by introducing trade books, regional titles, photography collections, and books with the potential for classroom use.

William A. Wood of the University of Minnesota Press said of this

deviation from purest scholarship, "Like everyone else, we find the traditional monograph an endangered species, and so we seek textbooks
and reference books and trade books for the larger and sustaining audiences they will find. A few years ago, 70 percent or more of the titles we
published were classified by us as monographs; now we run closer to 50
percent."[1]

University press officials acknowledge that nonmonographic titles have
an appeal, because they often have the potential to help recoup the financial losses sustained by monographs. But the expansion of the title mix
should not be viewed as a purely financial decision. Officials contend that
the expanding title mix serves the life of the intellect, by filling voids left in
the wake of commercial publishers' obsession with bestsellers. Since certain nonmonographic works no longer appeal to commercial publishers,
these works—be they trade books, regional studies, fiction, or poetry—
might well go unpublished if university presses did not step in. So, again,
a mixture of altruistic and financial considerations is at work in deviations
from purest scholarship.

❦ Trade Books for the Nonspecialist

Trade books differ from scholarly monographs in both content and
writing style. While monographs are on narrow subjects and are
aimed at the specialist, trade books are on subjects of broader interest
and are aimed at the nonspecialist. Trade books are designed to be read
by persons without specialized knowledge of a subject.

John Ryden, director of Yale University Press, defines a trade book as
"a work which meets all the appropriate standards but which, because of
its import and the skills with which it is written, is of interest to more
than the specialist in the field, more than the author's colleagues."[2]

For instance, in 1986, Harvard University Press published *Untangling
the Income Tax*. Rather than being just for economists, the book is billed
by the press as "highly readable" and "nontechnical" in its description of
how tax laws affect the real sharing of tax burdens and the performance
of the economy. The author is a Princeton professor who served in the
Treasury Department during the Ford administration.

A considerable difference of opinion exists concerning the place of
trade books in scholarly publishing. In the polling of fifty-two univer-

sity press directors, ten responded that trade books comprise less than 10 percent of their new titles, referred to as the frontlist, yet another ten directors said that trade books comprise 40 percent or more of their frontlists.

Unfortunately, no definitive demarcation exists between scholarly monographs and trade books. The marketing staffs at some presses encourage frequent use of the trade designation because it allows them to offer larger discounts as inducements to bookstores. Other presses shun the trade designation on titles because they see it as at odds with their mission to publish scholarly works. In addition, a few presses automatically designate a title as a trade book if it is published simultaneously in cloth and paper, with the cloth edition sold primarily to libraries and the paper edition sold primarily to individuals.

A debate over the appropriateness of trade publishing was evident in the written comments of university press officials who responded to our survey. Chris Kentera, director of the Penn State University Press, replied, "We do not consider ourselves a 'trade' publisher. We feel university presses that consider themselves such are not really scholarly publishers and should incorporate and not be associated with a university. . . . After all, it is the publication of scholarly books 'to advance knowledge' that is the reason for the existence of tax-free, university-connected university presses."

Another director responded, "We feel that most university presses are not really completely involved in the publication of scholarship, but that they view themselves as 'trade' publishers who must publish trade and regional books in order to 'make a profit' so as not to anger their university controller/business manager. We feel that the real business of a university press is to publish books and journals that are contributions to further research and scholarship and are thus a great benefit to higher education throughout the world."

Yet another director responded, "University presses can no longer afford to publish monographs so specialized that they cannot reach an audience of at least 1,000. There are other outlets for such studies. We must continue to publish books of real scholarship, but we need to reach also into the gray area that once was a marginal trade market for commercial houses—to do books that are thoughtful, where the scholarship has been digested and is evidenced in clarity rather than in footnotes—on important national and international issues."

J.G. Goellner, director of Johns Hopkins University Press, does not believe that university presses are on the verge of becoming true trade publishers. He wrote, "University press people have always referred to their 'trade books,' but for the most part that term has merely designated books sold to dealers at larger discounts in the hope that the dealers will purchase copies for stocking and displaying on their shelves. I do not believe university presses are equipped to do real trade publishing consistently." [3]

A university press's definition of a trade book is far different from the meaning assigned to this term by the large New York commercial trade publisher. In New York a trade book may be a book by an actress who believes in reincarnation; or a book on the sex habits of Americans, based on interviews with volunteers; or a book by a business consultant on how to maintain power within the corporate world. University presses do not publish such genres of "trade books." The trade books published by university presses and the smaller specialized houses are of a more serious nature.

In recent years, the New York commercial trade publishers have virtually abandoned the serious nonfiction book, because it typically has a low profit ratio. The key to making a profit in commercial trade publishing today is subsidiary rights—book clubs, mass market paperbacks, television spin-offs, and other media tie-ins. If a trade book does not have strong potential for mass sales or for subsidiary rights, then it likely will not be considered worth the big trade publisher's effort. New York trade publishing has become a hostage to the bestseller and to subsidiary rights.

But the serious trade book, with anticipated sales perhaps no higher than a few thousand copies at best, is attractive both to university presses that operate with no profit expectation, and to the growing number of smaller specialized publishers now scattered across the United States that often use camera-ready printing techniques. Such trade books not only are financially feasible, but also are considered of value to society because they are written with the aim of communicating with the general public. Sociologist Walter W. Powell, who studied two commercial scholarly houses in detail, concluded:

Changes in the structure of trade publishing have created new opportunities. University presses and commercial scholarly houses are moving into the territory the larger trade houses have vacated in their quest for blockbusters. As trade publishers have increased expectations of the number of copies a book needs to sell in order to be deemed successful, they have become less willing to take on books that are eminently worthwhile but have modest sales potential.[4]

The serious trade book has become enticing to university presses. Not only do such books typically sell better than scholarly monographs, but also they provide greater visibility for a publishing program, since book reviewers emphasize titles that appeal to the general reading public. One result is that the outlets for serious, nonmonographic fare increasingly are located not in New York City but in such cities as Baton Rouge, Ann Arbor, Minneapolis, Chapel Hill, and Berkeley. An implication of this emerging shift is that the understanding of what interests the reading public now encompasses wider geographic diversity.

❦ General, Topical, and Regional Books

Most university press books that carry the trade designation can be grouped in one of three categories: general-interest scholarship, topical studies, or regional titles.

General-interest trade books typically have the traditional scholarly apparatus but appeal to other readers in addition to specialists in a field. These books, because of their broader appeal, could easily find a place on a bookstore shelf. For instance, Columbia University Press published *How to Deep-Freeze a Mammoth*, a collection of light-hearted essays that examines the extinction of dinosaurs, the history of the Mediterranean Sea, the origin of birds, the theory of the continental drift, and the discovery of the Piltdown Man fossil forgery that fooled scientists for more than forty years. And, true to its title, the book offers a humorous recipe for freezing a mammoth. The Columbia press calls it a book "written for the lay reader." The author is a professor of paleontology at the University of Helsinki.

Trade books, by nature, are on topics of interest to a broad group of readers. Few outside academia may be interested in an analysis of Keats or in peasant protests in feudal Japan, but a considerable number are interested in such topics as alcoholism, the Peace Corps, and Christmas. *Becoming Alcoholic: Alcoholics Anonymous and the Reality of Alcoholism* (Southern Illinois University Press), written by a sociologist, contends that AA affiliation parallels religious conversion because reformed drinkers embrace a radical lifestyle change similar to that undertaken by the convert. *The Bold Experiment: JFK's Peace Corps* (University of Notre Dame Press), written by a World Bank staff member, is based on hundreds of interviews with volunteers and on newly declassified documents at the JFK Memorial Library and the Peace Corps library and archives. *The Making of the Modern Christmas* (University of Georgia Press), written by two British historians, chronicles the history and rituals of Christmas from the mid-winter Saturnalia of pre-Christian Europe to the present day. All take a scholarly approach to a popular topic.

Trade books published by university presses seek to merge the scholarly care given the monograph with the nontechnical prose needed to appeal to a general audience. This can create an awkward federation, which is why some in scholarly publishing believe trade books fall outside the university press mandate. For instance, *Love and Love Sickness: The Science of Sex, Gender Difference and Pair-Bonding*, published by Johns Hopkins University Press, is like two books in one, part of it being too technical for a lay readership to comprehend and another part being a highly opinionated polemic with little scientific support. This combination of monographic specificity and trade book generalizations drove a reviewer for the *New York Times* to call the book "profoundly disagreeable to read because of its overuse of jargon, its disorganization, and its pretentiousness." The review added, "It is simply astonishing that this book is published by a university press." Of the author, the reviewer wrote:

> John Money is a well-known medical psychologist, a professor at Johns Hopkins, the author or editor of 14 books and an important contributor to the understanding of hormonal anomalies in sexual behavior and gender differentiation. That is the good John Money. There is also the bad John Money, who fancies himself a philosopher of sexual conduct (or a "sexosopher," to employ one of the several neologisms he has invented), a scourge of the church, a staunch foe

of the "sexual dictatorship" of our time and the author of some of the wildest generalizations seen since the heyday of Charles Reich. In his new book, the bad Money drives out the good Money. The scientist is at first edged out, then rudely shoved aside by the zealot, so much so that . . . one begins to entertain serious doubts about the goodness of the good Money, that is, about the merits of the scientific work itself.[5]

University press trade books, though, aren't always destined for such controversy. Trade titles range from *Modern Winemaking* (Cornell University Press) to *Fund-Raising: The Guide to Raising Money from Private Sources* (University of Oklahoma Press) to a book on protest singers called *Guerrilla Minstrels: John Lennon, Joe Hill, Woody Guthrie, and Bob Dylan* (University of Tennessee Press). These three books all happen to have been written by scholars with a Ph.D. degree. But, unlike scholarly monographs which are written almost exclusively by those within the academy, a number of trade books come from persons outside the academy. *The Teacher Rebellion* (Howard University Press), written by a three-term president of the American Federation of Teachers, details the story of union building and teacher activism in the public schools and provides glimpses of behind-the-scenes strategy sessions. *Once They Were Eagles: The Men of the Black Sheep Squadron* (University Press of Kentucky) was written by a retired Marine Corps colonel who served as the intelligence officer of what became the most famous aerial combat squadron in World War II. Although such works do not fall within the definition of pure scholarship, they do represent contributions to knowledge by offering scholars insight into the early years of collective bargaining and the wartime years in the Pacific.

Topical studies constitute another genre of university press trade books. These are books written and published in relation to an event or issue of some timeliness. An acquisitions editor gave this illustration: "A book on Iran at the time of the American hostage crisis would be a trade book. A book published now on the history of Iran would be a scholarly book." Writing style is another key determinant in whether a book represents a topical study.

In 1983, Duke University Press published *Afghanistan and the Soviet Union*, outlining the significance of the Soviet Union's 1979 invasion of its southern neighbor. The author, Henry S. Bradsher, was a *Washington Star* correspondent in Afghanistan and also served in the 1960s as the Associated Press bureau chief in Moscow. He wrote the book while serving as a guest scholar at the Kennan Institute for Advanced Russian Studies in the Smithsonian Institution's Wilson Center. His manuscript was turned down by the first university press that considered it. "We published it," Duke director Dick Rowson said, "because it was authoritative and the subject was topical, and we thought it would remain so." Sure enough, with the Soviet occupation of Afghanistan continuing, the Duke press published a new and expanded version in paperback two years later. But, says Rowson, "We go low-key on trade books because we don't want to undermine our basic scholarly mission."

Indiana University Press published *Bitburg in Moral and Political Perspective* within one year of President Reagan's controversial 1985 visit to the cemetery in Bitburg, where Nazis are buried. The edited volume includes a chronology of events; a selection of news accounts, cartoons, and photographs; and the speeches of Reagan and others. The book covers Germany's struggle with its Nazi past, the importance of symbols in politics, the moral concept of reconciliation, and the failure of historical memory in both Germany and the United States. The editor, Geoffrey Hartman, an English professor at Yale, wrote in the book's introduction:

> The theme of memory haunts us increasingly. As events "pass into history," and they seem to do so more quickly than ever, are they forgotten by all except specialists? "Passing into history" would then be a euphemism for oblivion, though not obliteration. That something is retrievable in the archives of a library may even help us to tolerate the speedy displacement of one news item by another.

The recent rise of prominent black politicians has spawned scholarly studies of a topical nature. *Chicago Divided: The Making of a Black Mayor* (Northern Illinois University Press), written by a professor of history and political science, chronicles the 1983 election of Harold Washington. *The Jesse Jackson Phenomenon* (Yale University Press), written by an assistant professor of political science and Afro-American studies, argues that Jackson's 1984 campaign for president hurt rather than helped the development of a viable black political movement in the United States.

The 138-page book on Jesse Jackson was published as a Yale Fastback. These are shorter books that are published speedily, in cloth and paper simultaneously, because of their timely nature. University presses are known for having a slow, deliberate publication process. Even after editorial acceptance, it can take a year or more before a book is published. This pace works against the publication of topical studies. So, for timely studies, Yale has a speeded-up process.

One of the best-known achievements of the Fastback series came in 1974, when the nation was aswirl with talk of President Nixon's Watergate troubles. A Yale Law School professor, Charles L. Black, Jr., proposed to the press a short handbook on the impeachment process. Yale's Committee on Publications just happened to be meeting within a few days, and the committee approved the project. The manuscript was drafted in three days. Five weeks later, an eighty-page *Impeachment: A Handbook* was printed and bound. By good fortune, the American Booksellers Association was holding its annual convention in Washington, D.C., the weekend following approval. The Yale sales force took advance orders for 5,000 copies of *Impeachment* in a couple of days. Another 8,000 advance orders came in before publication. By the time Nixon resigned, a total of 35,000 paperbacks were in print.[6]

Black's handbook simply explained the process of impeachment, without taking an advocacy stance. But a number of topical trade books today blur the distinction between scholarship and opinion. Another Yale Fastback is *The Long Darkness: Psychological and Moral Perspectives on Nuclear Winter*. The book, published in 1986, consists of essays by Carl Sagan, Stephen Jay Gould, Henry Steele Commager, and six others. The Yale press describes the authors as "some of the most articulate and respected opponents of the escalating arms race."

Regional titles represent a third genre of nonmonographic books published with frequency by university presses. Regional books appeal to individuals who live or have an interest in a specific geographic area. "We can't fill the insatiable desire of people to read about themselves," said Ann Haugland, formerly sales and publicity manager at the University of Minnesota Press.[7] One Minnesota press title that has evoked strong regional interest is *Where We Live*, a detailed geographic study of the Minneapolis–St. Paul area. Although the book takes an academic approach—for instance, it uses the term "residential zone" instead of "neighborhood"—Haugland said it has been popular among residents of the Twin Cities.

A buyer for the B. Dalton Booksellers chain considers a regional title to be "a crossbreed" between trade books and monographs, since regional books are written in a trade style yet are specialized like a monograph in their marketability: "If a non-fiction trade book is an attractive, informative and interestingly written volume likely to sell well in bookstores, a regional trade book is all of these with a geographic fence built around it. . . . The market for regional books, in other words, is limited and identifiable, and therefore within reach of the marketing capabilities of even the smallest publisher."[8]

Since university presses are not concentrated in a single geographic region, as a group they publish studies covering almost every geographic area of interest. Southern presses, for instance, publish regionally-oriented titles such as *Southern Folk, Plain and Fancy: Native White Social Types* and *Media-Made Dixie: The South in the American Imagination*, both by the University of Georgia Press. Western presses, in particular, emphasize regional environmental issues.

But university presses also recognize the benefit of serving the specific home state and even local community. Exploiting local cultural connections can have a positive effect on the place of the press within the university and community. The University of Hawaii Press publishes an abundance of trade titles, including an underwater guide to the islands and a book entitled *A Practical Guide to Divorce in Hawaii*. The University of Texas Press put out *Lone Stars: A Legacy of Texas Quilts, 1836–1936*. The University Press of Virginia is the publisher of *Virginia Cemeteries: A Guide to Resources*. The University of Utah Press brought out a seventy-two-page guide for joggers entitled *Running in Salt Lake City*. The University of Tennessee Press published *Big Orange: A Pictorial History of University of Tennessee Football*.

The three broad groupings of nonmonographic studies, then, are general-interest scholarship, topical studies, and regional titles. Some nonmonographic books fall in no one clear category. Louisiana State University Press published, to acclaim, C. Vann Woodward's *Thinking Back: The Perils of Writing History*. Woodward has won the Pulitzer Prize and the Bancroft Prize, among others, in a career spanning more than half a century. The book is his retrospective view of his experiences as a historian.

An increasingly popular hybrid literary form is called "creative nonfiction." An example is *Mountain Blood* (University of Georgia Press), a collection of yarns and recollections of mountain life written by an English professor.

Another type of trade book is exemplified in *Plaintext* (University of Arizona Press), a series of essays in which Nancy Mairs describes what it means to be a woman battling the debilitating effects of agoraphobia and multiple sclerosis in a patriarchal world. Mairs writes of the joy of romance and the trauma of rape, the despair of institutionalization and the tenderness of motherhood. In one essay, she writes of her health:

> I am a cripple. I choose this word to name me. I choose from among several possibilities, the most common of which are "handicapped" and "disabled." I made the choice a number of years ago, without thinking, unaware of my motives for doing so. Even now, I'm not sure what those motives are, but I recognize that they are complex and not entirely flattering. People—crippled or not—wince at the word "cripple," as they do not at "handicapped" or "disabled." Perhaps I want them to wince. I want them to see me as a tough customer, one to whom the fates/gods/viruses have not been kind, but who can face the brutal truth of her existence squarely. As a cripple, I swagger.

Mairs's book is not scholarship. But it makes for serious reading and, in the view of editors at the University of Arizona Press, was within the press's publishing mandate.

As one of the strangest offerings by a scholarly publisher, the University of California Press decided to publish a Japanese comic book. "Japan, Inc." is an introduction to that nation's economics, featuring the business dealings of two junior executives—the well-meaning Kudo and the ruthless climber Tsugawa. Despite the comic book format, the book offers a serious look at trade competition with the United States, the rise of the yen, and deficit financing. The idea of publishing a comic book bothered California director James Clark: "I thought, 'A university press shouldn't be publishing comic books.'" But scholarly experts disagreed. Besides, the comic book has been a bestseller in Japan since 1986. One can't argue with economics like that.[9]

Each university press, then, creates its own sense of what legitimately falls within its editorial mission. Trade books that virtually all university presses find difficult to reconcile with their mission include cookbooks, self-help books, books of inspiration, and how-to books. But beyond that, university presses have diverging concepts of what appropriately may be considered scholarly publishing. That divergence is nowhere more evident than in the decision by some university presses to publish original fiction and poetry.

❦ Publishing Fiction and Poetry

Dennis Gossen is dead, his career in economics cut short by the Harvard Promotion and Tenure Committee and an apparent suicide. But when two members of the tenure committee are killed, Harvard economics professor Henry Spearman finds himself on the trail of a murderer.

This is the plot of *The Fatal Equilibrium*, a mystery novel that provides a grasp of basic economics on the way to solving a murder case. The publisher is the scholarly MIT Press. Amid the economics lessons, the book is full of academic intrigue, as readers try to pinpoint the murderer. Was it Morrison Bell, mathematics star and inventor of devices to defeat the squirrels in his birdfeeders? Was it owl-like Oliver Wu, the distinguished sociologist who harbors deep resentments? Was it Valerie Danzig, supposedly Gossen's former lover? Or Foster Barrett, gourmet Harvard classicist? What about Cristolph Burckhardt, infatuated employer of Gossen's fiancee? Or Russian emigre Sophia Ustinov, *aficionado* of American poetry and Borzoi hounds?

The fictional Professor Spearman applies the hypothesis of diminishing marginal utility to solve the mystery. A *New York Times* book review said, "Using the logic of a rational consumer, Spearman explains why apparently similar jobs pay different salaries, why soda machines differ from newspaper dispensers, and why—everything else being equal—Dennis was not likely to kill himself."[10]

The Fatal Equilibrium is listed in an MIT Press catalog amid such scholarly monographs as *The Structure and Reform of the U.S. Tax System* and *The Political Economy of International Monetary Interdependence*. The mystery book's predecessor, *Murder at the Margin*, was a success, with the *Wall Street Journal* calling it a "painless way to learn economic principles." The author of both novels is "Marshall Jevons," the pseudonym for the team of William Breit, professor of economics at Trinity University, and Kenneth G. Elzinga, professor of economics at the University of Virginia.

A few university presses now are publishing serious fiction, described as literary works that require an intellectual reading. These books may be experimental novels, or works by new writers who do not write category fiction.

"There seems to be a diminishing outlet for good, high-quality fiction," said Beverly Jarrett, director of the University of Missouri Press. "As more and more New York houses are purchased by conglomerates, we've seen more and more formula fiction, the quick, easy read where the characters are the same and the plot is the same."

Commercial houses still publish novels by "name" authors, but fewer novels by first-time authors. Jarrett said that New York publishers report rejecting some excellent novels by first-time authors because the novels likely would not sell ten thousand copies. Some university presses view it as a legitimate role to step into the gap to assure the continuation of quality fiction.

"If the so-called 'bottom line' is defined solely by accountants, as it is in conglomerate publishing, then one, of course, moves toward the common denominator of the most buyers," Jarrett said. "But if the bottom line encompasses the fullest existence one can live as a human being, then there are considerations outside the domain of accountants. The shareholders of serious writing are all the citizens of the republic."

In the 1970s, Robert Emmitt, then managing editor of the Vanderbilt University Press and a novelist himself, faulted university presses for eagerly publishing analyses of existing literature but shunning the opportunity to publish new literary works. He argued that university presses should begin publishing "primary sources" of literature:

We know, too, that as long as we stick to publishing what the scholar calls his "secondary sources," we are on safe ground as university publishers: nobody can accuse us of playing fast and loose with the word "scholarship," of trying to undermine our profession or of starting revolutions; we are secure, proper, respectable, and righteous in the eyes of the community we publish and serve—so long as we go on publishing, say, stylistic and/or thematic analyses of William Faulkner but never venture to publish what we believe and hope will be another William Faulkner.[11]

In the 1980s, an increasing number of university presses began publishing what they believe and hope to be other William Faulkners—often with literary and even financial success.

The legendary book that prompted dreams of literary success was John Kennedy Toole's novel *A Confederacy of Dunces*. The novel was published in 1980 by the LSU Press after being rejected by at least nine New York publishers. It went on to win the Pulitzer Prize for fiction and sold 55,000 copies in hardcover and another 750,000 in its Grove Press paperback.

The young author did not live to see his oft-rejected work acclaimed. As years passed without his finding a publisher, Toole became increasingly withdrawn. In 1969, in his early thirties, he committed suicide. The manuscript eventually came to the LSU Press through novelist Walker Percy. While teaching at Loyola University of New Orleans in 1976, Percy was accosted by a middle-aged woman who wanted him to read a novel written by her son. The mother said she had found no publisher willing to invest in a long, comic tale written by a man who would never write another book. Assuming the worst, Percy put her off. But one day she thrust a bulky, barely legible carbon copy of her son's novel in Percy's hands. He hoped that the first few pages would be so bad that he could reject it quickly. Instead, as he reports in his foreword to the novel, he "read on. And on. First with the sinking feeling that it was not bad enough to quit, then with a prickle of interest, then a growing excitement."

L.E. Phillabaum, director of the LSU Press, said that a paradox exists for first-time novelists, because it has become increasingly difficult to place full-length serious fiction with commercial publishers unless the author is a writer of substantial reputation. "It is, of course, nearly impossible to become a writer of such stature without having had books that have sold very well indeed. Catch-22," Phillabaum said, and he added:

It seems to us that there is a proper role for university presses in this world: to provide an additional outlet, albeit a modest one, for works of serious fiction. At LSU Press, we became convinced a few years before *A Confederacy of Dunces* was published that the commercial situation of picking books for market and subsidiary-rights potential would not reverse itself. We therefore decided, as a matter of policy, that publishing novels of high literary merit, regardless of sales potential, was an appropriate area for a university press.[12]

LSU publishes up to a half dozen original novels each year out of a list of about sixty new scholarly titles. First press runs of LSU Press novels average about 2,000 to 2,500 copies, all in hardcover.

However, the vast majority of university presses still consider fiction to be outside their editorial missions. Of the eighty American university members of the Association of American University Presses, only eighteen specified in 1989 that they accept fiction submissions. Most presses specifically state that they do not publish original fiction.

The publishing of original fiction is a point of debate among scholarly publishers. The director of an eastern university press responded to the survey by writing, "We do not feel that fiction falls within the province of a university press. If it is good, it will get published by one of the many, many trade publishers. A university press should not waste its resources on trade fiction publishing."

That sentiment is shared by many in scholarly publishing. Herbert S. Bailey, Jr., who retired in 1986 as director of Princeton University Press, told the *New York Times*:

> What bothers me when university presses do fiction is that it makes headlines. An occasional book of fiction may be okay, but things give way when people say "Isn't it wonderful? The university press is publishing novels." I have professional misgivings about a university press being seen as doing "wonderful things" instead of "stodgy things" that we do all along. And I don't think it's really "stodgy" if what you're doing is a specialized work of scholarship.[13]

Many others concur that university presses have no business publishing original fiction. "It's not our job. It's not our purpose. It's not what we know how to do," said Carol Orr, director of the University of Tennessee Press, adding that fiction demands a wholly different kind of publishing and a different marketing strategy as well.[14] In addition, fiction goes against the concept of specialized listbuilding. "In nonfiction, you build a list," an editor observed. "You can build a list in anthropology. In fiction, you have to build a list with each book." Fiction, then, offers new challenges in marketing.

A few in university publishing believe that fiction lies within the mission of a scholarly press. John Gallman, director of Indiana University Press, said in 1982:

> Our assumption is that serious fiction is as important to our culture and society as scholarship, and our subsidiary concern is that fiction needs help, that novelists need the same kind of support as do professors of history, literary criticism, or philosophy.
>
> If you wanted our rationale in twenty-five words or less, it would be this: We care about quality fiction. One must believe that there is an appetite, even a hunger, for serious, unpredictable new fiction. It is that very risk, the newness, the excitement that makes it important. Serious fiction is always something more than entertaining, though in our judgment it must be entertaining as well. We are not looking exclusively for experimental or avant-garde fiction. Nor are we particularly interested in the highest of highbrow material. We want our books to be good reads, exciting, funny, distinctive, and serious about life and feelings in the most fundamental sense.[15]

Today, Gallman still believes that quality fiction deserves quality outlets. But Indiana no longer encourages submissions of original fiction. Not only did the press find only a few novels it thought worth publishing, but also, Gallman said, the press wasn't able to do enough for the books in terms of promotion:

> An author works for two or three years on a novel and, then, even if he or she hasn't gotten accepted by Random House, still there are high expectations when a publisher takes it on, even a university press. When we are only able to sell seven hundred or eight hundred copies, usually because the *New York Times* and other major media have chosen not to review it, the author is understandably let down and disgruntled. If I were an author in that situation, I would be let down and disgruntled.

Still, success stories do exist. Considering the comparatively few novels published by university presses, a surprising number have achieved national prominence. In 1982, Ohio State University Press published a voluminous novel about small-town Ohio, a work fifty years in the writing, called . . . *And Ladies of the Club*, by eighty-eight-year-old Helen Hooven Santmyer. The press earlier had published her memoirs. Ohio State sold only 1,300 copies of the four-pound novel, but by chance it came to the attention of two Hollywood producers, who raised the issue of subsidiary rights. Weldon Kefauver, then director of the Ohio State press, engaged an agent to represent the press. In the wake of five months of negotiations, the press and the author became equal partners in a majority share of proceeds from the reborn novel, with G.P. Putnam's Sons as trade publisher and paperback rights set at a $250,000 minimum. The book became a main selection of the Book-of-the-Month Club, and Putnam sold 410,000 copies.[16]

Another recent success is *The Hunt for Red October*, published by the Naval Institute Press in 1985. President Reagan read the novel and pronounced it "the perfect yarn." The author, Tom Clancy, Jr., was invited to the White House. As a result, the book spent several months on the capital's bestseller list. "It never hurts to have a little advertisement, especially if it comes from the top," a bookstore trade buyer quipped.

The book is a sea thriller about a Soviet submarine captain who seeks to defect to the United States, bringing with him a special billion-dollar submarine named "Red October." Moscow dispatches fifty-eight attack submarines to hunt and destroy the special sub before its secrets fall into American hands.

Clancy was a Maryland insurance broker who never served a single day in the Navy, much less a day aboard a submarine. He studied the major unclassified books dealing with Soviet submarines and interviewed naval officers for background. Clancy conceived the idea for the book upon reading about an attempted mutiny aboard a Soviet frigate in 1976. "That mutiny rattled around in my head for years," Clancy said. Upon writing the manuscript, he went directly to the Naval Institute Press, because his total previous experience writing for publication had consisted of a letter to the editor and an article about MX missiles, both published in the press's monthly magazine. The press specializes in books such as *Dictionary of Naval Abbreviations*. But as it happened, the editors had decided to publish original fiction, provided it was "wet"—about the sea.[17]

Although most university presses avoid publishing original novels, many publish another form of fiction—novels which are old, out of print, or in another language, and are considered worth perpetuating. Presses have individual lists in such reprint arenas as Latin American literature, American Indian writings, and Third World and other non-mainstream fiction. As an example, the University of Nebraska Press began a "Modern Scandanavian Literature in Translation" series in 1986, with the publication of *Winter's Child*, the first English translation of the 1976 novel by a Danish writer. A number of university presses who do not seek original novels, then, reprint existing ones.

Historically, most university presses also have considered the publication of poetry to be incongruous with their mission to provide an avenue for scholarship. While literary criticism of poetry is published, original poetry itself typically is not. This once prompted an editor to compare the academic preference for literary criticism over literary production to "a farmer who prefers discussing his crops to planting them." [18]

Of the eighty American university members of the Association of American University Presses, only twenty-two specified in 1989 that they accept poetry submissions. A few more publish a volume of poetry each year, with someone outside the press screening submissions. But most presses specifically state that they do not publish original poetry.

An eastern university press director responded, "We do not believe a scholarly publisher/university press should publish poetry. There are more than enough publishers of poetry in the United States to take care of the little good poetry written." An editor for a university press in the Southwest added, "Poets who are good, I maintain, get published." But others disagree. As trade publishers have become less receptive to poetry without mass appeal, some university publishers have started to take up the literary slack by adding more volumes of poetry to their lists.

University presses which are recognized as leading publishers of poetry include Wesleyan, Pittsburgh, LSU, and Arkansas. Yale University Press has its Younger Poets Series, founded in 1919. That series competition is open to American writers under age forty who have never published a volume of poetry. Previous winners include James Agee, Adrienne Rich, and Muriel Rukeyser.[19] The press traditionally receives more than eight hundred manuscripts a year from new poets.

Asked to rank the houses that published the best or most significant poetry, 158 American poets ranked the University of Pittsburgh Press second nationally, following the commercial press Atheneum, and ranked Wesleyan University Press fourth. Other university presses receiving more than a dozen citations included Yale, Princeton, and Georgia.[20]

Most university presses, however, avoid publishing poetry because so many people write it yet so few buy it. A quip common among editors is that books of poetry would be consistent bestsellers if only every person who wrote poetry would buy one book of poetry a year. Editors at university presses that publish poetry acknowledge that it sells poorly, but one of them said, "We publish it anyway because it deserves to exist." LSU Press publishes half a dozen or so books of poetry each year, about 10 percent of its new titles. One of LSU's successful poets is Miller Williams, himself the director of the University of Arkansas Press. Williams holds the academic rank of University Professor at Arkansas and has won the Prix de Rome of the American Academy of Arts and Letters. He is the author or editor of more than twenty books, the latest being *Patterns of Poetry: An Encyclopedia of Forms* (LSU Press). His love of poetry is reflected in the listbuilding directions of the Arkansas press. About 25 percent of the press's new titles each year are poetry collections, poetry criticism, or poetry in translation. Even allowing for overhead and other expenses, Arkansas's poetry list more than pays for itself. "Our poetry program is in the black. We make money on our poetry books," Williams said. "Presses that explain their failure to publish poetry because it isn't profitable to them are probably being honest. But the myth that poetry never sells—people ought to be disabused of that."

University press directors and editors are hesitant to undertake the massive manuscript screening that would be required for poetry. A former poetry program official outlined the cause for this concern:

> University press directors are afraid of poetry, and for good reasons. First, they know from their own experience, or from the directors at other presses, that there is a tremendous volume of manuscripts waiting to be considered, and, like a reservoir, the number grows each year. . . . If a university press announces that it will begin reading poetry manuscripts, it can expect to receive at least two thousand the first year, and these collections are not easily categorized and eliminated. With scholarly publications, university presses can decide conscientiously that they will read no more manuscripts

dealing with Melville or Faulkner or Hemingway, and an editorial assistant can return the submissions without considering them. But with original creative writing, there are few categories, and the press must make arrangements to screen many excellent volumes.[21]

Some presses, such as Arkansas, do their own soliciting and screening of poetry collections. Other presses depend on an outside mechanism. The University of Alabama Press publishes two books a year for the Alabama Poetry Series. But rather than handle the selection process, the press publishes works selected by the creative writing faculty in the university's English Department. The University of Hawaii Press has an annual poetry contest run by an independent editorial board. The University of Illinois Press appoints a professor who is a published poet to choose one annual publication. An editor with the University Press of Virginia said, "We publish one volume a year for the Associated Writing Programs. Submissions go to them, not us. We don't let any poetry manuscripts in our door."

The Associated Writing Programs (AWP), with headquarters at Old Dominion University, has proved successful at encouraging the publication of books of poetry as well as other genres of creative writing. The AWP assists with the most taxing phase of the process by handling an annual competition in four genres—poetry, fiction, short stories, and creative nonfiction. The AWP assures publication of winning entrants, while a university press absorbs the costs of production and sale. The AWP solicits manuscripts and sends them to screeners, who are published writers in the four fields. These screeners narrow the lists in each category to twelve to fifteen finalists. The work of each of these writers is sent to a prominent writer in the appropriate genre, who selects the winner.

Currently, Texas Tech University Press publishes the winning poetry collection from about five hundred entries sent to the AWP each year. The University of Iowa Press publishes the winning entry among novels, the University of Missouri Press the winning short story entry, and the University of Georgia Press the winner in creative nonfiction. The work by the dozen or so other finalists in each category also typically is circulated to interested presses. Many manuscripts eventually are published, since presses have the assurance that they have been rigorously screened. With this process, the AWP solved the university press's largest problem, by making quality manuscripts available without the trouble and expense of evaluation.

❦ Texts, Reference Books, and Series

Those in university publishing may disagree over the publication of fiction and poetry, but they are in agreement on the need to attract books suitable for classroom use. At most presses, the bestselling titles are those which professors, year after year, assign for use by students.

University presses, though, seldom publish conventional textbooks that serve as the basic informational source for a course. The books they publish with classroom appeal serve primarily as required or supplemental readings in upper level courses with limited enrollments. These books are written to be understood by students as well as by scholars. "We don't want to publish textbooks, but if we can get a book in a classroom, fine," a western university press editor said. The director of an eastern university press added, "We don't want to get into the textbook business and become a profit-making press. We don't want to detract from our scholarly mission by getting into that."

For commercial presses, the biggest publishing profits—not including subsidiary rights income—come from textbooks. University presses, as nonprofit entities, are not expected to have a profit motive. Once, the head of a large commercial textbook publisher in New York came to a university press meeting as an invited speaker, heard a rumor of conventional textbook publishing among those tax-exempt presses, and threatened to draw down all of the powers of the Internal Revenue Service.

University presses cannot become blatant profit-seekers. Yet presses recognize that a book with a classroom application can help pay for scholarly monographs that do not recover their costs. At the Johns Hopkins press, all but one of the twenty bestselling titles have found substantial course-related markets. The one exception is *The 36-Hour Day*, a handbook for families or victims of Alzheimer's disease. The handbook has sold about 400,000 copies. The next leading seller is *The Johns Hopkins Atlas of Human Functional Anatomy*, now in a third edition, with sales approaching 200,000 copies. The book is for students learning to be paramedical technicians and learning to fill other health-care positions. The atlas, with 210 color illustrations depicting all organs and systems of the human body, even makes its way into high-school science classrooms.

In looking for books that might be used in courses, editors at the Johns Hopkins press monitor trends in education. For instance, the press published the atlas just as new fields of paramedical training were being developed and required appropriate course materials. In fact, the press is quite open in making an effort to acquire titles that combine scholarly merit with solid potential for classroom sales. "I find nothing at all wrong with this. It used to be asserted that university presses should not publish course or textbooks, but that's nonsense," director J.G. Goellner said. "Now, every time we consider a new book, we raise the question: Will it have any kind of course application? It has to be a good book judged by scholarly standards, but we also have bills to pay." [22]

Few presses are as direct in their marketing for classroom use as the Johns Hopkins press. In advertising its *Introduction to the Theory of Social Choice*, the press called the book "the first textbook on the topic suitable for use in undergraduate courses in economics, political science, and political sociology."

Usually, nonprofit university presses employ a subtler approach. Harvard University Press told prospective buyers that sections of *The Israeli Economy: Maturing Through Crises* would be "ideal for course use." Columbia University Press promoted *The Freudian Body: Psychoanalysis and Art* by saying its "challenge to established thought will be fascinating reading for students of literature, psychoanalysis, critical theory, and women's studies." Stanford University Press said that its *Politics and Paradigms: Changing Theories of Change in Social Science* will "be of interest to students of political philosophy as well as of comparative politics." Indiana University Press called *Committed Journalism: An Ethic for the Profession* a book "for every practicing journalist or student of journalism. It is destined to set standards for the industry and to be *the* book on journalism ethics for the foreseeable future." And Duke University Press promoted *Polanyian Meditations* by saying that it "gives promise of starting an entirely new debate among students at the leading edge of philosophic thought."

University press officials justify the publication of such course-related books by saying that if teaching, like research, is indeed a proper function of the university, then the publication of books useful in teaching surely is a proper function of the university's press.

University press books can even influence curricular development. The University of Pennsylvania Press published an edited anthology by Valene Smith called *Hosts and Guests: The Anthropology of Tourism*. The work had been offered to eighty-six different houses and repeatedly turned down, usually with comments about the risky future of the subject or the lack of regular university courses. Nelson H.H. Graburn, professor of anthropology at the University of California at Berkeley, wrote, "Since its publication, however, large courses have been introduced for undergraduates on a regular basis; it has been possible to teach such courses only since this book came into existence."[23]

University presses also are prime publishers of reference books needed by libraries and students and within the professions. Reference works have a large base market among libraries, and library budget cuts seldom affect reference book purchases as they do monograph purchases. Reference works also typically have a long life.

At the University of Chicago Press, the all-time bestseller is *A Manual for Writers of Term Papers, Theses, and Dissertations*, which is approaching five million copies sold since it first appeared in 1937. A fifth edition was released in 1987. The previous four were written by Kate L. Turabian, who also wrote the second best-selling publication of the Chicago press —*A Student's Guide for Writing College Papers*, which still sells fifty thousand copies a year. Richmond Lattimore's translation of *The Iliad of Homer* is Chicago's third best seller, and the fourth is another reference work, *The University of Chicago Spanish Dictionary*. Another steadily selling reference book is *The Chicago Manual of Style*, which first appeared in 1906. In that first edition, the appendix offered ten pages of hints, beginning with, "Manuscripts should be either typewritten or in a perfectly clear handwriting. The former is preferable."[24] The current thirteenth edition is 738 pages long—almost 200 pages longer than the twelfth edition.

Harry Church Oberholser's *Bird Life of Texas* is a monument in the annals of reference book publishing. Shortly after Frank Wardlaw became director of the University of Texas Press in 1950, he was advised that one of his first acquisitions should be Oberholser's bird book. But this work almost became the book too big for Texas. The manuscript weighed in at 105 pounds, and it contained 3,200,000 words. Published in 1974, the book was seventy-three years in the making. In 1901, the U.S. Biological Survey sent two young scientists to Texas to make a survey of bird and mammal distribution. One of the scientists published his survey in a 1906 government bulletin. The other, Oberholser, delayed publication until he could accumulate more data. Accumulate he did, until the manuscript reached such proportions that its size virtually precluded publication. Oberholser was unwilling to allow surgery on his creation, so the project languished for another decade. Finally, when Oberholser was ninety-two years old, all parties agreed to a plan to pare the manuscript to about one million words. Oberholser died the following year, never getting to see his bird book in print.[25]

Examples of newer reference works include the eight-volume *Encyclopedia of Materials Science and Engineering* (copublished by the MIT Press and Pergamon Press), a seven-volume work in progress called *Dictionary of North Carolina Biography* (University of North Carolina Press), and *The Sucking Lice of North America* (Penn State University Press), written for entomologists, parasitologists, public health workers, veterinarians, and zoologists. Even smaller university presses can undertake reference book publishing. In 1986, the University Press of Kansas published *Flora of the Great Plains*, a reference work on plants, covering about one-fifth of the United States. The one-volume work is the biggest book the press ever has published; it has 1,408 pages, weighs more than four pounds, and contains about one million words. The book is the product of more than thirty-five years of plant collecting, research, and writing. Funding support came from the National Science Foundation and participating universities. The work will serve as a sourcebook for naturalists and for plant taxonomy classes.

University presses also have a predilection for creating series. Many editors dislike series, complaining that they take an inordinate amount of time to organize and that they place responsibility more on an academic supervisor than on an editor. But other editors say there is no better way to establish a reputation in a field than by offering a series.

The University of Wisconsin Press is up to sixteen volumes in its *Studies in Eighteenth-Century Culture*. Stanford University Press has established a new series called *Comparative Studies in History, Institutions, and Public Policy*. One of the oldest book series emanates from the Sather Lectures in classical literature, given annually on the Berkeley campus and published for more than sixty years by the University of California Press.

The mechanism for creating a series of scholarly books can vary. A distinguished lecture series may be converted into a series of books. Or the work of several scholars presented jointly in a regular symposium may be published as an edited volume. The increasing frequency of edited volumes is a byproduct of the specialization of knowledge. No single scholar is likely to possess the breadth of knowledge and the tools of research needed to explore a single topic in the full range of relevant approaches. Still another form of edited work is the volume of homage referred to as the *festschrift*. This is a volume of essays honoring a retiring scholar and written by the scholar's former students. Most university presses discourage the submission of *festschrifts* because such works frequently have little unity of content.

A series typically is conceived by a university press as an acquisition tool, or else a prominent scholar willing to be the series editor proposes the concept to a press. The offerings still go through the traditional peer review and editorial committee processes, but the scholar may serve as a commissioning agent to encourage the writing of manuscripts that would fit the series.

Most university presses avoid directly commissioning books themselves. As director J.G. Goellner of the Johns Hopkins press wrote:

> The press may sort through the fruits of scholarship, rejecting the underripe and the overripe, the misshapen and the wormy. But this sorting is limited to whatever fruits are made available. Scholarly publishers do not for the most part "commission" books of scholarship the way textbook publishers commission textbooks. Doing so would mean directing the research of scholars. Good scholars do not permit that—and I wouldn't trust one who did.[26]

Sheldon Meyer of Oxford University Press also opposes commissioning works. "Many presses in the 1960s were commissioning. That's terrible," he said. "The best work comes out of the scholar's own interests." Charles Grench, executive editor at Yale University Press, said that he may mention to scholars, while on a scouting trip, a topic of interest to the press. "We don't steer people into writing specific books," he said, "but we all have a bright idea now and then."

Through the years, though, some university press books have been commissioned, with good results. The first book ever commissioned by

Columbia University Press was Ernest F. Scott's *The Literature of the New Testament*, published in 1932.[27] More recently, the University of Nebraska Press commissioned a book of essays on western military leaders, and the University of Illinois Press commissioned a book entitled *Black Leaders of the 20th Century*, in both cases in response to perceived voids in those areas of scholarship.

Commissioning can help a press establish a new listbuilding area. When the University of Illinois Press decided to start a list in American music, the press assigned eight books in the field and attracted two more. "You establish an identity, so that authors say, 'Here's a place that is receptive to manuscripts in this area,'" said director Richard Wentworth. The University of Illinois Press now has published more than two dozen books in American music. One book—on the western swing music of Bob Wills —sold fifteen thousand copies within a month of publication, with Wills attending promotional autograph parties in Texas and Oklahoma.

🐚 Publishing the Grand Projects

A dozen or so university presses are large enough and gutsy enough to take on the grand projects that would terrify most commercial publishers, since they involve large expenditures with no corresponding assurance of large returns.

One form of grand project is publication of the edited papers of prominent individuals. The intent is to provide future scholars with a chronicle of the correspondence and papers of such historical figures as James Madison and Edmund Burke.

In the late 1970s, Columbia University Press completed publishing *The Papers of Alexander Hamilton* in a twenty-seven-volume set. Hamilton's writings had been published in two previous editions—a seven-volume edition by his son, put out in 1850, and a twelve-volume edition by Henry Cabot Lodge, reissued in 1904. The Columbia press decided that a new edition was needed to make the work comprehensive and to establish a record of Hamilton's writings that would meet the critical standards of the twentieth century. The press undertook the $1.6 million challenge, upon completing *The Works of John Milton* in 1938.[28]

At Princeton University Press, publication of the papers of Thomas Jefferson is now complete. The press currently is publishing the papers of Woodrow Wilson, at the rate of about three volumes a year, and is more than halfway through a complete Thoreau. With the end of long litigation involving the Einstein estate, Princeton now is publishing the papers of Albert Einstein, scheduled to appear in twenty volumes stretching into the late 1990s.

At Yale, the papers of Benjamin Franklin have been appearing one volume a year for more than two decades, with at least two more decades to go. Yale also has begun work on the papers of an entire family—the Peales. In a showdown of families, Harvard is planning at least one hundred volumes for the Adams family papers. Harvard also plans to publish all of the papers of Sigmund Freud.

The University of California Press is publishing an eight-volume edition of the papers of Marcus Garvey, founder of the Universal Negro Improvement Association. The history professor who is editing the work said that Garvey, in some ways, is to black Americans what George Washington is to white Americans.[29]

Besides correspondence, university presses like to publish the complete works of literary writers. Cornell is publishing the works of William Butler Yeats; California a critical Mark Twain.

Political documents aren't overlooked. In 1987, Chicago marked the bicentennial of the U.S. Constitution with the publication of a five-volume documentary history called *The Founder's Constitution*. The work is an anthology of primary documents from the seventeenth, eighteenth, and early nineteenth centuries that bear on the writing of the Constitution and the application of its principles.

Translations also are published in multi-volume sets. The University of Toronto Press is publishing an English translation of the writings of Renaissance scholar Erasmus. Editor Ron Schoeffel went to a library one day in 1968 to look up something on Erasmus and found that not all of his writings had been translated from sixteenth-century Latin. "I didn't realize what we were taking on," he said. "I thought it'd be sixteen or eighteen volumes. It now will be eighty-five." The target date for completion of the project is 2010 A.D.

Of this desire among scholarly presses to publish complete works, the *New York Times* commented:

One is reminded of the clerics who started this publishing tradition, especially of the Benedictines of the French Abbey of St. Maur, who 350 years ago, at the suggestion of Erasmus, began to collect, edit and publish all the works of the Fathers of the Church, both Latin and Greek, in giant folios that came from the abbey for more than 100 years in ivory vellum covers, like a long procession of robed abbots.[30]

The University of Chicago Press has taken on some particularly ambitious projects lately. One project that will run well into the twenty-first century and is expected to cost three million dollars, not allowing for inflation, is *The Complete Works of Giuseppe Verdi*. This heavily subsidized, thirty-seven-volume edition is to be published at the rate of about one volume a year. It will include all of the composer's oeuvre—operas, sacred music, songs, and chamber music. Scholars allowed into Verdi's archives found not only variations in the scores but different versions of entire sections of works. The first volume off the press, published in 1983, provided an annotated score of *Rigoletto* with a companion volume of textual notes. A performance of the new *Rigoletto* premiered soon thereafter in Vienna, under the baton of Riccardo Muti. "That is a very dramatic story in itself," said director Morris Philipson of the University of Chicago Press. "While the Vienna Opera was determined to have the premiere performance, it didn't publicize what it was doing, and therefore each time there was a difference from the accustomed performance, the audience booed."[31]

Another of Chicago's grand projects has been sidetracked, perhaps permanently. In 1973, the Chicago press began publishing a translation of *The Mahabharata*, a complex epic known as the wellspring and mirror of ancient Indian civilization. The translator, J.A.B. van Buitenen, a Sanskritist, died in 1980 in his fifties, having seen three volumes to press —with only a third of the 100,000 couplets in the vast poem. It is unlikely that the press will be able to find another skilled translator who will dedicate a lifetime to the work.

Some of these grand projects have become landmarks of scholarship and editing. One of these megabooks is *The Children of Pride*. At a Thanksgiving Day dinner in New Orleans in 1952, a young English teacher at Tulane University learned from his hostess that she had in her attic a journal and some letters written by her ancestors. The teacher, Robert Manson Myers, asked to see them. The correspondence revealed a family's efforts to keep in touch before, during, and after the Civil War. Charles Colcock Jones was a Presbyterian minister and owner of three Georgia plantations. He and his wife corresponded with a son at Harvard Law School, in the heart of Abolitionist country; there were notes from daughter to mother about the nice young preacher she was to marry; there was the mother's harrowing account in her diary of how Yankee soldiers stormed their Georgia house.

Although Myers was an eighteenth-century English literature specialist and not a Civil War specialist, he was intrigued by the writings and resolved to compile them into a book. When nearly finished, he stumbled upon another cache of Jones family letters—a huge one—at the University of Georgia Library. So he decided to start over and incorporate the best of them, too. In all, Myers typed 6,000 letters and ultimately chose 1,200. He arranged the letters to form an "epistolary novel" whose pace and clarity would engage the reader just as a narrative does.

Fifteen years after that Thanksgiving dinner, Myers had completed a 2,140-page manuscript. He submitted it to the University of Georgia Press, which turned it down. So did others, aghast at its size. Yale University Press invited it in, with this response:

> For a few days after that five-box manuscript landed with us, we treated it like a beached whale; we circled it cautiously, poked at it gingerly, and almost called a truck to haul it away. But then three or four of us began reading it and we were hooked, including Joan Kerr, wife of the director of the press, who read the entire manuscript while recuperating from surgery. Vann Woodward, pre-eminent historian of the period and a member of our Publications Committee, was enormously enthusiastic; so was our outside reader, Eugene Genovese, another historian uniquely qualified to judge its scholarly value.[32]

Myers turned out to be one of the most exacting authors that Yale has ever had. He read proofs by examining them under a magnifying glass, picking up typesetting flaws not apparent to the naked eye.[33] Yale published the book in 1972 and sold more than 25,000 copies in the first year. The book won the 1973 National Book Award in history.

An even larger megabook is *The Lisle Letters*, researched and edited by Elizabethan scholar Muriel St. Clare Byrne over a period of fifty-one years. The six published volumes contain two million words and 3,953 pages. In 1930, Byrne first suggested editing the sixteenth-century correspondence of Viscount Lisle, Edward IV's illegitimate son. Her project earned the support of T. S. Eliot, then a director of the British publishing house of Faber & Faber, which signed her to a contract in 1941. The project grew too big, though, and the British publisher pulled out. The University of Chicago Press took over the project in 1975, with Byrne then eighty years old.

The Tudor letters span seven years, 1533–40, a period encompassing Henry VIII's break with the pope, his divorce from Catherine of Aragon, and his marriages to Anne Boleyn, Jane Seymour, Anne of Cleves, and Catherine Howard. Those years also saw the dissolution of the monasteries, the rise and sudden fall of Thomas Cromwell, and the execution of Sir Thomas More. All of these served as background for the Lisle story and were mentioned, almost casually, in the letters. Lord and Lady Lisle, separated for a brief time, wrote some remarkable love letters. At the end, Lord Lisle was sent without warning to the Tower of London for treason he did not commit.

Byrne found the letters in the Public Record Office four hundred years later. Trained in history and languages, she recognized the value of the letters. Already a published writer with a special appreciation of the stage, especially Shakespeare, she saw in the letters a fascinating drama with a classic beginning, middle, and end.

The manuscript that arrived at the Chicago press had 4,799 pages—all typed single-spaced. Some of the pages were brown and fragile with age, having been typed thirty or more years earlier. Some pages had been cut apart and glued together to make room for additions.[34] The work was published to acclaim in 1981, when Byrne was eighty-six years old.

A megabook that University of California Press director James Clark calls "a perfect metaphor for what a university press does" is *The Plan of St. Gall.* The book, considered a classic in medieval scholarship, is an architectural, historical, and anthropological study of a Carolingian monastery plan preserved in the Convent of St. Gall, Switzerland, for 1,100 years.

The project began in 1967 as a book of seven hundred pages with 561 illustrations. By the time it came out in 1980, its size and cost had doubled. The book cost $359,749 to produce, and overhead was estimated at $281,000. Sales of the two thousand sets at $250 apiece brought in $500,000, and the book received $152,000 in subsidies. So it could be argued that the book made $11,000. But there were incalculable human costs. The traditional roles of author and publisher blurred. The authors —Walter Horn, professor emeritus of art history at the University of California, and architect Ernest Born of San Francisco—ultimately brought with them more than $100,000 in funding, and they assumed an active decision-making role. Born selected the typeface and redesigned one of its characters. He chose the paper and the cloth for the cover. He determined the layout of every page. The authors' involvement at times reduced the publisher's role to that of bill-payer.

Clark chronicled the fascinating history of the book by reproducing letters between the authors and then-director August Frugé:[35]

> Frugé to Horn, September 1967: "There remains one worry: the finances of the project. . . . I don't like to be so cautious before committing myself to a royalty, but we are buying a pig in a poke, especially when we are dealing with Ernest, who is excellent on quality but not overconcerned about other people's money."

> Frugé to Horn, October 1973: "I am acutely embarrassed by the high cost of this one project. You know, I am sure, that I like the idea of putting out one super handsome book—a kind of monument. But I do not have the right to spend the University's money on a monument to you or to the Press."

> Horn to Frugé, October 1973: "You have written in your letter of October 8 what I have heard you state more than once in informal conversation: that with the St. Gall book Ernest and I are out to set a 'monument'—to ourselves, to you, and to the Press. You must allow us to correct this impression because it is erroneous. Neither Ernest nor I is interested in a monument."

At this point, it became evident that matters concerning the project probably would be made public. Correspondence began to take on the character of documentation.

> Frugé to Horn, December 1974: "In the year since my letter of 8 October 1973 the cost of printing, paper, and binding appears to

have gone up by about $22,000. This is in addition to the $21,000, which I mentioned in the earlier letter and which had largely to do with the new material, text and illustrations, that you and Ernest wish to add to the book. I simply cannot steer the Press into what appears to be a large financial disaster. Nor can I leave this project as a sort of time bomb to be defused or exploded by my successor. . . . This is formal notice, then, that the Press will not continue with the project under present circumstances."

Horn to Frugé, January 1975: "In your handling of the St. Gall book you have appeared inactive and timid. . . . You suffer from a ludicrous misconception that Ernest and I are hell-bent to set ourselves 'a monument.'"

Frugé to Horn, January 1975: "You keep coming back to my jest about a monument to you and Ernest. I had not dreamed that so lighthearted a thrust could strike so deep. In any event, I have no objection to a monument provided it not also become a tombstone for the Press."

Horn to the President of the University of California, January 1975: "I consider Mr. Frugé's action to be an affront to me as author of this work."

Frugé to the university's vice president, February 1975: "I am grateful for the offer to help in my little duel, as you call it, with Walter Horn. . . . We are jockeying for position, as you will see. He is trying to get me off balance and I am trying to retain what leverage I have."

Frugé to Born, January 1977: "In spite of our little difficulties, which were inherent in our differing responsibilities, I am proud to have worked with you and Walter on a remarkable project."

With this note, Frugé retired. Three years later, *The Plan of St. Gall* was published to critical acclaim.

To reach larger audiences with these works, university presses have published significantly abridged versions. Popular among general readers are California's abridgement of *The Plan of St. Gall*, Yale's abridgement of *The Children of Pride*, and Chicago's abridgement of *The Lisle Letters*.

❦ Bestsellers and Reprints

Through the years, university presses have had some surprising best-sellers—books with sales above 100,000 copies. Most bestselling titles have been trade books or reference works.

Mark Girouard's *Life in the English Country House* (Yale University Press) is a social and architectural history that evidently is the only American university press book ever to make the *London Times*'s bestseller list.[36] Another unlikely bestseller was *The Mushroom Hunter's Field Guide* (University of Michigan Press), by Alexander Smith, who at the time of publication in 1958 was the curator of fungi at the University of Michigan herbarium. A reviewer at *The New Yorker* was so taken by the book that he devoted several pages to it, writing, "Dr. Smith has done for the hunter of mushrooms what Mr. Hemingway did for the hunter of big game."

In 1975, a University of Texas Press editor discovered in the archives of the university's Humanities Research Center a 150-page manuscript written by T.H. White in 1941 as the original conclusion to his King Arthur legend, chronicled in *The Once and Future King*. In 1977, the manuscript was published by the Texas press as *The Book of Merlyn*. White, then, posthumously ended his Arthurian epic as he had wished thirty-six years earlier—with the king, discouraged by the disbanding of his Round Table, having returned to the tutelage of his childhood mentor, Merlyn, for a final lesson about war, human society, and the reasons for hope. The book made the *New York Times*'s bestseller list, with sales of one million copies in hardcover and paperback together.

As university presses publish titles with more general appeal, these works are making their way into the reprint rights market. Such books tend to be trade books and others in the expanding title mix, not scholarly monographs. Paperback reprint rights to Harvard's all-time bestseller, *One Writer's Beginnings*, by Eudora Welty, were sold to Warner Books for $50,000. Harper & Row paid the University of California Press $100,000 for *Habits of the Heart: Individualism and Commitment in American Life*, by Robert Bellah and others. The University of Kentucky Press sold reprint rights to *The Twenty-Five-Year War: America's Military Role in Vietnam* by Gen. Bruce Palmer, Jr., to Simon & Schuster's trade paperback imprint called Touchstone. The Arkansas press sold *In the Land of Dreamy Dreams*, a collection of short stories by Ellen Gilchrist, to Little, Brown. Berkley

Books paid almost $50,000 for paperback rights to the Naval Institute Press's *The Hunt for Red October*. Increasingly, however, scholarly publishers are choosing to reprint their own titles in paperback rather than sell rights to the large New York commercial paperback houses. "We're becoming more competitive with the commercial paperback houses, so there really isn't any reason to sell most paperback rights," said Claire Silvers, publicity manager for Harvard University Press.[37]

University presses also are adding titles that commercial publishers let go out of print because of the 1980 Internal Revenue Service ruling that eliminated the ability of profit-making publishers to take tax writeoffs for overstock. Scholarly publishers do not need the same sales volume as commercial publishers do to make a book worthwhile. Before adding a reprint, a university press typically contacts professors in the relevant academic discipline, asking whether the book still has any appeal for classroom use. For instance, when advised by several journalism professors that Myron Farber's 1978 book, *Somebody is Lying*, probably had little course application anymore, Princeton University Press opted not to add the book to its reprint list.

One of the most successful reprint series is the Bison Books trade paperback series published by the University of Nebraska Press. First published in 1960, the more than six hundred Bison Books still in print now account for 50 percent of the press's annual sales. Nebraska publishes three or four new Bison Books each month. Examples include *Billy the Kid: A Handbook*, *Adventures of a Mountain Man*, and *Historic Sketches of the Cattle Trade of the West and Southwest*, which updates a 1940 edition.

Reprint series usually don't have great reputations. Press catalogs almost always list trade books first, then scholarly monographs, then, almost as an afterthought, reprints. But David Holtby of the University of New Mexico Press said, "The value of a reprint can be a powerful acquisition tool, not just as an afterthought." Darla Beckman, former marketing manager at the Nebraska press, noted that a Bison Book played a major role in acquiring one particular manuscript. A scholar noticed a Bison Book at Albertson's Grocery Store in Clarkson, Washington. Said Beckman, "He figured that any university press that could get a book into a grocery store, next to the *National Enquirer*, could successfully market his book."

University presses, then, have expanded the title mix considerably from the days when they published only dissertations and scholarly mono-graphs. University presses still view the publication of monographs as their essential mission as scholarly publishers. But few limit their role to monographs. They publish trade books and reference books, some pub-lish original fiction and poetry, others go heavily into reprints—all in the belief that they are helping to advance knowledge while staying solvent.

7. Pursuing

the Frontiers

of Knowledge

Scholarly publishing serves not only as a transmitter of ideas but also as an intellectual agent of society and even as a shaper of the cultural agenda. The role of intellectual gatekeeper involves far more than simply publishing received knowledge. The gatekeeper also should keep abreast of intellectual currents, define and redefine fields of inquiry, challenge preconceived notions, and, in so doing, stimulate the intellectual advancement of the culture.

University presses, as a leading vehicle for intellectual discourse, seldom serve as passive gatekeepers. Instead, they actively shape the cultural agenda by defining their role in the scholarly enterprise through list-building and aggressive acquisition methods. By being on the frontiers of scholarship, a press can help direct the cultural agenda, rather than merely reenforce existing values, beliefs, and practices.

Knowledge, after all, is not static. Neither is the pursuit of knowledge. As scholars shift their research attention from one area of study to another, intellectual pursuit itself shifts. New fields of inquiry arise while old ones decline. The frontiers of knowledge continually expand. This shift in intellectual pursuits is reflected in what eventually reaches publication.

For instance, a current area of inquiry among historians is cultural and intellectual history, which addresses the impact of ideas on culture, and of culture on ideas. While cultural and intellectual history has grown in popularity, a receding area of inquiry has been traditional narrative history. Although no linear relationship necessarily exists between the two, the illustration shows the evolving nature of scholarship. If a press fails to perceive current "cutting edge" research interests, then it will be publishing narrative histories at a time when historians no longer consider them to be on the frontier of knowledge. "This is an evolution within the discipline itself," a university press editor said. "Publishers try to get in step with that."

Intellectual currents not only result in evolution within a discipline, but also can create hybrids of specialization—new areas of inquiry that cross disciplinary lines. Publishers try to recognize these newly arising fields because publishers want to be at the forefront of scholarly evolution. As an editor at a prestigious university press put it, "Scholarly publishing plays a role in helping a new field establish an identity or in helping to legitimize it. The university press doesn't do it; the books do."

For example, scholars currently are mining the territory that lies between history and geography. Historical geographers, as they are called, look at history from the perspective of space and region, land and environment. Two of the largest projects in this field are being published by university presses. Yale University Press is publishing a three-part study called *The Shaping of America*, by geographer Donald Meinig of Syracuse University. The study emphasizes the human creation of places, networks, and intercontinental systems. In Canada, two university presses united to publish a multi-volume work called *The Historical Atlas of Canada*. The University of Toronto Press published an English version, and the University of Montreal Press published a French version. The atlas traces, through a series of maps, both the development of Canadian boundaries and the social, economic, and cultural evolution of the country.

So far, the work of historical geographers appeals more to historians than to geographers, perhaps because geography itself is such a hybrid field. Geography initially began in geology, with human and cultural dimensions added later to the study of the physical earth. Now, the research of geographers ranges from the spread of populations to the spread of diseases and from drawing maps to forecasting climate trends.

"If you look at geography in the last twenty-five to thirty years, you see it exploding," said Sam B. Hilliard, professor of geography at Louisiana State University. "The end result is that the field looks like a wheel: people sit on their own spokes and talk less and less to those on the other side. Eventually, the wheel may become a doughnut, with a huge intellectual hole in the middle. We have already reached the point where we look at some of the titles of research papers, and not only do we not know why they are geographic, we don't even know what they are talking about."[1]

Another hybrid field is sport history—a cross between the remarkably diverse areas of physical education and history. Schools such as the University of Maryland, Ohio State, and Penn State now offer Ph.D. programs in sport history in their physical education departments. "Today, scholars realize that sport can and should be studied systematically," said Marvin Eyler, professor emeritus of sport history at the University of Maryland at College Park. But in 1972, when Eyler helped found the North American Society for Sport History, "I would tell other scholars I was a sport historian, and they would say, 'What do you do? Count the baseballs in the World Series?'"

The research in sport history tends to be interdisciplinary, with subjects ranging from the presentation of the "tomboy" in American fiction to analyzing rituals in American sport to studying the role of baseball in transmitting the dominant values of capitalism. "In the early years of the field, physical educators looked at history from a traditional standpoint: this was the event, these were the great leaders, this was how they played sports. In the last few years, the research and the methodology have changed dramatically. They are becoming more interdisciplinary, more quantitative, and more like social-history research in general," said Steven Riess, a historian at Northeastern Illinois University and editor of the *Journal of Sport History*. "What is happening is that sport historians think of themselves as labor historians, or urban historians, or immigration historians, or economic historians—with a special interest in sports."[2]

Some university presses recognized this new field of inquiry and began listbuilding in sports. The University of Illinois Press has a new series called "Sports and Society," billed as encompassing biographical and historical studies as well as those using psychological, sociological, anthropological, political, and economic approaches.

Another growing area in historical scholarship is business history. The Bell Telephone system is the subject of a new series of books published jointly by Johns Hopkins University Press and the American Telephone and Telegraph Company. AT&T has opened to scholars its extensive archival records, dating from the invention of the telephone and its patenting in 1876 up through World War II. AT&T is helping to finance publication of books in the series. The general editor of the series is Louis Galambos, a professor of history at Johns Hopkins University. Despite the corporate sponsorship, Galambos said that the books go through standard editorial channels, including outside review and approval by the faculty editorial board. "As the series develops," Galambos said, "there will be more and more authors with different points of view."[3] Galambos said that AT&T is prepared for scholars whose viewpoints disagree with its own on such issues as labor relations and the political and economic history of AT&T.

Of course, not all new directions in scholarship emanate from university presses. Commercial scholarly houses play a vital role in the distribution of knowledge, too. In combination, profit-seeking publishing houses and nonprofit university presses have a significant impact on the advancement of many academic disciplines.

❦ Emerging and Receding Agendas

The freedom that scholars have to set their own research agendas results in the growth of some fields of scholarship and the decline of others. In scholarly publishing today, the social sciences are flourishing while the humanities are suffering. One reason is that there are more economists than European historians, more sociologists than philologists, and more clinical psychologists than Shakespeare scholars.

Not only do social science books sell more consistently, but both research and publication in the social sciences—compared with the humanities—are more frequently subsidized by foundations or the government. Studies in the humanities seldom generate the types of subsidies available for "hard" or "soft" scientific and technological research and publication. After all, a book analyzing Henry James may invigorate the mind, but it does nothing to stimulate an economy or set in motion any practical, as opposed to intellectual, discoveries. "The humanities are having a tough time," one editor said. "Presses are necessarily having to look at the bottom line."

Literary studies are the ones most in trouble. Editors said that the highest percentage of submissions at their presses is in literary criticism and that up to a third of all scholarly books published today are literary studies. Yet they cited literary criticism as the most overpublished area of inquiry and reported that, because of declining sales, they are cutting back significantly in the literary field.

A university press director in the Midwest who went through a Ph.D. program in English himself has not made literary criticism a priority at his press. "I may have been weaned from some of my intellectual predilections by seeing the market for literary criticism," he said.

In the words of a Princeton University Press editor, sales have "dropped off incredibly" in literary criticism. As a result, editors say that university presses are publishing proportionately less in literary criticism than a decade ago. "Because so much is written in that field compared to what is published, we can set very high standards," a West Coast editor added. "People in that field write a lot, but they don't buy a lot of books themselves."

Because of supply and demand, fierce competition exists to have manuscripts in literary criticism published by university presses. Manuscripts that have become particularly difficult for authors to get published include studies of a single work, studies of works by less prominent authors, studies of foreign literature, studies of premodern literatures, and highly technical studies in such areas as linguistics and philology.

Another type of difficulty exists in the publishing of Native American studies. While books of literary criticism at least have an identifiable audience, university press editors cited the extraordinary difficulty in defining the audience for Native American studies. "Indians aren't really 'Indians' at all," an acquisitions editor at a western press said. "They are Apache, Sioux, Cherokee, and Navajo. They are individual and distinctive groups. So we tend to get narrow works with a limited audience." Another complicating factor is that the two disciplines with the most active interest in Native American studies—historians and anthropologists—have different research approaches. Historians primarily study written records, while anthropologists do field research. In fact, a common joke among editors is that the typical Indian family consists of a mother, a father, two children, and an anthropologist. In fact, the difference in methodological approaches causes real problems for scholarly publishers. "Historians and anthropologists speak different languages," one editor said. "They don't communicate. It leads to conflicts. There is definitely a fear on the part of scholars to attempt a broad synthetic work." It also is difficult to get suitable readers for crossdisciplinary works. "There's a difficulty in having a manuscript by a historian and sending it to an anthropologist," the editor said.

Ethnohistory serves as an academic bridge between history and anthropology, but not all scholars appreciate that approach. Said Beth Hadas, director of the University of New Mexico Press, "Their research methods differ greatly. Openmindedness should be emphasized. The historian and the anthropologist need to work together more. We really can't study the Navajo culture without studying Navajo history. Then there are art historians and anthropologists. Getting readers' reports can be difficult. They think they are encroaching on each others' territory."

Despite the listbuilding difficulties, Native American studies remains a popular listbuilding field in the West. At a convention of western university presses in 1985, Hadas reported that, because of Indian land-claim issues, the *New York Review of Books* had declared Indians "in" this year. Hadas quipped, "In scholarly publishing in the West, Indians are always 'in.' But sometimes we have to go to New York to find out if Indians are *really* 'in.' "

However, books in Native American studies are not consistent sellers. A University of Nebraska Press editor pointed to a declining interest in Native American studies. Minority programs at colleges and universities that began in the 1960s and 1970s are dying. "Students who once took Native American studies courses are now doing computer programming," he said. "A year ago I was really pessimistic. Sales on Indian monographs were disappointing. Today I'm a little more optimistic. The key seems to lie in the topic." But editors complained that even the Native American books that win critical acclaim still have mediocre sales—defined by them as sales totaling only in the hundreds.

In fact, sales have declined precipitously for scholarly monographs in general. Princeton University Press statistics indicate that hardback books that on the average sold 1,660 copies in five years in 1969, sold 1,003 in 1984 —a decline of nearly 40 percent.[4] Editors reported major declines in sales for the more specialized books in the humanities such as classical studies, modern languages, Latin American history, philosophy, art history, art criticism, and the fine arts. Books in these fields typically sell in the hundreds instead of the thousands. Sales in European history have plummeted as well, perhaps because fewer students in higher education have been taking foreign languages. One university press director said that his press, with the help of a five-thousand-dollar subsidy, published a title in European history and discovered first-hand the lack of a market. The book dealt with Polish foreign diplomacy. "It's a significant book," the director said. "That's why we published it." The book sold fewer than five hundred copies.

Herbert S. Bailey, Jr., director emeritus of Princeton University Press, worries that scholarly publishers quite naturally may gravitate away from subject areas that do not provide a good buying public. Using Latin American studies as an example, Bailey wrote:

> Lack of publication channels can discourage scholarship and can deprive the public of knowledge. Can our country afford, for example, to let Latin American studies decline, or let the publication of Latin American studies decline? Obviously not, and I believe the leadership in university press publishing must make the scholarly world, and the world of public and private foundations, aware of what is happening.[5]

Because sales are an indication of vitality in scholarly areas, university presses do look at sales figures in determining the rise and fall of subject areas. Editors said that religious studies are on the ascent, and political science monographs are on a slight decline. Books with a Soviet theme are selling, and so are titles dealing with the American presidency. But black studies, in the words of a university press director, "had its boom years and then dropped off."

Editors worry about the perception that they build their lists based on sales potential. That perception is not wholly untrue. But the reasoning goes deeper than that. A monograph that makes little contribution to knowledge usually will not sell, and a monograph that does not sell will be unable to fulfill its purpose of satisfying intellectual hunger.

The key to scholarly communication is publishing in areas where there exists a large enough intellectual constituency to support publication. This level of publication support typically is identifiable through book purchases. William A. Wood of the University of Minnesota Press wrote:

> We deliberately are eschewing "soft" subject areas, especially those in the humanities and social sciences in which the press has

no strong backlists. Instead, we are moving into new fields where the chances for us seem brighter because of strong departments at our parent university, or because numbers of graduate students are rising, or because the fields are ones in which scholars buy lots of books.[6]

University presses, then, find themselves with a mixed motivation in the decision to publish. They seek to contribute as fully as possible to intellectual life, within the natural constraints of budgetary reality. August Frugé, director emeritus of the University of California Press, wrote, "The university press . . . exists to publish learned works; when it uses commercial methods and when it seeks books that will sell, it is walking close to the moral edge. And it *must* walk close. If it finds too few saleable books, it can go broke. If it finds too many, it can lose its soul."[7]

❦ Evolution in Listbuilding

Listbuilding continually evolves, because intellectual pursuit and scholarly publishing operate within a cyclical dynamic. Scholars do pioneering work in a field. Editors take note of that interest and start publishing in the new field. Publication encourages more research; more research means more publishing. The cycle continues until, eventually, the new field is incorporated into existing disciplines, becomes dormant, or becomes an established entity of its own.

Women's studies, for instance, constitutes a broad field of inquiry spanning less than two decades of intensive scholarly pursuit. Scholarly publishers believe that women's studies will remain a strong listbuilding area for years to come, because this field's perspectives are now becoming integrated into other disciplines. But women's studies also has retained an independent vigor of its own by branching out in new directions and creating new areas of inquiry.

A major offshoot in recent years is the integration of racial and economic issues into women's studies. "The women's movement is accused of being white and middle-class," Gloria Bowles, lecturer in feminist studies at Stanford University, told university press editors at a regional convention. "Books which are able to integrate race, class, and sex issues are needed. We are turning down books for our classes that have only a white perspective."

The first known women's studies program began at San Diego State University in 1970, occupying the forefront of the Women's Movement. At first, scholarship consisted of an "add women and stir" approach, with study of a token woman author or a female scientist casually tossed into the traditional subject matter. Next, women's studies sought to integrate women fully into existing disciplinary studies. Women writers were brought into the canon, with the intent of challenging the contours of the literary disciplines and looking at history from an other-than-male perspective. For instance, the Renaissance historically has been viewed as a high point of artistic and intellectual activity. That was true for men but not for women, Bowles said. Today, women's studies is becoming more crossdisciplinary or multi-disciplinary, challenging the rigorous boundaries between disciplines. There are integrationists who want to get women into the existing male-focused studies in order to achieve more balance, and there are separatists who strive for a new discipline centered on studies of women.

There's a lot in a name. In the early "add women and stir" days, the field frequently was called "female studies." But Bowles said that that designation had too biological a cast. Today most programs are called "women's studies," although that name is criticized for its possessive cast. San Francisco State University calls its program "women studies." Others use the term "gender studies." Researchers in this field often are social scientists and sociologists for whom "gender" is a comfortable word, since they are interested in studying both men and women. The criticism directed toward gender studies is that it doesn't recognize the power imbalance between men and women. Lately, a name growing in popularity is "feminist studies"—the most radical name, because of its political and philosophical connotations.

As women's studies emerged as an area of intellectual inquiry, scholarly publishers began building lists in the field. Kathleen Ketterman, assistant director for marketing at Indiana University Press, said that in 1972, when the press published its first women's studies book, *Suffer and Be Still: Women in the Victorian Age*, the press had a book whose potential audience barely was conscious of its own existence. As that audience developed, the Indiana press became known by the discipline's adherents as a publisher at the forefront of women's studies. Books on women's studies now comprise about 15 percent of the frontlist at the Indiana press. Billing itself as a leader in women's studies publishing, the press packs its direct-mail brochures with such titles as *Soviet Sisterhood* and *If All We Did Was To Weep At Home: A History of White Working-Class Women in America*. Another, called *We've All Got Scars*, argues that in this nation's elementary schools, little girls become second-class citizens and little boys become victims of a "macho" tradition. *Plains Woman: The Diary of Martha Farnsworth, 1882–1922*, is another Indiana book, which the press's brochure calls "an intriguing look at how it felt to be a woman in a male-defined world that was undergoing tremendous cultural and technological change."

Once a press establishes a reputation in a field, prospective authors flock to it with related manuscripts. "Indiana was my first choice as a press," said Bowles, who has published with the Indiana press. "The reason was, they had published such excellent manuscripts in the area of women's poetry, and I wanted my book to be among those books that I respect and that I had drawn on for my own research."

At the University of California Press, about one hundred of its more than three thousand titles are in women's studies. All but nine of those have been published since 1980. Two California editors solicit manuscripts in the area of women's studies, in such fields as history, politics, and sociology. "Women's studies books do sell, and there is a growing market for them," said Sheila Levine, a California press editor whose specialties are history and Asian studies.

Much of women's studies publishing partakes of feminist advocacy, Levine said, noting that university presses frequently debate the appropriateness of advocacy publishing. Ketterman of the Indiana press is a believer in advocacy publishing. "Most of what we have published and called women's studies over the years can be loosely defined as any book about women, or written by a woman, or thought to have a female audience, whether written by a man or woman. It's the add-women-and-stir theory of publishing," Ketterman said. "Feminist studies are quite another thing. They are books written from a feminist political perspective, incorporating or attempting to evolve a whole new feminist theory."

Bowles of Stanford said that she, too, is a proponent of advocacy publishing. She said that universities have not been value-neutral but have influenced the structure of knowledge through the years. "Man had been the norm, the universal. That kind of a legacy of over two thousand years is not going to be erased in a few year's work," she said, adding that she views women's studies as a critique of the structure of knowledge. "I don't see women's studies as an academic exercise—academic in the sense of useless. I look for books that seek to forge some bridges between learning and the lives of women."

People in publishing often see themselves as social change agents. By publishing books that overturn or challenge existing theory, editors can take their press's lists in directions that influence the cultural agenda. Thus they assume the role of gatekeepers of ideas.

Traditionally, the role of university presses has been to preserve and disseminate the results of scholarly research. These tasks remain the primary justifications for their existence. But through the years, university presses have developed a reputation for social conscience. The University of North Carolina Press published books on the post-Reconstruction South that challenged the traditional southern viewpoint. The University of Oklahoma Press published pioneering studies on the American Indian. Temple University Press has a reputation for publishing advocacy works with such titles as *The Feminist Case Against Bureaucracy* and *Chaos on the Shop Floor: A Worker's View of Quality, Productivity, and Management.* Naomi Pascal, editor-in-chief at the University of Washington Press, cited two lists developed at her press—one in Native American studies and the other in Asian American studies—that might be said to "reveal a certain bias on the part of the press and its editors." Nevertheless, she said:

> What the university press imprint means—or ought to mean—is that the book will not be an unsubstantiated polemic but a carefully reasoned and meticulously documented presentation. These criteria permit a wide range of points of view but would exclude, I believe, a defense of racism, creationism, or any other of the persistent idiocies of our time. There may, however, be less clear-cut instances, where an editor's own convictions affect what a press publishes.[8]

❦ A Penchant for Controversy

Just as some university presses welcome feminist studies because they overturn existing thought, scholarly publishers look for provocative works in philosophy and economics and sociology. The word "controversial" is a popular one among both nonprofit and commercial publishers. A book that becomes controversial not only may sell well, but it likely will challenge the intellectual contours of a discipline.

Cornell University Press calls its book *Speculum of the Other Woman* a "profoundly controversial book." Harvard University Press predicts that its book *The Contentious French* is "bound to be controversial" because it offers a "dazzling new interpretation of four hundred years of modern French history." Of the book *Contemplating Music*, the Harvard press says it "will spark controversy among musicologists of all stripes." LSU Press calls its book *The Normative Basis of Culture* "undeniably ambitious and potentially controversial" among philosophers and social scientists.

University presses believe in publishing works that push a discipline in new directions. For instance, legal scholars have been debating two dominant themes in twentieth-century jurisprudence: legal positivism and utilitarianism. Legal positivism holds that the only rights and duties that exist are those explicit in the law. Utilitarianism holds that judges should decide cases on the basis of what is good for society—in the words of nineteenth-century philosopher Jeremy Bentham, what is the greatest good for the greatest number. Harvard University Press has advanced this debate by publishing three books within a decade by Ronald Dworkin, a scholar who divides his time between Oxford University and New York University. In his 1977 *Taking Rights Seriously*, Dworkin provided a defense of the view that law is based not on public policy but on moral principle. In his 1985 book, *A Matter of Principle*, Dworkin discussed the interplay of politics and moral philosophy and the balancing of individual rights and the common good. Then, in his 1986 *Law's Empire*, Dworkin presented a theory of law that the Harvard press modestly predicted "will be studied and debated—by scholars and theorists, by lawyers and judges, by students and political activists—for years to come." University press editors believe that it is part of their mission to publish reasoned works that cause debate in intellectual circles and so foster the intellectual development of the culture.

But university presses are not immune to subject-matter intimidation. One editor who worked at an Ivy League university press in the 1970s remembered witnessing the editorial committee's rejection of a manuscript by Harvard geneticist Arthur Jensen, whose controversial thesis suggested that blacks may be genetically inferior to whites. "We got eight readings, all wildly different," the editor recalled. "We even sent it to a black biologist at Stanford. He wrote an impressive report strongly in favor of publication." But the editorial committee decided not to publish the book. "They were afraid of publication—physically afraid," he said. "One board member said he didn't want young blacks, who wouldn't understand why the school published the book, attacking him." Jensen's book eventually was published by Harper & Row.

Editors wrestle with ethical issues in publishing. In 1985, Duke University Press published *High Treason*, an account of the purges in the Red Army during the Stalin years. The manuscript, smuggled out of the Soviet Union, was the product of two Russians who gained access to secret documents. One is a computer engineer who now lives in New York; the other remains anonymously in the Soviet Union. The manuscript raised scholarly questions because, as the Duke press director Dick Rowson said, "Our peer reviewers said the manuscript couldn't be authenticated since the material comes from Soviet archives." But it was published because it offered insights that could not be constructed in any other fashion.

Ethical dilemmas come in other forms as well. A University of California Press editor recalled sponsoring a work on a new technique for the artificial filtering of human sperm so as to produce offspring of the preferred sex. Several members of the editorial committee argued that the book should include a discussion of the ethics of the new procedure. But a philosopher on the committee disagreed, arguing that, to be consistent, the editorial committee would need to impose the same requirement of ethical discussion on the Los Alamos Scientific Laboratory Series concerning weapons research.[9]

University presses also can face political pressure. To avoid such possible pressure, many university presses avoid studies dealing with contemporary politics or political issues. Political pressures can influence a list in other ways, too. One university press, after publication, was asked by its administration to provide readers' reports on certain books dealing with Marxism and other controversial topics. The administration never said anything, yet the request sent a message to the editorial staff. Editors said they also have been asked to consider manuscripts written by wealthy alumni and potential benefactors, but none reported being forced to publish the works.

Another dilemma involves publication of books critical of the parent university. In 1979, the University of Washington Press published *Cold War on the Campus*, which told the story of academic freedom at the University of Washington during the McCarthy era. The book portrayed one of the current members of the editorial committee in a somewhat unfavorable light. The staff made the manuscript available to all editorial committee members in advance. The manuscript was approved unanimously.

Similarly, in 1986, Yale University Press published a book that investigated Yale's anti-Semitic policies through the years. The book, *Joining the Club*, began as a sophomore term paper by Dan Oren, a 1979 Yale graduate who is the son of Israeli immigrants. Oren had discovered in the Yale archives a folder labeled "Jewish Problem," containing a 1922 memo from the admissions chairman urging limits on "the alien and unwashed element." In 1923, the admissions committee enacted an informal quota that would hold Jewish enrollment to about 10 percent. The university's 1945 annual report said, "The Jewish Problem continues to call for the utmost care and tact. The proportion of Jews among the candidates who are both scholastically qualified for admission and young enough to matriculate has somewhat increased and remains too large for comfort." The restrictive policy was phased out beginning in 1960. Today, Jewish students account for about 30 percent of the Yale enrollment.

University presses welcome the scholarly debate that books may create, but they do not want to see the books themselves become controversial through challenges to their academic integrity. That type of controversy reflects negatively on the review process in scholarly publishing.

One of the more remarkable controversies concerned David Abraham's *The Collapse of the Weimar Republic: Political Economy and Crisis*, published by Princeton University Press in 1981. The book argues that German big business played a role in the downfall of the Weimar Republic, paving the way for Nazism. The book contends that German businessmen came to favor Hitler—a view that scholars have squabbled about for decades. At the time of publication, Abraham was an assistant professor of history at

Princeton. Eighteen months after publication, a Yale professor charged that Abraham had rewritten quotations and selected only those portions of source documents that suited his purposes. For instance, Abraham had cited a German banker as calling the Nazis a "positive force" and telling associates that "we should contribute to them and their efforts." Critics said that the source documents showed that the banker did not use the word "positive" or urge direct contributions. A University of California professor charged, "What Abraham has done disqualifies him as a member of the profession." Critics of Abraham wrote letters to universities where Abraham had applied for work after being denied tenure at Princeton, and job opportunities evaporated. Other historians then entered the fray, charging that Abraham's critics had gone too far and had turned their criticism into a personal vendetta.[10]

Another unwanted controversy centered on a special Soviet edition of the *Oxford Advanced Learner's Dictionary of Current English*, published by Oxford University Press. The Soviet edition of the dictionary defines capitalism as a social system "based on the exploitation of man by man, replacing feudalism and preceding communism." Communism is defined as "a theory revealing the historical necessity for the revolutionary replacement of capitalism." Socialism is defined as "the first phase of communism, a social system which is replacing capitalism." The Soviet edition gives no indication that the definitions have been altered, so users have the impression that the definitions are those that appear in Western editions of the dictionary. "We were very anxious that this dictionary should be published. We were in negotiations for ten years," said an Oxford spokesman. "In the end, the Russians would only agree to publish if we allowed changes to some sensitive definitions. Our negotiator considered that no Russians learned their politics from dictionaries, and a reasonable compromise was made."[11]

❦ The Impact of New Technology

The frontiers of knowledge are not the only frontiers expanding in scholarly publishing. Technology, too, is creating new frontiers in the publishing world.

An increasing number of university presses are taking the author's original "keystrokes" all the way through to bound book. Although no press now requires that manuscripts be submitted in machine-readable form, many university presses encourage authors whose manuscripts have been accepted for publication to submit the final work in a format suitable for direct conversion to type. Numerous other presses, though, are adopting technological innovation more slowly, saying that the money saved by capturing the author's keystrokes and converting them to type is fairly minimal at present. Smaller university presses, for example, deal with considerably less copy in a year's time than other print media, so economies of scale do not result. In addition, a book publisher faces the dilemmas resulting from lack of computer standardization. At a computerized newspaper or magazine, textual matter goes from reporter to copyeditor to graphic designer to the production staff, all within a standardized system with compatible equipment. But book publishing is organizationally diffuse and, until various computer manufacturers standardize the design of their systems and software, each word-processed book constitutes a new logistical puzzle for a book publisher. No single coding structure exists for such basic elements as paragraph indentation, italics, and boldface. An author's word-processing, then, may offer relief from typesetting costs, but the cost savings, editors said, are partially countered by word-processing conversion costs. Moreover, since authors can so easily create new edited versions, text-editing on computer tends to invite constant changes in each stage of preparation after acceptance. As a result, a number of university press officials say that the new technology is not yet worth the effort. An eastern press director said, "It is a greatly overrated factor. It rarely saves dollars and creates additional proofing problems." A midwestern director said, "We encourage it only if fully compatible with our typesetter's equipment." The computer age, critics say, is turning authors into typesetters and editors into proofreaders.

The computerization of writing, however, also has advantages for publishers and authors. Desktop publishing allows for the elimination of composition, and software makes bibliographic control and indexing easier for authors. Moreover, electronic publishing has the potential to influence the dissemination process as well as the composing process. With a manuscript on disk, a publisher has the text in a transmittable form, in the event that it needs to be shared with an audience—even an audience of one. "On-demand publishing" entails producing copies to order instead of producing for inventory. In avoiding speculative printings, the on-demand publisher assumes no inventory risk and defers all manufacturing expense until sales occur. By taking an author's original keystrokes to bound book and by deferring all printing costs until the time of sale, the new technology makes it possible to undertake low-risk publishing of books that have some scholarly value but little market promise.

Scholarly publishers see a dark underside to the glitter of this new technology. Amid potential savings both before and after publication, publishers recognize the potential for an author's work to be transmitted to users without regard for the traditional gatekeeping process. Electronic publishing permits elimination of the middleman between the author and the consumer—the publisher. A bulletin-board concept of knowledge-sharing has no quality control mechanism, and editors say that such direct source-to-user transmission of scholarship would doom publishing as it now exists. Not only do scholarly publishers collectively regulate what enters the channels for intellectual digestion, but also, editors say, the books they publish are considerably better than the manuscripts they receive. It is the selection and editing process which separates publishing from mere printing.

Advances in technology are forcing a reappraisal of what publishing actually is. The Latin root of the word "publish" is *publicare*—to make public. In the past, publishing was the monopoly of a few. Today, every person potentially is both a producer and a transmitter of information. In an essay on the impact of technology on scholarly publishing, a Rutgers sociology professor and a commercial publishing business manager jointly wrote, "Today, anyone can make anything public simply by affixing words to a piece of paper and photocopying it. The same individual may distribute the paper or add it to a databank where it may be retrieved by users. Publishing can be performed by anyone who has the opportunity and ability to use the new technology to enter and retrieve information, from librarians to researchers in industry."[12]

Technological innovation has influenced the very notion of property rights in intellectual discovery. The U.S. Copyright Law of 1978 acknowledges the implications of technological change by stating that copyright protection exists from the moment that an idea is made permanent.

Technological innovation also is changing the character of relationships among authors, publishers, and the marketplace. Libraries, as a primary marketplace for scholarly books, traditionally have been viewed as storehouses for books and as depositories for the written word. A futuristic vision anticipates that the duplicating library someday will supersede the circulating library. Rather than being a storehouse for books designed to be bought, shelved, and lent, libraries would produce and then give away or sell copies of their holdings. Theoretically, the cost of making and disseminating copies "on demand" and then paying royalties would be less than the cost of storing and maintaining copies for circulation. This would make copyright and royalty control essential to the creation of a duplicating library.

As traditionally understood, publishing entails selecting works, printing them, and then disseminating them. Increasingly, scholarly publishing cannot keep up with the growth in research and writing. August Frugé, director emeritus of the University of California Press, recommends a two-tiered system of publication.[13] He said that the most significant studies, and those most in demand, would deserve traditional publishing. For other types of research and writing, another form of permanency—such as microform, video disks, electronic journals, or computer databases—would be suitable, so long as the material could be accessed by others. At some point, the evaluation of research, especially in the humanities and social sciences, may no longer be tied to the book. Frugé predicts that those who today want to evaluate young scholars on the basis of published books one day might use an equivalent standard, the publishable manuscript; at that time, forms of access other than book publication may be regarded as respectable avenues of "publication."

Several university press directors said that the academic review boards at some colleges and universities already have accepted books published in microform as credentials for promotion. The Office of Scholarly Communication within the American Council of Learned Societies reported that 43 percent of more than three thousand scholars surveyed said that tenure committees should consider referred material such as microform as comparable to conventionally published material. The percentages of survey respondents agreeing with this idea ranged from 32 percent among political scientists to 53 percent among those in languages and linguistics, where publication is more difficult.[14]

Although authors face challenging odds in getting books published, at least university presses are publishing more books than ever before.

Omitting the Cambridge and Oxford presses, which both have acquisition offices in New York City and which together publish a third of all university press books, American university presses still recorded a healthy 25 percent growth rate in new titles in three years. In 1987, the latest year for which complete figures were available, American university presses produced 4,130 new titles, compared with 3,295 titles in 1984. University press directors and editors forecast continued expansion into the 1990s. Editors cited more aggressive acquisition, more trade publishing, and the creation of more series as key strategies for expanding their publishing programs.

The 1960s was a decade of growth in scholarly publishing, thanks to library prosperity and foundation subsidies. But the byword in the 1970s was "crisis," as university presses had to retrench in an effort to become more self-supporting. The 1980s became another decade of growth, as university presses adopted commercial management techniques and sought titles with broader sales appeal while reducing the size of lists in areas that consistently failed to recoup publishing costs. Such strategies, however, have not made university presses mere commercial presses in disguise, as a glance at the latest ten titles from a typical New York publisher and from a typical university press will show.

Scholarly publishing has grown exponentially within a single generation. More books have been published worldwide since 1950 than in all preceding years of civilization.[15] That fact is of concern to scholars and editors alike, because the book explosion makes it increasingly difficult for scholars to stay abreast of intellectual currents, potentially forcing them into further specialization in their reading. Some people have suggested that too much is being published, and that scholarly publishers should not be so expansion-oriented. These critics suggest the need for a "literary birth control." The suggestion recalls T.S. Eliot's 1933 admonition, "If people only wrote when they had something to say, and never merely because they wanted to write a book, or because they occupied a position such that the writing of books was expected of them, the mass of criticism would not be wholly out of proportion to the small number of critical books worth reading."[16]

Opinion is divided over what this expansion in publishing has meant to the quality of what is published. One university press director in the Midwest said that he fears for the future of scholarly publishing because he feels that the number of published titles has increased while the pool of quality manuscripts has declined. He believes that it is easier to publish now than five years ago, because almost every press is expanding. "Every press is trying to maintain current levels or higher. They need numbers," he said. "That has nothing to do with the merit of the manuscript." Another director added, "The educational system doesn't require as much as it used to. For instance, texts used to contain Latin phrases. Now, many scholars know no Latin." In contrast, an editor at an East Coast press said that he doubts that less-worthy books are being published today. He worries, though, that manuscripts are being rushed to completion. "The pressure in academia to publish is real," he said, leading to a tendency to cut research short. Other editors believe that the quality of manuscripts is as high as, or even higher than, in the past, because of improved standards of scholarly research. The challenge for them, these editors say, comes in the screening process. With so many quality manuscripts to choose from, editors must be careful to properly perform their roles as gatekeeper, so as to ensure that only what is considered the best of scholarship and writing is published.

❦ The Future of Acquisitions

The acquisition process is more of an art than a science. In it, much depends on the press's editorial personnel, the changing marketplace, and the evolving nature of scholarship itself. There is an art to successful listbuilding that both fulfills a scholarly mission and satisfies financial obligations.

It is now possible to specify several future directions in the university press acquisition process. First, university presses will fill increasing portions of their frontlists through active acquisition, leaving even less room for author-initiated manuscripts and proposals. To get the best works, presses no longer can rely on reputation, but instead must actively solicit.

Second, a larger percentage of university press lists will be built on advance contracts. As editors compete to publish the work of senior scholars, advance contracts will become a popular mechanism to attract the established scholar. But this will require the cooperation of editorial committees willing to take risks with editors.

Third, the proportion of specialized scholarly monographs directed toward narrow academic audiences will decrease, particularly in the over-published area of literary criticism. If it is to shape the cultural agenda, scholarly publishing no longer can remain so specialized that it fails to reach the general reader.

Fourth, scholarly publishers will search for works that synthesize rather than particularize. Without works that show the relationship among disparate parts, scholarship risks becoming like the spokes of a wheel with no hub. Works that synthesize are desired by scholars in all fields and usually are good sellers. But typically, only senior scholars have the insight to do such broadly encompassing works.

Fifth, more university presses will gravitate into the uncharted waters of serious trade publishing. As commercial publishers abandon serious but nonscholarly works because of the quest for bestsellers, university presses will consider these works as falling within their purview.

Sixth, the number of revised dissertations published as books will remain steady—simply because such projects represent the first publishable work of the junior scholars who are destined to become tomorrow's senior scholars. But as publication becomes more necessary for academic advancement, doctoral students will need to select dissertation topics with broader appeal. Each work will need to address the question, "So what?"

Seventh, university presses will rely more on series to establish a presence in listbuilding. To do so with typically small editorial staffs, these presses will lean more heavily on decentralized decision-making. The selection process may become the full responsibility of a press-appointed scholar within a university department or at another university.

Eighth, competition for publishable manuscripts will become keener among university presses. As presses expand their title counts and their scholarly missions, the genteel profession will assume a more outwardly competitive nature. As the director of a smaller university press put it, "It won't be the Yales of the world that will succumb. Young scholars tend to migrate to those presses with prestige. The Yales of the world will keep expanding. It's the smaller presses I'm worried about. If they haven't established a presence in a field, they'll be left out in the cold. The competition is growing even keener."

University presses also are expected to continue to adopt the ways of commercial publishing within the context of a scholarly list. On the business side, this will mean increased export sales, more emphasis on subsidiary rights income and book clubs, and more cooperative ventures in promotion and distribution.

University presses expect to lose money on at least some of the books they publish. Deficits on some titles are considered to be the price of disseminating new knowledge. But presses do try to achieve overall budgetary stability within the concept of subsidized publishing. As one university press official said, "Scholarly publishers are under a compulsion to achieve a rigid operating deficit as much as commercial publishers are under a compulsion to provide a profit to stockholders."

The mission of the university press is evolving in part because the mission of the commercial publisher has evolved. No matter how worthy a manuscript may appear, the serious commercial publisher needs sales in the thousands for a manuscript to be financially practical. University presses, because of their nonprofit status and dependable book-buying audiences, can afford to publish manuscripts with far fewer anticipated sales. Many books being published by university presses today would have appeared on commercial lists in an earlier time. University presses are coming to resemble the serious commercial houses of a quarter of a century ago, such as Knopf. As university presses fill the void left by commercial publishers, they leave a void of their own—the small-sales scholarly monographs whose too-frequent publication, because of rising production costs and declining library sales, constitutes economic suicide. Many such monographs now are published by commercial monograph houses that may require camera-ready copy and stipulate other cost-saving procedures. This type of scholarly publisher has emerged to publish many of the books that once might have been published by university presses when deficits mattered less. Such role shifts reflect a restructuring of the relations between commercial and nonprofit presses. In the future, the roles could become more distinct, with major commercial houses publishing potential blockbusters, university presses and large scholarly houses publishing qualified manuscripts for which anticipated sales are modest, and smaller commercial monograph houses, using costsaving efficiencies, publishing the limited-market books.

Amid these changes, scholars seem particularly concerned about financial influences on editorial judgments. Editors, too, worry about this.

Beverly Jarrett, when with the LSU Press, told her colleagues at a university press convention:

Our publishing programs are not commercial undertakings whose value is measured on balance sheets. And we are not editors whose survival is dependent upon the economic and popular successes that occasionally come our way. We don't get fired if none of our books sells out this season. . . .

Keeping those legitimate functions of the university press clearly in focus will, of course, help us to avoid sinking into the kind of ethical quagmire that one often associates with college athletics. From an initially very wholesome goal of cultivating the bodies as well as the minds of students, the vision of many athletic departments became so muddied that only lip-service was paid to that original goal. Actions soon demonstrated another definition of purpose, when college athletes were excused from maintaining academic standards and paid or rewarded by another measure of success. This kind of duplicity—the kind that says A is what's vital, but then rewards B—created a moral wilderness that breeds first confusion, then cynicism.

For the university press, then, . . . we must not say that scholarship and serious creative work come first whereas money or prizes or big names come second, if the way we conduct our operations says the opposite.[17]

Not only do university presses publish works that could not be published commercially, but also these presses are considered indispensable components of higher learning and, indeed, of the creation of new knowledge. The raison d'etre of a university press, after all, is to serve the world of scholarship and learning, with the academic community as its primary constituency.

In publishing for a narrow constituency, university presses serve the academic community primarily by validating the scholarly efforts of authors. Philip G. Altbach, director of the Comparative Education Center at the State University of New York at Buffalo, wrote of the important role of the university in this process:

Universities constitute a key validation process for knowledge. In a sense, these mechanisms decide what knowledge is legitimate and what is not. To a considerable degree, they determine what gets published and what does not. If knowledge is not certified by these academic networks, it may never see the light of day, or if it does, it may not be considered valuable. . . .

The universities, through these mechanisms of review, provide a mandatory service. Qualitative judgments need to be made because all knowledge is obviously not of equal value. The exercise of judgment is particularly important as the knowledge explosion proliferates information beyond the capacity of individuals to absorb it. Thus, reliable means of making evaluations are the key to both knowledge creation and dissemination.

But the fact that such a large part of the evaluation and gatekeeping function takes place in institutions of higher education is cause for some concern. Although the process is decentralized within the institution, the overarching norms and orientations of the university will tend to underlie most of the decision-making structures. Universities are conservative institutions. They are slow to change their structures, values, and orientations.

It may well be that the basic approach to validating knowledge is also conservative and that the gatekeepers are slow to accept innovative ideas. Anti-establishment ideas may take a long time to seep into the consciousness of the academic gatekeepers and thus achieve legitimacy. The fact that the universities hold something close to a monopoly on the validation of knowledge gives them enormous power and also special responsibilities in these matters.[18]

Some scholarly publishers believe that university presses are too timid editorially, in their role as academic gatekeepers. Kenneth Arnold, director of Rutgers University Press, worries that too many monographs are written more to advance a scholar's career than to advance the frontiers of knowledge. Complicity in the tenure and promotion process, Arnold contends, is one reason why university press books do not sell. Many of them were not meant to. He suggests that university presses, instead, should view themselves as Socratic gadflies in the system, opening gates to alternative points of view. He wrote of university presses in general:

A conservative streak persists. Presses are still publishing hundreds of monographs, at a time when the exchange of information is becoming increasingly computerized, and when the value placed on those monographs, even among the scholars to whom they are addressed, is diminishing. . . .

For too long, university presses have been subservient to the academic system and way of thinking, to organizations with money (and their agenda), to the public relations needs of universities, and to their own institutional neuroses. Collectively, they must begin to conceive of themselves as an active cultural force and an agent of change within the educational system if they are to grow and survive. The primary challenge facing them today is to take control of their future on their own terms. That is called maturity. It is time for the university press to grow up.[19]

To appeal to a broader market, Arnold said that university presses will need to publish books that are intended to be read, not merely consulted, and they must assume responsibility for interpreting scholarship for the nonacademic market. If they do that, Arnold said, university presses can become the cultural force for change and enlightenment they were meant to be.

Chester Kerr, former director of Yale University Press, calls gatekeeping the one indispensable function performed by publishers—one that must not be surrendered to the libraries or to technology. Gatekeeping, as one press director put it, entails deciding what is to be published, let through the gate, and backed by an investment decision. The director added:

And what's more important, gatekeeping is deciding what is *not* published. If we think there are too many new books being published now, just wait until technology opens the floodgates, when every research scholar can put his findings directly into some database and can even go on-line with it. Unless there is some agency charged with sifting, the system is going to be filled with junk and scholar-readers will have very little in the way of guideposts to point them toward what is worth consulting and what can safely be ignored.[20]

Citing the significance of the gatekeeping role in scholarly publishing, a Northwestern University professor, however, warned of the care that editors must take to assure equity: "The scholarly press is a guardian of received knowledge as well as the expanding frontiers of knowledge. Thus, decisions about which manuscripts do and do not get published play a major role in what gets defined as knowledge, what is thus preserved or presented to a wider audience, and what is dismissed as trivial or not worthwhile."[21]

The relationship between received and emerging knowledge is a precarious one, especially when emerging ideas sharply challenge received wisdom. Works that contradict, criticize, or reject dominant paradigms and traditions often take shape within a developing arena or school of thought little known or accepted by establishment scholars.

Interestingly, university presses operate within a system that, at least theoretically, balances the interests of received knowledge and emerging knowledge. The editors themselves, who make that initial in-house evaluation of a manuscript or proposal, have a bias toward emerging knowledge. They prefer works that challenge the status quo because these will be the books with the most potential for influencing intellectual currents. After all, without challenges to the status quo, scholarship would be a stagnant repetition of what already is known. Because of this, the acquisition process encourages nontraditional ideas. The traditional way of looking at history or literary criticism or economics comes to be viewed as the conservative, status quo approach.

Yet the scholarly publishing enterprise also is biased toward the status quo. Peer reviewers and editorial committee members tend to be established scholars in a field—the very ones, in fact, who may have built their careers on what is now called the status quo in their disciplines. Particularly in the selection of peer reviewers, editors must remain cognizant of this potential conflict of purposes. But the editors, who get to select the peer reviewers for each manuscript under consideration, look for scholars who would be open to new directions within their discipline as long as the work measures up to the standards of scholarship. Thus editors, with their preference for emerging knowledge, and scholars, who play an essential role in preserving the quality of the imprint, combine to chart a course toward expanding disciplines within an acceptable scholarly framework.

Nothing reaches print at a university press without meeting some acknowledged standard of scholarship. Ostensibly, the more prestigious the press, the higher the standards. The problem, however, is not with what *is* published, but with what is *not*. The gatekeeper not only selects what is permitted to enter the marketplace of ideas but, by default, denies entry to other works. This crucial determination influences the flow of knowledge within a culture. To the benefit of scholarship, scholarly publishing has a variety of gatekeepers. If one publisher chooses not to place a manuscript in the marketplace of ideas, another publisher can do so. With the availability of dozens of highly competitive university presses, as well as a number of commercial houses that publish serious scholarship, a worthy manuscript, given perseverance by its author, should find a publisher.

All paths to university press publication have certain constant features —for instance, the three-stage process of in-house evaluation, peer review, and editorial committee approval. But decision-making is individual. No two presses have identical sets of criteria for assessing manuscripts, and no two manuscripts are considered in an identical manner.

Unquestionably, how a manuscript comes to the attention of an editor plays a significant role in decision-making. Senior scholars who serve as brokers for the work of junior scholars boost chances for publication simply by persuading an editor to place a manuscript in the decision-making channels. After that, the manuscript is on its own. But for junior scholars, the hardest task simply is getting that initial consideration. Of course, some over-the-transom submissions and some blind proposals do eventually reach publication. But any technique that can lead an editor to make the initial overture—such as presenting a paper at a major convention or writing an article for a leading journal—will enhance the chances of eventual book publication.

The acquisition process, frankly, is not egalitarian and never will be. Ann Orlov, a former behavioral sciences editor at Harvard University Press, said that not all well-researched and well-written manuscripts have equal chances to be considered and published. Nevertheless, most editors and many authors prefer to view the process as egalitarian. Orlov wrote, "I suspect that editors and naive authors hold to the equal-chance myth for the same reason that most of us teach our children that all men in the United States are equal before the law: it is an important ideal with an important social function. What really happens is sometimes fair and sometimes unfair, but without the ideal things would probably be worse."[22]

The scholarly publishing enterprise certainly is imperfect, fraught with the risk that worthy manuscripts may be overlooked. But university presses do exhibit a commitment to intellectual discovery, and this commitment pervades the acquisition process. University presses seek to publish the works that best fit their perceived missions, best present quality scholarship, and best satisfy the demands of the scholarly marketplace. By standing at the junction of intellectual discovery and its public consumption, scholarly publishers serve as important gatekeepers for the mental life of a culture.

Appendix

Listbuilding Areas of

University Presses

Presses provided the following listings to the Association of American University Presses for inclusion in the 1988–89 Directory. Each press's 1987 new-title output (the latest year available) is listed in parentheses. The AAUP Directory also lists press personnel, phone numbers, mailing addresses, and special series for the eighty American university presses listed below, as well as the Canadian, international, institutional, and associate members. In addition, an author wanting to know which university presses publish in a particular academic discipline will appreciate a comprehensive listbuilding grid in the directory. The annual directory is available from the AAUP, 584 Broadway, New York, NY 10012.

The University of Alabama Press (43)

History, political science, public administration, Judaic studies, linguistics, southern regional studies, literary criticism, history of American science and technology, anthropology, and archaeology.

University of Arizona Press (41)

Anthropology, space sciences, southwestern Americana, arid-lands studies, natural history, Mexican studies, Native American studies, Asian studies, and creative nonfiction.

The University of Arkansas Press (15)

Biography, short fiction, poetry, translation, literary criticism, history, regional studies, and sociology.

University of California Press (240)

African studies, anthropology, arts and architecture, Asian studies, biological sciences (anatomy, botany, entomology, zoology), classical studies, economics, film and theater, folklore and mythology, geography, geology, history, labor relations, language and linguistics, Latin American studies, literature, medicine, music, natural history and ecology, Near Eastern studies, philosophy, physical sciences (astronomy, chemistry, engineering, mathematics, physics), political science, religious history and interpretation, sociology, urban studies, and women's studies.

Cambridge University Press, American Branch (886 overall)

The humanities, the social sciences, the biological and physical sciences, mathematics, music, psychology, religious studies, reference works, and English as a second language.

The Catholic University of America Press (13)

American and European history (both ecclesiastical and secular), Irish studies, American and European literature, philosophy, political theory, social studies, and theology.

The University of Chicago Press (208)

Sociology, anthropology, political science, business and economics, history, American and foreign literatures, literary criticism, biological and physical sciences, mathematics, conceptual studies of science, law, philosophy, linguistics, geography and cartography, art history, classics, architecture, education, psychiatry, psychology, and musicology.

Colorado Associated University Press (8)

Physical sciences (especially theoretical, atmospheric, and space physics), natural history, ecology, economics, American history, agriculture, political science, and regional studies.

Columbia University Press (144)

Reference, history, philosophy, American and foreign literatures, Asian studies, film studies, women's studies, journalism, music, art, archaeology, anthropology, social work, sociology, political science, political economy, international affairs, business and economics, law, psychology, life sciences, geology, astronomy and space science, evolutionary studies, and computer science.

Cornell University Press (124)

Anthropology, Asian studies, classics, history, literary criticism and theory, nature study, philosophy, political science, and veterinary science.

Duke University Press (58)

The humanities, the social sciences and related science subjects, with lists in American and English literature and criticism, American and European history, policy studies, Soviet and East European studies, Latin American studies, sociology and gerontology, economic history and theory, environment and energy, political philosophy, ethics and religion, psychology, music, cultural criticism, urban and regional planning, and anthropology.

University Presses of Florida (20)

History, archaeology, regional concerns, philosophy, and literary theory. Each of the nine universities has its own editorial program.

Fordham University Press (17)

Principally in the humanities and the social sciences.

Gallaudet University Press (14)

Publications related to hearing loss and deafness in such areas as linguistics, sign language, law, history, education, audiology, speech pathology, gerontology, and medicine, in addition to instructional materials and children's fiction.

Georgetown University Press (11)

Languages and linguistics (especially Romance linguistics) and ethics studies.

University of Georgia Press (60)

American and English literature, southern literature, American and European history, medieval and Renaissance studies, eighteenth-century studies, folklore, American studies, women's studies, civil rights, Afro-American studies, critical theory and film, photography, anthropology, natural history, and regional studies.

Harvard University Press (115)

The humanities, the social and behavioral sciences, the natural sciences, and medicine.

University of Hawaii Press (45)

Asian and Pacific studies in history, art, anthropology, sociology, philosophy, languages and linguistics, literature, political science, and the physical and natural sciences.

The Howard University Press (5)

Afro-American and African studies, the humanities, visual arts, history, literature, sociology, anthropology, and psychology.

University of Illinois Press (106)

American history, American literature (especially twentieth-century), American music, Black history, sport history, religious studies, communications, film studies, law and society, social sciences, western history, women's studies, working-class history, short fiction, and poetry.

Indiana University Press (105)

African studies, anthropology, Arab and Islamic studies, art, Black studies, business, cultural and literary theory, environment and ecology, film, folklore, history, Jewish studies, linguistics, literary criticism, military studies, music, philosophy, politics and international relations, public policy, religious studies, semiotics, Soviet and East European studies, state and regional studies, translations (especially Russian and Chinese), Victorian studies, and women's studies.

University of Iowa Press (28)

Literary criticism and history, short fiction, American history, regional studies, poetry, early music, archaeology and anthropology, natural sciences, Victorian studies, history of photography, aviation history, biography, and autobiography.

The Iowa State University Press (62)

Aviation, agriculture, journalism, design, engineering, home economics, education, sciences and humanities, veterinary medicine, and regional history.

The Johns Hopkins University Press (127)

American and European history, Caribbean studies, classics, earth and planetary sciences, economics and economic development, environmental studies, geography, health policy administration, history of science and technology, history of medicine, international relations and security, literary theory and criticism, medicine and public health, natural history, psychology and human development, regional books of general interest, and U.S. government and public administration.

University Press of Kansas (21)

American history, American studies, presidential studies, social and political philosophy, political science and public policy, military history, agriculture, sociology, and the Great Plains and the Midwest.

The Kent State University Press (15)

American cultural, military, diplomatic and Civil War history, art history, women's history, medieval studies, American and British literature and criticism, science fiction and utopian studies, music studies, and North American (particularly midwestern) archaeology.

The University Press of Kentucky (40)

American and European history, literature and criticism, political science, international studies, folklore, women's studies, anthropology, Black studies, sociology, Romance languages, and studies concerning the Appalachians and the South.

Louisiana State University Press (57)

The humanities and the social sciences with particular emphasis on southern history and literature, southern studies, French studies, Latin American studies, poetry, fiction, and music (especially jazz).

The University of Massachusetts Press (40)

American studies and history, Black and ethnic studies, women's studies, cultural criticism, architecture and environmental design, literary criticism, philosophy, poetry, political science, sociology, and books of regional interest.

The MIT Press (165)

Architecture, design arts, photography, economics and finance, computer science and artificial intelligence, cognitive science, neuroscience, materials science, formal linguistics, aesthetics and art criticism, continental philosophy, history and philosophy of science, and general science (astronomy, biology, mathematics, physics).

Mercer University Press (27)

Religion, theology, philosophy, and history, with an emphasis on biblical studies, New Testament, church history, southern history, Civil War history, and regional studies.

The University of Michigan Press (27)

Literature, classics, history, theatre, women's studies, political science, anthropology, economics, life sciences, regional books, and textbooks in English as a second language.

University of Minnesota Press (38)

Literary and cultural theory, biology and the earth sciences, personality assessment, clinical psychology, psychiatry, health sciences, philosophy, Nordic area studies, Upper Midwest studies, American culture, and feminist studies.

University Press of Mississippi (27)

American literature, American history, American culture, southern studies, Afro-American studies, women's studies, social sciences, political science, popular culture, folklife, art and architecture, natural sciences, and other liberal arts.

University of Missouri Press (36)

Art history, conservation, ecology and natural history, history, literary criticism, regional studies, social sciences, poetry, and short fiction.

Naval Institute Press (35)

Naval biography, naval history, oceanography, navigation, military law, naval science textbooks, sea power, shipbuilding, professional guides, nautical arts and lore, and technical guides.

University of Nebraska Press (88)

English literature, American literature, translation, political science, music, the American West, the Great Plains, the American Indian, food production and distribution, agriculture, natural history, psychology, modern history of western Europe, and Latin American studies.

University of Nevada Press (10)

History, biography, anthropology and natural history of the west, Basque peoples of Europe and the Americas.

University Press of New England (35)

History, Judaica, literature and criticism, folklore, regional studies, philosophy, psychology, life sciences, and academic strengths of the nine sponsoring universities.

University of New Mexico Press (71)

Social and cultural anthropology, archaeology, American frontier history, western American literature, Latin American history, history of photography, art and photography, and Southwest and Rocky Mountain studies including natural history and land-grant studies.

New York University Press (104)
Economics, history, politics, psychology and psychiatry, New York City and State regional affairs, literature and literary criticism, Middle East Studies, Judaica, women's studies, and the performing arts.

The University of North Carolina Press (67)
American and European history, American and English literature, American studies, southern studies, political science, sociology, folklore, religious studies, legal history, classics, women's studies, music, urban studies, public policy, Latin American studies, business and economic history, anthropology, health care, and regional studies.

Northeastern University Press (16)
American history, literature and literary criticism, American studies, poetry, criminal justice, women's studies, music, and regional studies.

Northern Illinois University Press (15)
American history, European history, Russian history, Latin American history, political science, British literature, and American literature.

Northwestern University Press (25)
Literary criticism and theory, philosophy, theatre studies, drama, Eastern European literature, Renaissance studies, media criticism, South American literature, African literature, Chinese literature, Russian literature, Jewish studies, political science, poetry, and classical studies.

University of Notre Dame Press (48)
Philosophy, ethics, sociology, political science, history, theology, medieval studies, liberal arts, law, and business.

Ohio University Press (60)
Nineteenth-century British literature and literary criticism, history, nineteenth- and twentieth-century continental philosophy, health sciences, African studies, and Western Americana.

Ohio State University Press (27)
Afro-American studies, business history, criminology, early modern European history, Eastern European and Russian history, politics and literature, human development, international women's studies, modern literature and literary theory, philosophy and cognitive studies, political science, regional studies, sports history, U.S. history, urban studies, Victorian studies, fiction, poetry, and belles lettres.

University of Oklahoma Press (66)

Western U.S. history, American Indian studies, classical studies, language and literature, philosophy, energy studies, women's studies, art and archaeology, and regional studies.

Oxford University Press, American Branch (1,444 overall)

Scholarly monographs, general nonfiction, Bibles, college textbooks, medical books, music, reference books, and children's books.

University of Pennsylvania Press (56)

American and British history, anthropology, art, architecture, biological sciences, business, computer science, economics, folklore, history of science and technology, law, linguistics, literature, medicine, music theory, women's studies, and regional studies.

The Pennsylvania State University Press (52)

Art and architectural history, literature and criticism, music, philosophy, religious studies, history, political science, sociology, anthropology, archaeology, psychology, computer science, science, engineering, natural science, and agriculture.

University of Pittsburgh Press (40)

The humanities, the social sciences, and public health (especially mental health).

Princeton University Press (134)

American, Asian, European, Latin American, Middle Eastern, Russian and Eastern European history, archaeology, classics, art history, architecture, music, philosophy, literature, translation, poetry, religious studies, anthropology (especially European), demography, economics, constitutional and international law, political science, sociology (especially historical), astrophysics, biology, chemistry, computer science, engineering, geology, history of science and medicine, mathematics, ornithology, and physics.

Rice University Press (3)

Literary theory and criticism, photography, Texas studies, and the social sciences.

The Rockefeller University Press (1)

Primarily biomedical sciences, along with science-oriented historical, philosophical and biographical studies.

Rutgers University Press (60)

Literary criticism, film, art history and criticism, American history, women's studies, anthropology, sociology, life and health sciences, mathematics, history of science and technology, and regional studies.

University of South Carolina Press (35)

Rhetoric and speech communication, religious studies, international relations, contemporary literature, southern history and culture, military history, maritime history, international business, industrial relations, physical education, and marine science.

Southern Illinois University Press (58)

American and English literature, philosophy, speech and rhetoric, First Amendment studies, journalism, education, sociology, political science, archaeology, anthropology, linguistics, botany, and zoology.

Southern Methodist University Press (7)

American studies, anthropology and archaeology, ethics and human values, film and theatre, folklore, regional fiction and nonfiction, religious studies, rhetoric and composition, and sport.

Stanford University Press (71)

The humanities, the social sciences and the natural sciences with particular emphasis in anthropology, health policy, history, literary criticism and theory, linguistics, political science, psychology, sociology, systematic botany and zoology, women's studies, and studies involving China, Japan, Latin America, and Russia.

State University of New York Press (103)

Philosophy, religion, Middle East studies, Jewish studies, Asian studies, work and labor studies, women, linguistics, and education.

Syracuse University Press (42)

New York State and regional studies, Iroquois studies, special education (with emphasis on learning disabilities and rehabilitation), contemporary Middle East, international affairs, American history, and environmental management studies.

Teachers College Press (36)

Scholarly, professional, text and trade books on education and related areas.

Temple University Press (62)

American studies and history, sociology, political science, health care, women's studies, comparative policy, philosophy, photography, ethics, social theory, work, sexuality, political economy, urban studies, Black and ethnic studies, educational policy, and Philadelphia regional studies.

The University of Tennessee Press (19)

American studies, history, political science, religion, anthropology, folklore, vernacular architecture and material culture, literature, women's studies, sports studies, African American studies, Native American studies, Caribbean studies, and Appalachian studies.

University of Texas Press (61)

The humanities, the social sciences and the natural and physical sciences, regional studies, translations of Latin American literature, photography, classics, architecture, film, American studies, Eastern European studies, Latin American studies, Mexican American studies, and Middle Eastern studies.

Texas A&M University Press (35)

Texas and the Southwest, American and western history, natural history, the environment, military history, economics, business, architecture, art, and veterinary medicine.

Texas Christian University Press (7)

Texas and southwestern history and literature, American studies, rhetoric and composition, fiction, and young adult books with emphasis on Texas and the Southwest.

Texas Tech University Press (14)

Biological sciences, medical sciences, museum science, regional studies, classical studies, American and European history, literary criticism and theory, philosophy, poetry, and women's studies.

Texas Western Press (7)

American southwestern history, northern Mexico and U.S.–Mexican border studies, and regional studies with a social, physical, scientific, cultural or linguistic approach.

University of Utah Press (15)

Anthropology, western history, regional studies, Mormon studies, Mesoamerican studies, Middle East studies, philosophy and ethics, poetry, and fiction.

Utah State University Press (5)

Folklore, western history, agricultural history of the West, biography, political science, and regional culture and economy studies.

The University Press of Virginia (42)

U.S. colonial history, literary criticism, bibliography, architectural history, American decorative arts, and regional studies.

University of Washington Press (66)

Anthropology, Asian-American studies, Asian studies, art, aviation history, forest history, marine sciences, music, art history, history and culture of the Northwest, Native American studies, and Scandinavian studies.

Washington State University Press (5)

Pacific Northwest history, social sciences relating to the Northwest, minority studies, Asian-American studies, communication arts, American literature, natural history, and the animal sciences.

Wayne State University Press (33)

African-American studies, Judaica, classics, folklore, literary criticism and theory, art and archaeology, urban and labor studies, health sciences, gerontology, regional studies, ethnic studies, and speech pathology.

Wesleyan University Press (45)
Interdisciplinary studies, history, literature, women's studies, government and public issues, biography, poetry, the social sciences, and the natural sciences.

University of Wisconsin Press (51)
The humanities, the social and behavioral sciences, and the earth sciences.

Yale University Press (199)
The humanities, the social and behavioral sciences, and the natural sciences.

🍏🍏🍏

Notes

INTRODUCTION

1. Almost all of the university presses that publish five or more new titles a year belong to the Association of American University Presses. The annual *AAUP Directory* contains staff rosters, addresses, and descriptions of the editorial programs of each member press. The directory is available from the AAUP, 584 Broadway, New York, NY 10012. A number of other university presses are in operation, but they serve primarily as institutional printers and seldom actively acquire manuscripts, thus they were not included in this study.

2. Herbert C. Morton, "Research on the Printed Word: A Review," *Scholarly Publishing* 11 (July 1980):368.

CHAPTER 1

1. Lewis A. Coser, "Publishers as Gatekeepers of Ideas," in *Perspectives on Publishing*, ed. Philip G. Altbach and Sheila McVey (Lexington, Mass.: Lexington Books, 1976), p. 17.

2. Jack Miles, "Intellectual Freedom and the University Press," *Scholarly Publishing* 15 (July 1984):291–300.

3. Chandler B. Grannis, "Scholarly Publishing," *The Book Publishing Annual* (New York: Bowker, 1984), p. 5.

4. Sheldon Meyer and Leslie E. Phillabaum, "What Is a University Press?", *Scholarly Publishing* 11 (April 1980):218.

5. Walter W. Powell, *Getting into Print: The Decision-Making Process in Scholarly Publishing* (Chicago: University of Chicago Press, 1985), p. 33.

6. Irving Rockwood, "Publishing a Scholarly Book," *PS* 20 (Summer 1987): 699.

7. Ibid., pp. 700–701.

8. Wendy J. Strothman, "On Moving from Campus to Commerce," *Scholarly Publishing* 18 (April 1987):161.

9. John Tebbel, *A History of Book Publishing in the United States*, vol. 2 (New York: Bowker, 1975), p. 535.

10. Robert Frederick Lane, "The Place of American University Presses in Publishing" (Ph.D. dissertation, University of Chicago, 1939), p. 17.

11. Ralph Barton Perry's defense of the Harvard press was reprinted as "Should

There Be a University Press?", *Scholarly Publishing* 17 (January 1986):109–17. The quotation appears on p. 111 of the reprinted version.

12. Chester Kerr, "The Kerr Report Revisited," *Scholarly Publishing* 1 (October 1969):15.

13. Roger W. Shugg, "Cui Bono?", *Scholarly Publishing* 10 (October 1978):7.

14. National Enquiry, *Scholarly Communication: The Report of the National Enquiry* (Baltimore: Johns Hopkins University Press, 1979).

15. Kurt Lewin, "Frontiers in Group Dynamics II: Channels of Group Life; Social Planning and Action Research," *Human Relations* 1 (November 1947):145.

16. David Manning White, "The Gate Keeper: A Case Study in the Selection of News," *Journalism Quarterly* 27 (Fall 1950):383–90.

17. Bruce Westley and Malcolm S. MacLean, Jr., "A Conceptual Model for Communications Research," *Journalism Quarterly* 34 (Winter 1957):31–38.

18. John Dimmick, "The Gatekeeper: An Uncertainty Principle," *Journalism Monographs* 37 (November 1974):1–37.

19. Gordon B. Neavill, "Role of the Publisher in the Dissemination of Knowledge," in *Perspectives on Publishing*, p. 50.

20. August Frugé, "Beyond Publishing: A System of Scholarly Writing and Reading," *Scholarly Publishing* 9 (July 1978):297.

CHAPTER 2

1. U.S. Bureau of the Census, *Statistical Abstract of the United States: 1986* (Washington, D.C.: Government Printing Office, 1986), pp. 158–59.

2. John Higham, "University Presses and Academic Specialization," *Scholarly Publishing* 10 (October 1978):40–41.

3. Curtis Benjamin, "Soaring Prices and Sinking Sales of Science Monographs," *Science* 183 (25 January 1974):282–84.

4. National Enquiry, *Scholarly Communication*, p. 30.

5. August Frugé, "Beyond Publishing," *Scholarly Publishing* 10 (October 1978):31–32.

6. Morris Philipson, "The Quality of Scholarly Writing and Scholarly Publishing Today," *Scholarly Publishing* 6 (October 1974):9.

7. Miriam Berkley, "Portrait of a Publisher: Morris Philipson," *Publishers Weekly* (6 July 1984), p. 33.

8. J.G. Goellner, "Specialization in Listbuilding," *Scholarly Publishing* 15 (October 1983):7.

9. Loren Hoekzema, "Repackaging Scholarly Books," *Scholarly Publishing* 15 (April 1984):237.

10. National Enquiry, *Scholarly Communication*, p. 111.

11. Goellner, "Specialization in Listbuilding," p. 9.

12. Ed Williams, "Publishing at North Carolina," *New York Times Book Review*, 18 October 1981, p. 13.

13. Chandler B. Grannis, "New Moves at Minnesota," *Publishers Weekly*, 29 July 1983, pp. 28–29.

14. The 1948 study by Chester Kerr was published the following year as *A Report on American University Presses* (New York: Association of American University Presses, 1949). His followup study 20 years later was summarized in Kerr, "The Kerr Report Revisited."

15. Goellner, "Specialization in Listbuilding," p. 6.

16. Michael A. Aronson, "Building the Science List of a University Press," *Scholarly Publishing* 5 (October 1973):53.

17. The Canadian study is cited in J.A. Morrison, "Scientists and the Scientific Literature," *Scholarly Publishing* 11 (January 1980):157–58.

18. Aronson, "Building the Science List," p. 56.

19. Anthony Parker, "The University Press as a Science Publisher," *Scholarly Publishing* 3 (April 1972):223.

20. National Enquiry, *Scholarly Communication*, p. 83.

21. Edward Tripp, "Editors and the Editorial Committee," *Scholarly Publishing* 8 (January 1977):101–102.

22. David H. Gilbert, "Getting There," *Scholarly Publishing* 13 (April 1982): 235–43.

23. Dan Davin, "Editor and Author in a University Press," *Scholarly Publishing* 10 (January 1979):125.

CHAPTER 3

1. August Frugé, "The Metamorphoses of the University of California Press," *Scholarly Publishing* 15 (January 1984):173.

2. Doug Mitchell, "First Person: A Book Acquisitions Editor is as Good as his Words," *Chicago Tribune Magazine*, 22 June 1986, p. 30.

3. Morris Philipson, "The Scholar as Publishing Author," *Scholarly Publishing* 8 (July 1977):292.

4. Kerr, *A Report on American University Presses* and "The Kerr Report Revisited."

5. August Frugé, "The Ambiguous University Press," *Scholarly Publishing* 8 (October 1976):4.

6. Ibid., p. 7.

7. Kenneth Arnold, "The Best Books Necessary," *Scholarly Publishing* 10 (October 1978):60–61.

8. Sanford G. Thatcher, "Competitive Practices in Acquiring Manuscripts," *Scholarly Publishing* 11 (January 1980):123.

9. Ibid., p. 113.

10. Beverly Jarrett, "Secrets of an Acquisitions Editor," *Scholarly Publishing* 15 (January 1984):151.

CHAPTER 4

1. Stephen Cox, "An Editor's Chrestomathy," *Scholarly Publishing* 15 (October 1983):24.

2. Eleanor Harman and R.M. Schoeffel, "Our Readers Report . . . ," *Scholarly Publishing* 6 (July 1975):339.

3. Willard A. Lockwood, "Standards and Performance in the Decision to Publish," *Scholarly Publishing* 8 (April 1977):217.

4. Miles, "Intellectual Freedom," p. 292.

5. A. Bartlett Giamatti, "Safeguard of Process: The Editorial Committee," *Scholarly Publishing* 7 (January 1976):130–31.

6. Tripp, "Editors and the Editorial Committee," p. 101.

7. Ibid., p. 103.

8. Robert Darnton, "A Survival Strategy for Academic Authors," *American Scholar* 52 (Autumn 1983):533.

9. Hugh Kenner, "God, Swahili, Bandicoots, and Euphoria," *Scholarly Publishing* 5 (July 1974):293.

10. Ibid., p. 295.

CHAPTER 5

1. Berkley, "Portrait of a Publisher," *Publishers Weekly*, p. 33.

2. Edwin McDowell, "Sometimes a Best Seller," *New York Times Book Review*, 10 May 1981, pp. 22–24.

3. Berkley, "Portrait of a Publisher," p. 33.

4. U.S. Bureau of the Census, *Statistical Abstract of the United States: 1986*, p. 159, and *Historical Statistics of the United States, Parts I and II* (Washington, D.C.: Government Printing Office, 1975), pp. 385–86.

5. Carroll G. Bowen, "The Historical Context of the University Press in America," *Scholarly Publishing* 2 (July 1971):345.

6. Ernest Cadman Colwell, "The Publishing Needs of Scholarship," *Publishers Weekly*, 1 February 1947, p. 516.

7. Ray Allen Billington, "Tracking the Covered Wagons," *Washington Post*, 1 April 1979, p. E1.

8. Elsie Myers Stainton, "A Bag for Editors," *Scholarly Publishing* 8 (January 1977):114.

9. Olive Holmes, "Thesis to Book: What to Get Rid of," *Scholarly Publishing* 5 (July 1974):341.

10. Robert Plant Armstrong, "The Dissertation's Deadly Sins," *Scholarly Publishing* 3 (April 1972):242.

11. Liz McMillen, "A Doctoral Dissertation is Not Yet a Book, Young Tenure-Seeking Scholars Are Told," *Chronicle of Higher Education*, 5 February 1986, p. 23.

12. J.G. Bell, "On Being an Uncompromising Editor," *Scholarly Publishing* 14 (February 1983):159.

13. Hoekzema, "Repackaging Scholarly Books," p. 254.

14. Darnton, "A Survival Strategy," p. 535.

15. Stainton, "A Bag for Editors," pp. 112–13.

16. Dan Davin, "Editor and Author in a University Press," *Scholarly Publishing* 10 (January 1979):123.

17. Robert T. King, "The Bivalent Economics of the University Press," *Scholarly Publishing* 1 (April 1970):268.

18. Ashbel G. Brice, "The Scholarly Monograph and the Hereafter," *Scholarly Publishing* 5 (April 1974):220.

19. William P. Germano, "Helping the Local Faculty with Publication Support," *Scholarly Publishing* 15 (October 1983):11–16.

20. Edward H. Berman, "On Publishing, Probably Perishing, and Surely Paying," *Scholarly Publishing* 16 (July 1985):308.

21. Ed Williams, "Publishing at North Carolina," p. 30.

22. John J. Corson, "How University Administrators View University Presses," *Scholarly Publishing* 9 (January 1978):112.

23. "Give & Take," *Chronicle of Higher Education*, 4 March 1987, p. 24.

24. Datus C. Smith, Jr., "An Anatomy of Subsidies," *Scholarly Publishing* 6 (April 1975):202.

25. Powell, *Getting into Print*, pp. 177–78.

26. Grannis, "Scholarly Publishing," p. 7.

27. Edwin McDowell, "University Presses Not United in Enthusiasm for Discounts," a *New York Times* syndicated story appearing in the *Kansas City Star*, 4 January 1987, p. 11D.

28. Quoted in Fred J. Dorn, "Do Scholarly Authors Need Literary Agents?" *Scholarly Publishing* 14 (October 1982):81.

29. James H. Clark, "The University Press and Sociology," *Society* 17 (November/December 1979):38.

30. A number of writings exist on the economics of publishing. They include J. Kendrick Noble, "Book Publishing," in *Who Owns the Media?*, ed. Benjamin M. Compaine (White Plains, N.Y.: Knowledge Industry Publications, 1982), pp. 95–141. Wendy Strothman, director of Beacon Press in Boston, also offered illuminating comments on this topic.

CHAPTER 6

1. William A. Wood, "Changing Editorial Direction," an article within a collection of articles titled "Stretching the Shrinking Dollar," *Scholarly Publishing* 14 (October 1982):32.

2. Eric Pace, "Yale University Press Prepares for the '80s," *New York Times Book Review*, 10 July 1979, p. 45.

3. J.G. Goellner, "The Future of University Presses," *Library Journal*, 15 September 1978, p. 1698.

4. Walter W. Powell, "Adapting to Tight Money and New Opportunities," *Scholarly Publishing* 14 (October 1982):10.

5. Joseph Adelson, "Sex Solemn and Kinky," *New York Times Book Review*, 10 August 1980, p. 13.

6. Jane Isay, "The Anatomy of a Fastback," *Scholarly Publishing* 6 (October 1974):81–85.

7. Chandler B. Grannis and John Mutter, "Targets for Scholarly Publishers," *Publishers Weekly* (29 July 1983), p. 25.

8. Patricia Blakely, "Selling Regional Books," *Scholarly Publishing* 12 (April 1981):269.

9. "Footnotes," *Chronicle of Higher Education*, 22 June 1988, p. 6.

10. Robert Krulwich, "The Cold Economist," *New York Times Book Review*, 20 October 1985, p. 55.

11. Robert P. Emmitt, "When the Well Runs Dry," *Scholarly Publishing* 2 (April 1971):247.

12. Herbert Mitgang, "Fiction: Yes and No," *New York Times Book Review*, 20 June 1982, p. 13.

13. Ibid.

14. Carol Sternhell, "Who Needs a Blockbuster? Another Way of Publishing," *New York Times Book Review*, 11 October 1987, p. 40.

15. Mitgang, "Fiction: Yes and No," p. 22.

16. "Cross Currents," *Publishers Weekly*, 27 January 1984, p. 30.

17. Patricia Blake, "One of Their Subs is Missing," *Time*, 4 March 1985, p. 82.

18. Jack Garlington, "Concerning the Little Magazine: Something Like a Symposium," *Carleton Miscellany* 7 (Spring 1966), p. 39.

19. "Footnotes," *Chronicle of Higher Education*, 23 July 1986, p. 7.

20. Mary Biggs, "Academic Publishing and Poetry," *Scholarly Publishing* 17 (October 1985):3–4.

21. Walton Beacham, "Finding Poets Publishers," *Scholarly Publishing* 9 (January 1978):160–61.

22. Stephen V. Roberts, "At Johns Hopkins," *New York Times Book Review*, 10 May 1981, p. 13.

23. Nelson H.H. Graburn, "University Press Books in the Classroom," *Scholarly Publishing* 13 (October 1981):77.

24. Catharine Seybold, "A Brief History of *The Chicago Manual of Style*," *Scholarly Publishing* 14 (February 1983):164.

25. Frank H. Wardlaw, "The Book That Was Too Big for Texas," *Scholarly Publishing* 6 (January 1975):159–63.

26. J.G. Goellner, "The Federation of the Book," *Scholarly Publishing* 12 (July 1981):293–94.

27. Henry H. Wiggins, "Early and Middle Years at Columbia," *Scholarly Publishing* 14 (July 1983):332.

28. Wiggins, "Publisher to Alexr. Hamilton Esqr.," *Scholarly Publishing* 9 (April 1978):196–97.

29. Angus Paul, "Inspiring and Controversial Marcus Garvey Lives," *Chronicle of Higher Education* (5 March 1986), p. 6.

30. D.J.R. Bruckner, "The Grand Projects," *New York Times Book Review*, 18 October 1981, p. 12.

31. Berkley, "Portrait of a Publisher," p. 32.

32. Dana J. Pratt, "Publishing *The Children of Pride*," *Scholarly Publishing* 5 (October 1973):30–31.

33. Ibid., p. 31.

34. Catharine Seybold, "The Lisle Letters at Chicago," *Scholarly Publishing* 13 (April 1982):245–62.

35. James H. Clark, "Publishing *The Plan of St. Gall*," *Scholarly Publishing* 13 (January 1982):101–17.

36. Edwin McDowell, "Sometimes a Best Seller," p. 23.

37. McDowell, "Books of Small Presses Key Source of Reprints," *New York Times*, 19 August 1985, p. C15.

CHAPTER 7

1. Karen J. Winkler, "New Breed of Scholar Works the Territory That Lies Between History and Geography," *Chronicle of Higher Education*, 24 September 1986, p. 7.

2. Winkler, "A Lot More Than Trading Baseball Cards: Sport History Gains a New Respectability," *Chronicle of Higher Education*, 5 June 1985, p. 8.

3. "Footnotes," *Chronicle of Higher Education*, 10 July 1985, p. 5.

4. Herbert S. Bailey, Jr., "The Future of University Press Publishing," *Scholarly Publishing* 19 (January 1988):63–64.

5. Ibid., pp. 64–65.

6. William A. Wood, "Changing Editorial Direction," p. 32.

7. Frugé, "The Ambiguous University Press," p. 9.

8. Naomi B. Pascal, "Freedom, Responsibility and the Agile Editor," *Scholarly Publishing* 16 (April 1985):258–59.

9. Miles, "Intellectual Freedom," p. 294.

10. Ezra Bowen, "Stormy Weather in Academe," *Time*, 14 January 1985, p. 59.

11. Richard Owen, "Who Says Capitalism is 'Based on the Exploitation of

Man by Man'? This *Oxford Advanced Dictionary of Current English*, That's Who," *Chronicle of Higher Education*, 10 April 1985, p. 1.

12. Irving Louis Horowitz and Mary E. Curtis, "The Impact of Technology on Scholarly Publishing," *Scholarly Publishing* 13 (April 1982):212.

13. Frugé outlined his concepts in a two-part series titled "Beyond Publishing: A System of Scholarly Writing and Reading," *Scholarly Publishing* 9 (July 1978): 291–311, and 10 (October 1978):17–35.

14. Robert L. Jacobson, "Scholars Fault Journals and College Libraries in Survey by Council of Learned Societies," *Chronicle of Higher Education*, 6 August 1986, pp. 21–23.

15. Horowitz and Curtis, "Impact of Technology," p. 213.

16. T.S. Eliot, *The Use of Poetry and the Use of Criticism* (London: Faber and Faber, 1933), p. 20.

17. Beverly Jarrett, "Doing Right by Your Author: Avoiding Duplicity in the Editorial Process" (paper delivered at meeting of Southern University Presses in Knoxville, Tennessee, September 1985).

18. Philip G. Altbach, *The Knowledge Context* (Albany, N.Y.: State University of New York Press, 1987), pp. 77–78.

19. Kenneth Arnold, "University Presses Could Still Become the Cultural Force for Change and Enlightenment They Were Meant To Be," *Chronicle of Higher Education*, 29 July 1987, p. 60.

20. Unnamed director quoted in Chester Kerr's "The Kerr Report: One More Time," *Publishers Weekly*, 5 June 1987, p. 22.

21. William H. Exum, "Affirmative Action and University Presses," *Scholarly Publishing* 14 (February 1983):125–26.

22. Ann Orlov, "Demythologizing Scholarly Publishing," in *Perspectives on Publishing*, pp. 240–41.

꙼꙼꙼

Bibliography

Adelson, Joseph. "Sex Solemn and Kinky." *New York Times Book Review*, 10 August 1980, p. 13.

Altbach, Philip G. *The Knowledge Context: Comparative Perspectives on the Distribution of Knowledge.* Albany, N.Y.: State University of New York Press, 1987.

Altbach, Philip G., and Sheila McVey, eds. *Perspectives on Publishing.* Lexington, Mass.: Lexington Books, 1976.

Alter, Nicholas A. "Scaled-Down Publishing for Small Markets." *Scholarly Publishing* 10 (January 1979):137–46.

Appelbaum, Judith. *How to Get Happily Published* 3d ed. New York: Harper and Row, 1988.

Armstrong, Robert Plant. "The Dissertation's Deadly Sins." *Scholarly Publishing* 3 (April 1972):241–47.

Arnold, Kenneth. "The Best Books Necessary." *Scholarly Publishing* 10 (October 1978):55–64.

———. "University Presses Could Still Become the Cultural Force for Change and Enlightenment They Were Meant To Be." *Chronicle of Higher Education*, 29 July 1987, p. 60.

Aronson, Michael A. "Building the Science List of a University Press." *Scholarly Publishing* 5 (October 1973):53–58.

Bailey, Herbert S., Jr. *The Art and Science of Book Publishing.* New York: Harper and Row, 1970.

———. "Economics of Publishing in the Humanities." *Scholarly Publishing* 8 (April 1977):223–31.

———. "The Future of University Press Publishing." *Scholarly Publishing* 19 (January 1988):63–69.

———. "On the Future of Scholarly Communication." *Scholarly Publishing* 17 (April 1986):251–54.

Banner, James M., Jr. "Preserving the Integrity of Peer Reviews." *Scholarly Publishing* 19 (January 1988):163–68.

Barzun, Jacques. *The American University: How It Runs, Where It Is Going.* New York: Harper and Row, 1968.

Battin, Patricia. "The Library: Centre of the Restructured University." *Scholarly Publishing* 17 (April 1986):255–67.

Beacham, Walton. "Finding Poets Publishers." *Scholarly Publishing* 9 (January 1978):159–66.

Bean, Donald P. "Discovering University Presses." *Atlantic Monthly* (December 1928):102–106.

———. "The Quality of American Scholarly Publishing in 1929." Reprinted in *Scholarly Publishing* 12 (April 1981):259–68.

Bell, J.G. "On Being an Uncompromising Editor." *Scholarly Publishing* 14 (February 1983):155–61.

Benjamin, Curtis. "Soaring Prices and Sinking Sales of Science Monographs." *Science* 183 (25 January 1974):282–84.

Berkley, Miriam. "Portrait of a Publisher: Morris Philipson." *Publishers Weekly*, 6 July 1984, pp. 30–33.

Berman, Edward H. "On Publishing, Probably Perishing, and Surely Paying." *Scholarly Publishing* 16 (July 1985):307–12.

Biggs, Mary. "Academic Publishing and Poetry." *Scholarly Publishing* 17 (October 1985):3–23.

Billington, Ray Allen. "Tracking the Covered Wagons." *Washington Post*, 1 April 1979, p. E1.

Blake, Patricia. "One of Their Subs is Missing." *Time*, 4 March 1985, p. 82.

Blakely, Patricia. "Selling Regional Books." *Scholarly Publishing* 12 (April 1981): 269–80.

Bledstein, Burton J. *The Culture of Professionalism, the Middle Class and the Development of Higher Education in America*. New York: Norton, 1976.

Bowen, Carroll G. "The Historical Context of the University Press in America." *Scholarly Publishing* 2 (July 1971):329–49.

Bowen, Ezra. "Stormy Weather in Academe." *Time*, 14 January 1985, p. 59.

Brice, Ashbel G. "The Scholarly Monograph and the Hereafter." *Scholarly Publishing* 5 (April 1974):219–25.

Brown, Carolyn T. "Scholarly Writing in a Department of English." *Scholarly Publishing* 15 (April 1984):205–21.

Broyard, Anatole. "The Author/Scholars." *New York Times Book Review*, 10 May 1981, p. 47.

Bruckner, D.J.R. "The Grand Projects." *New York Times Book Review*, 18 October 1981, pp. 12, 28–29.

Canby, Henry Seidel. "The University Presses." *Saturday Review of Literature*, 16 June 1928, pp. 968–70.

Carroll, Mark. "The Backpacker's Guides to Scholarly Publishing." *Scholarly Publishing* 16 (October 1984):59–63.

Chappel, Warren. *A Short History of the Printed Word*. New York: Knopf, 1970.

Clark, James H. "Publishing *The Plan of St. Gall*." *Scholarly Publishing* 13 (January 1982):101–17.

———. "The University Press and Sociology," *Society* 17 (November/ December 1979):38–41.

Cole, John Y. "Books, Libraries, and Scholarly Traditions." *Scholarly Publishing* 13 (October 1981):31–43.

Cole, Jonathan, and Steven Cole. *Social Stratification in Science.* Chicago: University of Chicago Press, 1973.

Colwell, Ernest Cadman. "The Publishing Needs of Scholarship." *Publishers Weekly,* 1 February 1947, pp. 516–19.

Compaine, Benjamin M. *The Book Industry in Transition: An Economic Study of Book Distribution and Marketing.* White Plains, N.Y.: Knowledge Industry Publications, 1978.

———. *Who Owns the Media?* 2d ed. White Plains, N.Y.: Knowledge Industry Publications, 1982.

Corson, John J. "How University Administrators View University Presses." *Scholarly Publishing* 9 (January 1978):107–14.

Coser, Lewis A. *Men of Ideas.* New York: Free Press, 1965.

———. "Publishers as Gatekeepers of Ideas." In *Perspectives on Publishing,* edited by Philip G. Altbach and Sheila McVey. Lexington, Mass.: Lexington Books, 1976.

Coser, Lewis A., Charles Kadushin, and Walter W. Powell. *Books: The Culture and Commerce of Publishing.* New York: Basic Books, 1982.

Cox, Stephen. "An Editor's Chrestomathy." *Scholarly Publishing* 15 (October 1983):17–37.

Cuningham, Charles E. "Up the Stairs and Over the Telephone." *Scholarly Publishing* 4 (April 1973):219–27.

Darnton, Robert. "A Survival Strategy for Academic Authors." *American Scholar* 52 (Autumn 1983):533–37.

Davin, Dan. "Editor and Author in a University Press." *Scholarly Publishing* 10 (January 1979):121–27.

Denham, Alice, and Wendell Broom. "The Role of the Author." *Scholarly Publishing* 12 (April 1981):249–58.

Dimmick, John. "The Gatekeeper: An Uncertainty Principle." *Journalism Monographs* 37 (November 1974):1–37.

Dorn, Fred J. "Do Scholarly Authors Need Literary Agents?" *Scholarly Publishing* 14 (October 1982):79–86.

"Editorial Use of Word Processors." *The Exchange* (a quarterly publication of the Association of American University Presses), Spring 1984, p. 5.

Eliot, T.S. *The Use of Poetry and the Use of Criticism.* London: Faber and Faber, 1933.

Emmitt, Robert P. "When the Well Runs Dry." *Scholarly Publishing* 2 (April 1971):247–53.

Exum, William H. "Affirmative Action and University Presses." *Scholarly Publishing* 14 (February 1983):123–38.

Fiering, Norman. *A Guide to Book Publication for Historians.* Washington, D.C.: American Historical Association, 1979.

Fletcher, Janet. "Defining the University Press." *Library Journal,* 15 September 1978, pp. 1700–01.

Flexner, Abraham. *Daniel Coit Gilman: Creator of the American Type of University.* New York: Harcourt, Brace, 1946.

Fox, Mary Frank, ed. *Scholarly Writing and Publishing: Issues, Problems, and Solutions.* Boulder, Colo.: Westview, 1985.

Frohlich, William. "Starting Small." *Scholarly Publishing* 14 (October 1982): 21–28.

Frugé, August. "The Ambiguous University Press." *Scholarly Publishing* 8 (October 1976):3–10.

——— . "Beyond Publishing: A System of Scholarly Writing and Reading." Two-part series. *Scholarly Publishing* 9 (July 1978):291–311, and 10 (October 1978):17–35.

——— . "Lectures into Books." *Scholarly Publishing* 12 (January 1981):158–66.

——— . "The Metamorphoses of the University of California Press." *Scholarly Publishing* 15 (January 1984):161–76.

——— . "Two Cheers for the National Enquiry: A Partial Dissent." *Scholarly Publishing* 10 (April 1979):211–18.

Garlington, Jack. "Concerning the Little Magazine: Something Like a Symposium." *Carleton Miscellany* 7 (Spring 1966):39.

Gaskell, Philip. *From Writer to Reader: Studies in Editorial Method.* New York: Oxford University Press, 1978.

Germano, William P. "Helping the Local Faculty with Publication Support." *Scholarly Publishing* 15 (October 1983):11–16.

Giamatti, A. Bartlett. "Safeguard of Process: The Editorial Committee." *Scholarly Publishing* 7 (January 1976):129–33.

Gilbert, David H. "Getting There." *Scholarly Publishing* 13 (April 1982):235–43.

——— . "An Interdepartmental Approach to Acquiring Computers." *Scholarly Publishing* 15 (April 1984):223–28.

Goellner, J.G. "The Federation of the Book." *Scholarly Publishing* 12 (July 1981):291–98.

——— . "The Future of University Presses." *Library Journal*, 15 September 1978, pp. 1695–99.

——— . "Mr. Bones." *Scholarly Publishing* 16 (January 1985):141–46.

——— . "Specialization in Listbuilding." *Scholarly Publishing* 15 (October 1983):3–9.

Graburn, Nelson H.H. "University Press Books in the Classroom." *Scholarly Publishing* 13 (October 1981):70–78.

Grannis, Chandler B. "New Moves at Minnesota." *Publishers Weekly*, 29 July 1983, pp. 28–29.

——— . "Scholarly Publishing." In *The Book Publishing Annual.* New York: Bowker, 1984.

Grannis, Chandler B., William Griffin, and John Mutter. "Riffs of Consensus and Practicality." *Publishers Weekly*, 19 July 1986, pp. 20–24.

Grannis, Chandler B., and John Mutter. "Targets for Scholarly Publishers." *Publishers Weekly*, 29 July 1983, pp. 22–27.

Greaser, Constance U. "Authors, Editors and Computers." *Scholarly Publishing* 12 (January 1981):123–30.

Haas, Warren J. "Research Libraries and the Dynamics of Change." *Scholarly Publishing* 11 (April 1980):195–202.

Harman, Eleanor, and Ian Montagnes, eds. *The Thesis and the Book*. Toronto: University of Toronto Press, 1976.

Harman, Eleanor, and R.M. Schoeffel. "Our Readers Report . . ." *Scholarly Publishing* 6 (July 1975):333–40.

Hawes, Gene R. *To Advance Knowledge: A Handbook on American University Press Publishing*. New York: American University Press Services, 1967.

Herbert, Rosemary. "Building a University Press from Scratch." *Publishers Weekly*, 7 June 1985, p. 28.

Higham, John. "University Presses and Academic Specialization." *Scholarly Publishing* 10 (October 1978):36–44.

Hill, Iris Tillman. "Workshop: The Publisher's Reader." In *Scholars and Their Publishers*, edited by Weldon Kefauver. New York: Modern Language Association of America, 1977.

Hoekzema, Loren. "Repackaging Scholarly Books." *Scholarly Publishing* 15 (April 1984):237–58.

Holmes, Olive. "Thesis to Book: What to Get Rid Of." *Scholarly Publishing* 5 (July 1974):339–49.

Holt, Patricia. "Scholarly—and Popular—Publishing from an Island Paradise." *Publishers Weekly*, 10 July 1981, pp. 27–28.

Holt, Patricia, and Chandler B. Grannis. "The Oft-Cited 'Crisis in Scholarly Publishing' Becomes a Way of Life." *Publishers Weekly*, 10 July 1981, pp. 22–26.

Horowitz, Irving Louis. *Communicating Ideas: The Crisis of Publishing in a Post-Industrial Society*. New York: Oxford University Press, 1986.

Horowitz, Irving Louis, and Mary E. Curtis. "The Impact of Technology on Scholarly Publishing." *Scholarly Publishing* 13 (April 1982):211–28.

Isay, Jane. "The Anatomy of a Fastback." *Scholarly Publishing* 6 (October 1974): 81–85.

Jacobson, Robert L. "Scholars Fault Journals and College Libraries in Survey by Council of Learned Societies." *Chronicle of Higher Education*, 6 August 1986, pp. 1, 21–23.

Jarrett, Beverly. "Doing Right by Your Author: Avoiding Duplicity in the Editorial Process." Paper delivered at meeting of Southern University Presses, Knoxville, Tennessee, September 1985.

———. "Secrets of an Acquisitions Editor." *Scholarly Publishing* 15 (January 1984):147–53.

Jeanneret, Marsh. "God and Mammon: The University as Publisher." *Scholarly Publishing* 15 (April 1984):197–204.

Johnson, Elmer D. *History of Libraries in the Western World*. Metuchen, N.J.: Scarecrow Press, 1970.

Joyce, Donald Franklin. *Gatekeepers of Black Culture: Black-Owned Book Publishing in the United States, 1817–1981*. Westport, Conn.: Greenwood Press, 1983.

Kefauver, Weldon, ed. *Scholars and Their Publishers*. New York: Modern Language Association of America, 1977.

Kenner, Hugh. "God, Swahili, Bandicoots, and Euphoria." *Scholarly Publishing* 5 (July 1974):291–95.

Kerr, Chester. "The Kerr Report: One More Time." *Publishers Weekly*, 5 June 1987, pp. 19–22.

———. "The Kerr Report Revisited." *Scholarly Publishing* 1 (October 1969): 5–30.

———. "One More Time: American University Presses Revisited." *Scholarly Publishing* 18 (July 1987):211–35.

———. *A Report on American University Presses*. New York: Association of American University Presses, 1949.

Kessel, Harlan R. "Marketing in the Eighties." *Scholarly Publishing* 13 (January 1982):135–41.

King, Robert T. "The Bivalent Economics of the University Press." *Scholarly Publishing* 1 (April 1970):261–73.

Krulwich, Robert. "The Cold Economist." *New York Times Book Review*, 20 October 1985, p. 55.

Lane, Michael. "Shapers of Culture: The Editor in Book Publishing." *Annals of the American Academy of Political and Social Science* 421 (September 1975): 34–42.

Lane, Robert Frederick. "The Place of American University Presses in Publishing." Ph.D. dissertation, University of Chicago, 1939.

Lewin, Kurt. *Field Theory in the Social Sciences*. New York: Harper and Row, 1951.

———. "Frontiers in Group Dynamics II: Channels of Group Life; Social Planning and Action Research." *Human Relations* 1 (November 1947):143–53.

Lockwood, Willard A. "The Decision to Publish: Scholarly Standards." In *Scholars and Their Publishers*, edited by Weldon Kefauver. New York: Modern Language Association of America, 1977.

———. "Standards and Performance in the Decision to Publish." *Scholarly Publishing* 8 (April 1977):211–21.

Luey, Beth. *Handbook for Academic Authors*. Cambridge, England: Cambridge University Press, 1987.

Machlup, Fritz, Kenneth Leeson, and Associates. *Information through the Printed Word: The Dissemination of Scholarly, Scientific, and Intellectual Knowledge*. 4 vols. New York: Praeger, 1979–80.

Macksey, Richard. *One Hundred Years of Publishing*. Baltimore: Johns Hopkins University Press, 1978.

Mann, Peter H. "Publishing the Scholarly Author." *Scholarly Publishing* 12 (January 1981):99–108.

McDowell, Edwin. "Books of Small Presses Key Source of Reprints." *New York Times*, 19 August 1985, p. C15.

———. "Sometimes a Best Seller." *New York Times Book Review*, 10 May 1981, pp. 13, 22–24.

———. "University Presses Not United in Enthusiasm for Discounts." *New York Times* syndicated story, in *Kansas City Star*, 4 January 1987, p. 11D.

McMillen, Liz. "A Doctoral Dissertation is Not Yet a Book, Young Tenure-Seeking Scholars Are Told." *Chronicle of Higher Education*, 5 February 1986, pp. 23–24.

Melko, Matthew. "Manuscripts in Progress." *Scholarly Publishing* 11 (April 1980):247–55.

Meyer, Sheldon. "Publishing Trade Books." *Scholarly Publishing* 10 (October 1978):65–71.

Meyer, Sheldon, and Leslie E. Phillabaum. "What Is a University Press?" *Scholarly Publishing* 11 (April 1980):213–19. Also in pamphlet form distributed by the Association of American University Presses.

Miles, Jack. "How to Lose Money Electronically: Word Processing and the Social Structure of Scholarly Publishing." *Library Journal*, 15 November 1984, pp. 2125–28.

———. "Intellectual Freedom and the University Press." *Scholarly Publishing* 15 (July 1984):291–300.

———. "The University Press and the American Mind." *Commonweal* 106 (25 May 1979):306–309.

Mitchell, Doug. "First Person." *Chicago Tribune Magazine*, 22 June 1986, p. 30.

———. "Reading Sociology: Editorial Semantics and the Rhetoric of Invention and Judgment." Paper delivered at meeting of Society for the Study of Symbolic Interaction, Chicago, August 1987.

Mitgang, Herbert. "Fiction: Yes and No." *New York Times Book Review*, 20 June 1982, pp. 13, 22.

Montagnes, Ian. "Perspectives on the New Technology." *Scholarly Publishing* 12 (April 1981):219–29.

Morrison, J.A. "Scientists and the Scientific Literature." *Scholarly Publishing* 11 (January 1980):157–64.

Morton, Herbert C. "Research on the Printed Word: A Review." *Scholarly Publishing* 11 (July 1980):361–70.

Nathan, Paul S. "Rights and Permissions," *Publishers Weekly*, 11 May 1984, p. 172.

National Enquiry. *Scholarly Communication: The Report of the National Enquiry.* Baltimore: Johns Hopkins University Press, 1979.

Neavill, Gordon B. "Role of the Publisher in the Dissemination of Knowledge." In *Perspectives on Publishing*, edited by Philip G. Altbach and Sheila McVey. Lexington, Mass.: Lexington Books, 1976.

Noble, J. Kendrick. "Book Publishing." In *Who Owns the Media?*, 2nd ed., edited by Benjamin M. Compaine. White Plains, N.Y.: Knowledge Industry Publications, 1982.

Orlov, Ann. "Demythologizing Scholarly Publishing." In *Perspectives on Publishing*, edited by Philip G. Altbach and Sheila McVey. Lexington, Mass.: Lexington Books, 1976.

Owen, Richard. "Who Says Capitalism Is 'Based on the Exploitation of Man by Man'? This *Oxford Advanced Dictionary of Current English*, That's Who." *Chronicle of Higher Education*, 10 April 1985, p. 1.

Pace, Eric. "Yale University Press Prepares for the '80s." *New York Times Book Review*, 10 July 1979, pp. 14–15, 45.

Parker, Anthony. "The University Press as a Science Publisher." *Scholarly Publishing* 3 (April 1972):223–29.

Pascal, Naomi B. "Freedom, Responsibility and the Agile Editor." *Scholarly Publishing* 16 (April 1985):255–61.

Paul, Angus. "Inspiring and Controversial Marcus Garvey Lives." *Chronicle of Higher Education*, 5 March 1986, pp. 4–6.

Penaskovic, Richard. "Facing Up to the Publication Gun." *Scholarly Publishing* 16 (January 1985):136–40.

Perry, Ralph Barton. "Should There Be a University Press?" Reprinted in *Scholarly Publishing* 17 (January 1986):109–17.

Philipson, Morris. "The Quality of Scholarly Writing and Scholarly Publishing Today." *Scholarly Publishing* 6 (October 1974):9–18.

———. "The Scholar as Publishing Author." *Scholarly Publishing* 8 (July 1977): 291–97.

———. "What Is a University Press Worth?" *Encounter* 40 (May 1973):41–49.

Powell, Walter W. "Adapting to Tight Money and New Opportunities." *Scholarly Publishing* 14 (October 1982):9–19.

———. *Getting into Print: The Decision-Making Process in Scholarly Publishing*. Chicago: University of Chicago Press, 1985.

Pratt, Dana J. "Publishing *The Children of Pride*." *Scholarly Publishing* 5 (October 1973):29–34.

Reitt, Barbara B. "An Academic Author's Checklist." *Scholarly Publishing* 16 (October 1984):65–72.

Reuter, Madalynne, John F. Baker, and Chandler B. Grannis. "Scholarly Publishers Meet in a Can-Fix-It Mood." *Publishers Weekly*, 30 July 1982, pp. 36–42.

Reuter, Madalynne, Chandler B. Grannis, and John F. Baker. "Scholarly Publishers Turn Their Eyes to New Markets." *Publishers Weekly*, 8 August 1980, pp. 20–27.

Roberts, Stephen V. "At Johns Hopkins." *New York Times Book Review*, 10 May 1981, pp. 13, 20–21.

Rockwood, Irving. "Publishing a Scholarly Book." *PS* 20 (Summer 1987): 697–706.

Rowson, Richard C. "Turning the Operation Around." *Scholarly Publishing* 16 (October 1984):39–48.

Schwartz, Barry. *Queuing and Waiting: Studies in the Social Organization of Access and Delay*. Chicago: University of Chicago Press, 1975.

Seybold, Catharine. "A Brief History of *The Chicago Manual of Style*." *Scholarly Publishing* 14 (February 1983):163–77.

———. "The Lisle Letters at Chicago." *Scholarly Publishing* 13 (April 1982): 245–62.

Shatzkin, Leonard. *In Cold Type: Overcoming the Book Crisis*. Boston: Houghton Mifflin, 1982.

Shugg, Roger W. "Cui Bono?" *Scholarly Publishing* 10 (October 1978):3–15.

Silver, Henry M. "The Conservative University Press." *American Scholar* 18 (Spring 1949):149–57.

Smith, Datus C., Jr. "An Anatomy of Subsidies." *Scholarly Publishing* 6 (April 1975):197–206.

Stainton, Elsie Myers. "A Bag for Editors." *Scholarly Publishing* 8 (January 1977):111–19.

Sternhell, Carol. "Who Needs a Blockbuster? Another Way of Publishing." *New York Times Book Review*, 11 October 1987, p. 40.

Strothman, Wendy J. "On Moving from Campus to Commerce." *Scholarly Publishing* 18 (April 1987):157–62.

Tebbel, John. *A History of Book Publishing in the United States*. 4 vols. New York: Bowker, 1972–81.

Thatcher, Sanford G. "Competitive Practices in Acquiring Manuscripts." *Scholarly Publishing* 11 (January 1980):112–32.

Tripp, Edward. "Editors and the Editorial Committee." *Scholarly Publishing* 8 (January 1977):99–109.

"University of Chicago Press: The King of the Least-Sellers." *Change* 16 (October 1984):38–48.

U.S. Bureau of the Census. *Historical Statistics of the United States, Parts I and II*. Washington, D.C.: Government Printing Office, 1975.

———. *Statistical Abstract of the United States: 1986*. Washington, D.C.: Government Printing Office, 1986.

Veysey, Laurence R. *The Emergence of the American University*. Chicago: University of Chicago Press, 1965.

Wallace, Ronald. "Shaping the Canon: The University Press and the Democratization of American Poetry." *Scholarly Publishing* 19 (April 1988): 144–56.

Walsh, John. "Einstein Papers Coming On." *Science* 222 (12 November 1983): 664.

Ward, John William. "How Scholars Regard University Presses." *Scholarly Publishing* 16 (October 1984):33–38.

Wardlaw, Frank H. "The Book That Was Too Big for Texas." *Scholarly Publishing* 6 (January 1975):159–63.

Webb, Thompson. "Author as Compositor: Word Processor to Typewriter." *Scholarly Publishing* 15 (January 1984):177–90.

Westley, Bruce, and Malcolm S. MacLean, Jr. "A Conceptual Model for Communications Research." *Journalism Quarterly* 34 (Winter 1957):31–38.

Weyr, Thomas. "UPs and the Trade Book." *Publishers Weekly*, 5 June 1987, pp. 23–24.

White, David Manning. "The Gate Keeper: A Case Study in the Selection of News." *Journalism Quarterly* 27 (Fall 1950):383–90.

White, Herbert S. "Scholarly Publishers and Libraries: A Strained Marriage." *Scholarly Publishing* 19 (April 1988):125–29.

Wiggins, Henry H. "Early and Middle Years at Columbia." *Scholarly Publishing* 14 (July 1983):327–36.

———. "Publisher to Alexr. Hamilton Esqr." *Scholarly Publishing* 9 (April 1978):195–205.

Williams, Ed. "Publishing at North Carolina." *New York Times Book Review*, 18 October 1981, pp. 13, 30.

Winkler, Karen J. "A Lot More than Trading Baseball Cards: Sport History Gains a New Respectability." *Chronicle of Higher Education*, 5 June 1985, pp. 5, 8.

———. "New Breed of Scholar Works the Territory that Lies between History and Geography." *Chronicle of Higher Education*, 24 September 1986, pp. 6–8.

Wood, William A. "Changing Editorial Direction." Within a collection of articles titled "Stretching the Shrinking Dollar." *Scholarly Publishing* 14 (October 1982):32–33.

Zuckerman, Harriet. "Stratification in American Science." *Sociological Inquiry* 40 (Spring 1970):235–57.

Index

Getting Published *was designed by Richard Hendel, composed by Tseng Information Systems, Inc., and printed and bound by Cushing-Malloy, Inc. The book is set in Ehrhardt. Text stock is 60-lb. Glatfelter Natural Antique, B-16.*